UNDER THE
Influence

By
Micah Paden

Under the Influence is a work of fiction. Names, characters, places, and incidents either are the product of the author's imagination or are used fictitiously. Any resemblance to actual persons, living or dead, events or locales is entirely coincidental.

Contents

CHAPTER 1

More Damned Secrets

"Emmarie Lynn, I can't believe we're still talking about this. The answer's NO." The woman scoots a straight-backed oaken chair away from the kitchen table and lets her body slump onto the leather padding.

The 17-year-old stands at the granite composite sink. She bites her lip and continues washing the breakfast dishes. Her mother's emphasis on the word 'still' signals her disinterest in rehashing the conversation, yet Emmarie knows her mother is not, in fact, done.

"Your father and I understand you've been accepted into Juilliard...That's such an honor. Honey, we're very proud of you. But you can't go this year. Maybe next."

Emmarie pauses from the dishes and turns to confront her mother. She detects a pleading in her mother's eyes that

1

immediately thrusts her into unfamiliar territory. It means something. She isn't sure what.

Steely eyes. Condescending eyes. Knowing eyes, and the rarer but real, 'I love you unconditionally' eyes. These looks she recognizes. But pleading eyes suggests her mother isn't telling her everything.

If that's true, the girl's no longer sure if her anger stems from the authoritarian 'no,' or from *more damned secrets.*

She aches to punctuate her anger, to signal her mother that she's no longer a little child. She considers briefly throwing the wet dishrag she holds, but instinctively knows this is a wrong choice.

"You're playing favorites! Danny's at Harvard." Determined not to let anything obstruct the killer daggers she imagines sending with her eyes, she brings a wet hand to wipe her auburn hair away from her face. "You didn't tell him to wait. My grades are just as good…"

"It's not your grades. You need to stay closer to home." Her mother's voice includes a pained sharpness and a certain finality. She lights a vanilla-cinnamon scented candle on the table in front of her and switches gears, much softer this time. "Smells like fresh-baked cookies, doesn't it? Look, honey, finish your senior year. Next fall, go to Portland State, U of O, or even WSU. You can always transfer later if you still want to."

Wait a year? Why do I always have to sacrifice? She doesn't understand the need to sacrifice at all. The family isn't poor.

Nor were they even *before* her mom became famous. Now they live in a $3.5 million estate on the Oregon Coast, which is not even close to what her parents can afford, she thinks.

"The right college is everything to me, Mom. You, of all people, should understand that."

"I do understand, honey. Believe me, I do. There are other factors to consider here, that's all."

She wants to ask, '*Like what?*' but that gives power back to her mother. Emmarie doesn't win arguments with her mother. Not against the great Dr. Janet Brooks Kelso, pop psychologist and one of the world's best-selling authors of self-help crapola on the Internet today.

"You don't know everything! You're too busy giving everyone else all your great advice. Telling them how to feel and what to do. You don't know how you are screwing up *my* life. No, I bet you *know,*" she emphasizes, "you just don't *care.* Do you!"

It isn't a question; it's an accusation. The words taste like venom in her mouth, and she regrets them instantly. But she can't take her words back, so she doesn't let a little regret stop her. She presses on.

"I'm sick of being the doormat in this family." She adds a staccato effect next to make sure her mother misses nothing. "It's. Not. Fair! Whenever Danny wants something, you and dad fork over the money."

Emmarie twists around enough to throw the dripping dishrag she finds herself still holding into the sink with the remaining dishes. It splashes water up and over the countertop when it lands.

The only education she feels will catapult her into the entertainment career she wants requires getting into Juilliard's musical arts and acting programs. She's done that. The prestigious school accepts less than six percent of their applicants, so she's beaten the odds already. Physically going to Juilliard is the hurdle now. Emmarie can't articulate it, but a Juilliard education would validate that she *matters*.

For the next few moments, she owns the stage. She uses her acting skills to orchestrate an exodus worthy of a Tony nomination if they have such a thing for 'best exit in a domestic drama.' Emmarie turns back around to her mother. "Tell me. Is it because he's your firstborn? Or because he's a *boy*???"

Her last question cuts a little too deeply. She can tell in the lines of her mother's face.

Emmarie licks a well-aged, hidden wound of her own. *Mother looks tired now. Frail even, like before. Doesn't matter. I can't help if what I say is true.*

"I'm outta here. I have to get ready for work."

"Don't take the Escalade. Your father wants it tonight. Take the Honda instead," her mother orders.

But I like driving the Caddy! Leaving her mother still resting at the table, Emmarie finishes her march out of the kitchen with her hand up dismissively as if to say, 'Whatever!' She rounds the corner, crosses the foyer, and takes the stairs up two at a time to her room. She'll feel better with a good hair brushing and some fresh lip gloss. Well, she thinks, at least she'll look better.

Slipping off her favorite sandals, she chooses a pair of blue canvas shoes with thick, cushy soles and a pair of socks she folds over at the ankles. Apparently, she inherited some of her father's practical nature. She learned early that sandals won't cut it, not when she stands forever waiting on customers to decide which goldfish to buy. Her willingness to suffer for fashion's sake has its limits, in contrast to her friend Amy who often works the same shift with her. Amy forgoes comfort to always look hot.

Emmarie grabs her phone from the charger and slips it into an outside pocket on her purse. Then fumbling a bit, she digs through the bag for her favorite lip gloss, Victoria Secret's Love Berry. When she has it in hand, she heads for the bathroom mirror and applies the berry pink tint to her lips. She blows a kiss to the image in the mirror.

She puts the gloss down and picks up her brush. With each stroke through her thick, shoulder-length hair, she fumes again. Ultimately, she brushes her hair much more than it needs. She selects a couple of barrettes from a drawer and uses them to pull her hair away from her face.

Maybe I should go to Jack's after work. Not come home. That'll tell them something…Tell them I won't put up with this shit!

She is acutely aware her parents are less than thrilled with her choice in boyfriends. They don't forbid her to see him, of course – even they are smart enough to know that would backfire. They caution her and say he doesn't have a lot of 'gumption.'

Well, maybe that's what she *likes* about him. *He's even keeled.* He doesn't get rattled, especially when she is. More than that, Jack wears polite and thoughtful like others wear shoes. Nevertheless, perhaps what her best friend Sophia says about Jack is true: His most attractive quality is that her parents don't care for him. Right now, he garners extra points for that.

She decides to call him on her way to work. She must hurry if she wants to get there early enough to prepare for her shift. She hates being late in general but being unprepared is the worst. Is that her father's practical influence again? Or her mother's sense of propriety? She isn't sure.

One more examination in front of the mirror. She tilts her head every which way to make sure she captured the right look. She has. *Voilà! Done.*

She slips the lip gloss and brush into her bag and throws it over her shoulder. Back in her bedroom, she decides on a jacket then bounces down the stairs. She needs to grab her insulated lunch bag off the counter, and the keys from the hanger by the door. *If mom is still in the kitchen, I'll ignore her.*

She is.

And she does.

Emmarie sets her jaw to avoid acknowledging her mother even faintly. Today, the woman is dead to her. She might stay dead, too. At least until she explains her double standard to Emmarie's satisfaction, or until Emmarie persuades her parents to change their minds.

And just how will I get them to change their minds if I'm not talking to them? Maybe I'll get Danny to advocate for me. He'll understand.

She refills her water bottle from the big side-by-side and snags the lunch she packed earlier, a chicken salad sandwich with grapes and pecans on nutty whole wheat, some carrot sticks, and an apple. In her peripheral vision, she sees her mother still sitting at the kitchen table. Her silent entrance disturbs her mother's reverie. *Good.* But now she feels her mother's eyes trailing her movements.

God knows they clash. *This fight feels different.*

If she could bring herself to read any of her mother's books, which she absolutely refuses to do, she believes they would say something to this effect:

'It is normal for children this age to assert their independence in preparation for leaving the nest.' And: *'Parents should be unconditionally loving, yet firm about their parenting roles. Remember, you are the parent. You are not supposed to be your child's best friend. Even though they won't admit it, they still need your guidance.'*

She reddens a bit when she remembers telling her mother, only recently in fact, that she isn't remotely interested in reading anything her mother ever writes. Well, she didn't say it exactly that way. If she remembers correctly, and she does, her exact words were:

"I'm glad the public buys it, Mom. But I don't. It's all pop-psychology BULLSHIT."

The memory re-triggers old emotions, which come flooding back. Unlike the current argument though, she can't remember what that one had been about. Not that it matters, because it's always something with a sandpaper mom. Try as you might to get along with that woman, you can never do enough, or do it well enough, to get out from under constant grating.

Emmarie believes she's a disappointment to both parents. She wishes that weren't true, but it is. It must be. She hates never measuring up and seeing that reflected in their eyes every day. Danny this and Danny that. This, at least, she understands — her big brother is perfect, and she adores him.

Her mother is also perfect or rather, the world thinks so. Of course, they don't see the Janet Brooks Kelso she knows. They only see the 'sanitized for your protection' version.

Why do I let her push my buttons?

Nevertheless, Emmarie determines to send a message to her parents, one they can't misinterpret or ignore. She brushes past her mother and doesn't say a word as she heads for the selection of car keys hanging in the alcove around the corner.

Reaching up, her mother's admonition echoes in her mind: *"Don't take the Escalade. Take the Honda."*

Exasperated, she reaches for the Honda keys attached to a gray alien keychain. She lifts the keys off the hook and the hard, flat rubber alien in her hand reminds her of better times. Like when on the spur of the moment over a long weekend, Dad had flown the family down to Roswell, New Mexico, in his Beechcraft Bonanza to see their aunt Julia. She'd treated them to tourist sites around town.

She pauses. Then with a wry smile, she promptly returns the keys to their place on the cast-iron 'Home Sweet Home' key rack.

This time she selects the brown Irish Setter keychain. With keys to the Escalade firmly in hand, she opens the garage door and sets off for the pet store where she works.

CHAPTER 2

When Worlds Collide

The notorious Oregon clouds arrive and push the blue from the sky. They bring raindrops too that wash away the last trace of real sun for the season. The predicted lack of an Indian summer proves true.

Depending on weather and tourist season, Emmarie can navigate the roads to enter Clatsop City in ten minutes. As she occupies her mind with the retorts she wishes she'd volleyed earlier, she spots something in the road. She slows the Escalade. Drawing nearer, she wonders what it could be. *A dead squirrel? No, not dead...*she swears she sees movement.

She halts the SUV a foot or two away from the gray whatever-it-is and leaps out to check. Not that she has the time, but the creature needs help. *Of course, if it's wild, it could have rabies… Better not touch it,'* her father's voice echoes in her thoughts.

'OMG, it's a kitty!' she says out loud. She abandons all caution and quickly bends over to check the animal's condition. Thank God, she didn't hit it, but someone had.

Much to her surprise, the fur-ball does not act feral. It plaintively cries, allowing her to pick it up and examine the skin and bones creature. She doesn't see much blood though, just some dirt and dried-looking stuff from small nicks. It continues to meow weakly, non-stop, as if it hasn't seen a person or food and water for days. This stretch of road experiences regular traffic, so Emmarie guesses it was hit not long ago. The driver must have twisted the steering wheel at the last minute, resulting in a 'side-swipe' that stunned it, she reasons.

She cradles the flea-bitten critter in her arms and walks back to the Escalade to find the emergency blanket they keep in the far back cargo area. She makes a little bed for it in the front passenger seat so she can monitor her charge, not unaware that the vehicle's interior now smells of pine air freshener, wet kitty fur, and feline diarrhea.

Her boss, Marta, a veterinarian-turned-pet store owner, splits her time between both businesses. *She'll know what to do.* At the very least, before Emmarie starts her shift, she'll make sure the little thing is cleaned up, receives food and water, and a place to rest.

Under the Influence

By the time Emmarie pulls the Cadillac into the parking lot that the Best Friends Pet Store shares with the Vet Clinic and a few other stores, it starts to rain again. Not enough to make her use the umbrella to cross the parking lot, but she takes it all the same. She might need it later. She cradles the kitten in her right arm while she shoves her purse, lunch, water bottle, and umbrella onto her left.

Darting through the drops while attempting to dodge the growing puddles, Emmarie spots Amy's blue Toyota Camry already there. *Shit, if she beat me here, I must really be late.*

Inside the store, she finds proprietor Marta Krates preparing to leave.

What a day to be running late!

Emmarie rushes in with her little bundle and immediately detects the familiar scent of pet feed and disinfectant. She apologizes profusely to Marta, accepting full responsibility for not leaving early enough. Expressions change into concerned smiles when she reveals the rescued kitten and relays details how she found it.

Marta dismisses the need for an apology altogether. She suggests some basic treatments using supplies readily found in the store and offers them to Emmarie. "If you need anything else, just write it down so I can take it off the inventory. Of course, I'll be next door if you need me." With one more quick inspection of the kitten and pat on its head, she turns her attention to Emmarie.

"Now, I have a favor to ask you. I was expecting to be back to close the store with Amy, but something has come up. Would you mind working a few hours past your shift to close for me? That keeps the store from being short-staffed and takes the pressure off."

"I don't mind staying if it helps," Emmarie says with ease.

Unlike Amy, Emmarie enjoys working when Marta shares the shift. Her boss acts like a mentor. When time allows, she explains marketing and business strategies and answers Emmarie's questions. They also discuss love and life. Marta is the mother figure Emmarie wishes her real mother would be. Due to Marta's tutelage, she would consider going into business if her entertainment dreams don't work out, but probably not. She knows she lacks the crystal ball that Marta seems to possess.

"I think I'll stick with my acting and music," she tells herself on more than one occasion.

"Hey, Emmarie," Amy calls as she approaches the end of the aisle where Emmarie hangs up chew toys. "We've got a cute guy in the reptile section. Could you help him? I would, but you know how I am with snakes...and he might actually want to *buy* one." Amy demonstrates her disgust with a controlled, yet highly animated shudder that makes her ample chest shake.

I see why boys like you, Amy!

"Sure. No problem. Tell him I'll be right there."

14

She finishes hanging the toys she has in her hands before she stands. Then uses her foot to push the rest of the box closer to the display, so no one trips over it. She locates the twenty-something man standing near the terrariums looking at all sorts of exotic creatures: Red-eared slider turtles, veiled chameleons, crested geckos, bearded dragons, Mexican red knee tarantulas, even Asian forest scorpions. And of course, snakes. They sell mostly fancy corn snakes and ball pythons. None of these creatures bother her, but she doesn't see their allure as pets, either. She prefers furry ones.

"May I help you?"

"I'm not home much so it doesn't seem fair to keep a dog in a bachelor's apartment. What do you know about that albino corn snake?"

"Have you owned a snake before?

He shakes his head 'no.'

"Do you already have a terrarium?" She waits for him to shake his head 'no' again, but he answers her instead.

"A friend gave me a 40-gallon tank with a lid."

She smiles at him and briefly covers the highlights of snake ownership: "You'll want a heavy reptile water bowl and to keep fresh water available at all times. Not just any bowl will do. Lighter bowls tend to tip over. You don't want it too deep either. Put it in a corner and keep it clean. Corn snakes move around mostly at night, so he'll find it when he's cruising the perimeter of his enclosure."

Emmarie notes that the man is muscular and tall. She can't imagine him being squeamish, especially since he's considering a reptile, so she asks, "Do you want to hold him?"

His gray eyes appear to change color to blue or hazel as they light up with the idea. Emmarie fishes the compliant snake out of the tank and gently offers it to the man. She finishes explaining snake care and answers his occasional question. The customer looks mesmerized. After he commits to the purchase, she sets about gathering the water dish, some Aspen bedding, and everything else she thinks he'll need, before walking with him and the snake to the cash register.

She rings up his purchase, so Amy doesn't need to get close to the snake. As she puts the prized animal into a travel box, she warns him: "Make sure your tank is escape-proof. Corn snakes are notorious for that. If you find it isn't, then come back and I'll help you find a more suitable enclosure."

He smiles at her for several beats, lowers his eyes to her name badge, then thanks her by name before leaving with multiple sacks.

"He's gorgeous," Amy says after he leaves. "His eyes!"

"Umm," Emmarie agrees with a slight nod.

Amy takes advantage of the momentary quiet to fill her co-worker in on her date the previous night. She punctuates it with play-by-play action. Different names and different places, but most of her tales end up with her in the back seat of a car or bedroom somewhere.

Emmarie discounts half of Amy's sexual escapades as 'just stories.' Even so, her fascination comes from hearing how different her friend's choices are from her own.

"What did *you* do last night?" Amy asks when she comes up for air.

"Extra credit homework. I want to show my parents I'm a serious student."

"Still not letting you go to Juilliard, huh?"

"My parents are punishing me for something. I just don't know what. But I'll get them to change their minds."

"Excuse me." A woman approaches and asks if the store has any Boswellia joint care products for her cats.

"Aisle 14, bottom shelf, the middle of the row. I think," Amy says. "Let us know if you don't find what you're looking for." Dismissing the woman, she turns back to resume her conversation. "What if you can't?"

"Can't what?"

"Change their minds."

"I will."

"I know. But what if you can't?"

"Then I'll find a way to pay for it myself, but I'm going."

Business for the remainder of the day stays steady at a slow pace. *Perhaps the threat of harder rain is keeping people home.* In any event, Emmarie finishes with the chew toys and does her best to ensure her customers leave satisfied, smiling, like the snake guy. Any extra time she has, she spends tending to the new kitten.

She forgot all about calling Jack earlier, but at least she remembered to square it with Marta to let the kitten recuperate at the store. That coup means she doesn't need to plead a case with her mother to keep a kitten.

What a mixed message that would send: *I want to keep this kitten, and oh, by the way, it'll become your cat when I leave for Juilliard in nine months.* She won't allow tugging heart strings to dilute her argument.

Emmarie now thinks only of heading to Jack's house while she and Amy work through the closing checklist for cleaning and securing the store for the night. She wants someone she trusts to tell her that everything will be okay. To convince her that even if she doesn't go to Juilliard, her life isn't over. No, that isn't right. She doesn't want someone. She wants Jack.

Having worked through the checklist, Emmarie now stands on the sidewalk, ready to lock up after Amy exits the building. Her co-worker makes a beeline to her car parked at the edge of the dimly lit lot. As she approaches her vehicle, she turns and waves, and gives Emmarie one of her usual admonishments. Tonight, it is: "Don't do anything I wouldn't do!" *As if that takes anything off the table, Amy,* Emmarie thinks. She smiles and waves.

She finds the right key for the glass door and twists it in the lock until she feels it catch. Then she withdraws the key and slips it into her bag. Out of habit, she grasps the door handle and tugs to confirm. *Yup, locked.*

Under the Influence

Surprisingly, the sky no longer spits, yet the asphalt looks black and shiny, especially where water pools. As she approaches the outer parking areas, only a few vehicles remain that she doesn't recognize as belonging to other strip mall employees. She notes an old, dark blue or black pickup she hasn't seen before, a light-colored van, and a Winnebago.

The evening air loses all semblance of the late autumn warmth that cradled the town only yesterday. Winter settles upon them, regardless of what the calendar indicates. She pulls her jacket tighter. *Hurry up and start the engine,* she tells herself. *I need to wear a warmer coat.*

She cranks the engine over to let it warm up a bit and catches KKOR in the middle of playing *You Say* by Lauren Daigle. She immediately joins in: *"You say I am loved when I can't feel a thing…"* Only when she senses heat on her feet does she buckle up. Now ready, she puts the vehicle in gear, eases off the brakes, and heads out of the lot.

Where is her phone? She locates it in the outside pocket of her purse, just where she put it earlier.

Her call to Jack goes to voice mail. *I'll head to his house anyway.*

Fortunately, at this time of the evening, traffic usually speeds along at a good clip unless there's an accident. The roads are okay but wet. Adele comes on the radio next. Emmarie turns up the volume and belts out a flawless rendition of *Someone Like You* right along with her.

She makes the turn toward Jack's house just as her smartphone rings. *Maybe that's Jack, calling me back.*

It isn't. She recognizes her mother's number. *Bet she's pissed about the Escalade.* Her mother knows she can't take calls at work, but she should have messaged her that she was working late. She knows she isn't doing herself any favors by not accepting the call, but she can't face her mother. She lets it ring. If she needs to, she'll apologize for not answering because she was driving. It wasn't safe to be on the phone. *Not a lie. Mom will understand that.*

In truth, traffic is negligible. Emmarie crosses a few major intersections when her phone dings. This time, it is Jack. For some reason, he texts instead of calls.

She has her phone in her right hand, focusing on what to text back to him. When the traffic signal on Tillamook Street changes from green to amber, she doesn't notice. The Porsche approaching on Peter Iredale Avenue, to her right, runs its light altogether.

Emmarie never hears the on-coming engine, crunching metal or breaking glass.

CHAPTER 3

Luck Be a Lady Tonight

—

"Don't move. Someone's called 911. Help is on its way." Emmarie can barely make out the man's voice, but she senses he's beside her. "Can you hear me? Do you understand?"

She manages a faint 'yes' while she takes mental inventory. The impact leaves her body twisted and facing out the driver's side window, or what's left of it anyway. Bits of broken auto safety glass lay everywhere. She smells engine grease, burnt rubber, and faint gasoline, mingling with pine and a stench she can't place. The disembodied voice keeps talking calmly.

She doesn't see much. Something blurs her vision, especially in her left eye.

There is blood. Lots of it. It seems to be coming from a gash somewhere. She thinks her body remains 'all in one piece.' At least she assumes so, as pain pulses from every limb. *What's happened? What's that smell?*

"My right arm and leg. I-I-I can't move them."

"Your arm and leg are pinned. Not to worry. I will stay here with you until the police arrive. What is your name?"

"Emmarie." Saying her own name forces her mind to focus, and in turn, unleashes thoughts. *Oh, God. The Escalade!* She starts to cry.

"No, Emmarie, listen to me. You will be okay."

"You d-d-don't understand. My— my parents will KILL me. Dad loves his Caddy. Not supposed to take it."

"Your parents will forgive you." The man's voice comforts her, telling her what she needs to hear, even if she doesn't believe him. "No doubt they love you more than this heap of metal. A vehicle can be replaced."

"Take the Honda—"

"You are resilient. Your kind makes your own luck."

'Luck.' Such an odd word. She doesn't feel lucky. The man's voice trails off to some distant recess. Emmarie rallies enough to realize he did not abandon her. She is fading. She renews her struggle to concentrate on his voice.

"Do you want me to call them for you?"

"Who?"

"Your parents."

"C-c-could you? I'm so c-cold."

The man bends down and looks around the mangled interior. "Where is your phone?"

"In my bag? I-I don't know."

"No worries."

No worries. No wor—

The front passenger side of the Escalade took the full force of the initial hit, spinning the vehicle until its grill rests crumpled against a now tilting metal light pole. The frame and the dashboard, both accordioned and askew, bare silent witness to the violence of the incident. Somehow her purse only tips on the seat, spilling most of its contents. Lighter items like pens and lip gloss lay on the floorboard.

The man walks around the tangle of pole and engine to the opening once filled by the front passenger window. He roots around in her bag with gloved hands, but the phone isn't there. He spies her wallet though. $32. Driver's license - Emmarie Lynn Kelso. 1730 Sea Breeze, Clatsop City, MINOR.

Emmarie groans.

"I am still here with you, Emmarie," he asserts. "Remember, do not move. All I am doing is looking for your phone. Your parents are more likely to answer a call from you. Okay? I am almost done."

He returns the wallet quietly. He elevates the entire handbag and looks underneath it. No phone. As he starts to set it down, he catches the glint of a pink metallic phone cover lodged between the passenger seat and the console. Leaning in and fully extending his arm, he fishes it out. The phone appears serviceable despite the shattered screen.

"Emmarie, what is your access code?

"My wha?"

"I need your home screen code so I can call your parents."

The bingo cage that is Emmarie's brain twirls, letting numbers fall at random into her consciousness. "Uh, 9-7-1-4? 9-1-7-3?" Somewhere in the distance, sirens signal coming help.

The man takes the glove off his right hand so that the touchscreen accepts the numbers he enters. He makes his way back to the driver's side. Time is running out.

"That works. What is the phone number?"

"My father's is…" She cannot produce all seven digits.

The man quickly scrolls to her settings and looks up her Apple ID information before checking her 'recents.'

When he finishes, he puts his glove back on and glances over his shoulder. Emmarie wouldn't see him, even if her eyes suddenly open. He removes a foil sanitizer packet from a coat pocket. Ripping it open, he uses the moist towelette to rub down every part of the phone as he strolls back around to the passenger window. He drops it next to her bag. The empty packet and used wipe go into his coat pocket.

A damp freeze sinks into her bones, mingling with the pain and fear lodging there. Her body shivers uncontrollably and she can no longer force her eyes to stay open. She allows them to close again — only for a moment.

The next thing Emmarie knows is that several ambulances are there, and paramedics are checking her over as best they can without moving her. They manage to put a brace around her neck. They place an EMS foil space blanket over her to conserve body heat, but the mylar does nothing to warm her. *So cold.*

Deputy Cooper with the Sheriff's department orders the traffic blocked off and starts interviewing bystanders, all the while making sure the paramedics have space and freedom to work.

Emmarie feels underwater. Everything fuzzy. Everything distant. Full thoughts are challenging if not impossible. *So many people now.* Her mind floats in and out of consciousness, amid orchestrated mayhem.

Someone mentions 'golden hour.' And she hears the words 'extricate' and 'Jaws of Life.' The paramedics stem the bleeding from the gash that turns out to be high on her forehead, just in her hairline, instead of directly above her left eye.

"That's going to need stitches, honey. But you're lucky. Do your hair right, and nobody will ever notice."

That word again: Luck-y.

Emmarie tries to smile, to let the paramedic know she appreciates her help. How she appreciates everyone's help.

Others move in and pry open the Escalade door from its frame with a thick pneumatic tool, a spreader. Quick and efficient, in a minute they have the door ajar and extended.

25

Then they use the tool as a cutter and slice right through solid hinges as if they were plastic, not steel. With the door completely off, the paramedics treat her more effectively.

"Is, is e-ri-won okay?" Emmarie asks.

"Let's focus on you right now."

Emmarie looks around as best she can without moving her neck. She can't find her helper anywhere. She wants to thank him.

Until police arrive…

The paramedics talk amongst themselves, but Emmarie finds it too difficult to focus, to process the jumble of conversation she hears. She recognizes words here and there though. Words like: Concussion and shock, and blood. Pressure. Dropping.

"We've got to get that dash off her. Now!"

The fire department's emergency response team pulls the vehicle away from the light pole to make more room to work. The man with the Jaws of Life has a ram attachment now. He expertly pushes the dashboard assembly away, while others work as a single unit to free Emmarie's pinned body from the wreckage.

"So cold…," she manages through bluish lips and clenched teeth. Her eyes begin to roll up beyond her fluttering lids.

"Stay with us, Emmarie. Open your eyes and stay with us." It is the same voice that tells her not to worry about a scar.

Somebody calls for a helicopter. "Hey, Cooper," a paramedic yells, "Can you give us a hand getting her into the chopper?"

He runs to help.

"One. Two. Three. LIFT."

Emmarie feels more than hears the thump, thump, thump of the blades.

CHAPTER 4

Deadly Consequences

Janet and Roger Kelso find themselves at 8:23 that Saturday night sitting in the all too familiar waiting room of Clatsop County Mercy Hospital, surrounded by smells of alcohol mingled with the body odor of exhausted and scared strangers. A few people text, whisper, or feign attention in old, tattered Field and Stream or People magazines. One woman rises and paces past the potted plant.

"Mr. and Mrs. Kelso?" As soon as Dr. Isvanhi Bajwa enters the room, Emmarie's parents jump to their feet. A copy of last June's Eating Well, long forgotten on Janet's lap, slides to the floor.

"Dr. Kelso—" Janet corrects. She feels Roger slip his left arm around her waist.

"Can we see her?"

Dr. Bajwa extends her hand to Janet first as a professional courtesy then to Mr. Kelso. "We're still assessing the extent of her injuries." She pauses momentarily to consult her notes.

Dr. Kelso feels her body tense, bracing for the worst. She grips Roger's right hand, which reaches out involuntarily to hold hers.

"Barring any surprises, I think Emmarie will be fine," Dr. Bajwa finally says.

Emmarie's mother almost crumples with relief, but her husband of 26 years steadies her. "Thank God," escapes her lips.

The doctor reviews Emmarie's condition. "In addition to obvious cuts and bruises, she has a comminuted fracture of her right tibia, a broken clavicle, and a concussion. We think her spleen ruptured as well. At this point, we've inserted pins and screws to reattach her bone, stitched her up, put a cast on her leg, and are monitoring her closely."

"Are you removing the spleen?" Dr. Kelso asks.

"That may not be necessary. We'll know more later. For the collarbone, it's a hairline fracture. We don't need to implant any plates or screws. She needs time for that to heal." Dr. Bajwa clears her throat from the effects of the busy evening before she continues. "From what I heard about the accident, your daughter is lucky to be alive, let alone in such good condition, considering everything."

"When can we see her?" her father asks.

"She's still asleep. I can have a nurse notify you when she's awake…"

"No. I want to be with her when she wakes up. Don't we, Roger?" Janet buries her face into the crook of her husband's neck. He smells faintly of the morning's Brut aftershave and dinner's garlic. Right now, for these few moments, she doesn't need to be strong. For the first time since that horrid phone call, she lets tears flow silently down her cheeks.

Room 214 is private, sparsely furnished with a bedside table, an over-bed stand, and a couple of armchairs with wood trim. Her hospital bed, illuminated by a bright streetlight outside the window, contains a sleeping mass of bandages and bruises named Emmarie.

Janet lets a heavy gasp escape when she sees her. Gathering herself, she immediately moves to her daughter's side to hold her hand. Except she can't. Emmarie's right arm and shoulder are fastened securely in a sling with only her fingers extending out. IV needles stick into the veins of her left hand.

Lacking the ability to comfort her sleeping daughter, Dr. Kelso shifts into her professional, 'let's-improve-the-situation' mode. She draws the curtains across the window to lessen the streetlight's glare. She directs her husband to fill a plastic pitcher with drinking water, then pours a glass and inserts the bendable straw she finds on the side table. She repositions the over-bed table within Emmarie's reach, sets her water there along with the remote for the wall-mounted television. When she can find nothing else to occupy herself, she begins clenching her jaw and expelling extended breaths as if gently inflating a low tire. Finally, she sits down and braces herself for more waiting.

Emmarie will wake up in her own sweet time, she tells herself. *She always did have a mind of her own.*

Roger breaks the silence. "You know, Janet, she isn't in a coma. She's just sleeping. Dr. Bajwa says Emmarie will be fine."

"That's not the point."

"Then I missed it."

"Seriously? We could have lost our daughter! She has no business being out after work, and no business taking the Escalade. She deliberately disobeyed me." Emmarie's mother digs her nails into her right hand until she catches herself. When she releases her grip, the hand with the half-moon imprints smooths wrinkles from her slacks. "Us, I mean. She disobeyed us."

"Why do you think she did that?"

"Who's the psychologist here?"

"I'm just saying. You fought. She stormed off to work. Jack lives in Warrenton. Put two and two together, why don't you."

"Don't you lecture me." Janet fights to keep her voice only slightly above a whisper. She longs for Emmarie to wake up, but not this way. Not to more fighting.

"What was the skirmish about earlier?

"The usual."

"Babe," Roger's tone shifts to encouraging his wife. "You know you need to tell her."

"I'm not ready."

"Emmarie is smart. She knows something's up. She'll keep baiting you and you'll keep playing into her hand. You have to tell her."

"What are we going to do about the Escalade?"

"Nothing. It's totaled," Roger declares. "I've already called our insurance."

"Roger! Emmarie disrespected us."

A tapping at the hospital door interrupts them. "Excuse me. Mr. and Mrs. Kelso? I'm Deputy Dashiell Cooper with Enforcement. May I have a word with you?"

"Police?" Without waiting for him to confirm, Mr. Kelso stands and steps back, making room for his wife to join them.

"Sheriff's Department. Let's step into the hallway if you wouldn't mind," Cooper says.

With a glance toward Emmarie to see if she is awake yet, Janet turns back to the officer. "Of course." She begins to perspire, a Pavlovian response triggered by the mere sight of law enforcement. She retains this vestige from her wilder youth, but it's as relevant now as a dewclaw on a dog.

Dabbing her brow with the sleeve of her blouse, she steps around the end of the bed, past her husband and into the hallway.

"I'm investigating your daughter's accident. I was one of the officers on scene."

"Good," Roger says. "Can you tell us anything?"

"How is your daughter? She looked pretty beat up."

"She has a concussion, broken bones and she hasn't woken up yet," Dr. Kelso offers. "But the doctors expect her to mend."

Officer Cooper smiles and lets out a brief sigh. "Emmarie's young and—" He cuts himself off, settling for a simpler, more professional comment. "I'm relieved to hear that." He pauses to signal switching gears. "Officially, it appears neither alcohol nor excessive speed is a factor on your daughter's part. However, her vehicle shows no sign of braking."

The deputy speaks with a slow and even pace. He's learned to do that to give families a chance to absorb what he tells them, something he's practiced during his three years working accident scenes and processing innumerable smashed bodies and broken lives. "It's a violation of Oregon law to go through a yellow light if a driver can stop. She may have been texting."

Dr. Kelso watches Cooper's face for clues as he speaks but finds none, so she looks at her husband for support. "Texting?"

"She may be cited. The vehicle that hit her—"

"Hit her? So, this isn't Emmarie's fault—"

"Ma'am—"

"Doctor," she corrects.

"Yes, Ma'am." He tries again. "We're still investigating. I mainly came to see how Emmarie is, and to let you know—" He doesn't have a good way to say this, so he clears his throat and proceeds: "The driver of the other vehicle, a Mr. Runyan Park. He didn't survive."

"Oh. God," her father gasps.

"But he's at fault, right? You said he hit her," Janet presses.

"He had a red light, which he ran. So technically, yes. But it's rarely that simple. The DA may get involved."

He doesn't say the words 'vehicular homicide.' He doesn't have to. Emmarie's mother pales at the thought. A beat or two later, blood reenters her cheeks, and she flushes with anger. "Roger, I told you she had no business driving to Jack's house in the Escalade. Now, there are consequences. A man's dead!"

"Take it easy, Mrs.—er, Dr. Kelso. Let's not get ahead of ourselves. We are a long way from determining that Emmarie is liable for Mr. Park's death." A law enforcement officer on any beat must be good at de-escalation, even at redirection. "Let's just be thankful your daughter survived with all her limbs intact. It's my opinion, if she had been in a lesser vehicle, she likely would have died too."

Janet blinks away tears at the thought. "All the same, when she wakes up, I'm going to kill her."

CHAPTER 5

Roses *and* Lisianthus

Emmarie's mother returns from the nurses' station carrying fresh flowers. "Honey, look! Aren't these pretty?" She picks up Jack's bouquet and moves it to the stand away from the bed. Then she sets the new vase directly in front of Emmarie on the over-bed table. "Oh, there's a card. Let's see who they're from, shall we?" Without waiting for permission, she slides her expertly manicured acrylic nail under the flap and pops it open.

Emmarie sighs. She resigns herself to being treated like she's ten and to her mother's bustling about with small talk to avoid real subjects. There's a dangerous rhino in the room that Emmarie wishes to avoid too; except she wonders if it might not be better to address the inevitable. *She's waiting to yell at me when the nurses can't overhear. There's no way she's letting this go.*

"Beautiful," Emmarie offers weakly. The bouquet truly is lovely, she thinks, brimming with aromatic red roses, accenting white lisianthus with pink tips, and the requisite gypsophila, more commonly known as baby's breath.

"Well, I think they are exquisite. Few people know this, but lisianthus flowers symbolize the joining of two people in a life-long bond," Janet explains as she rearranges a stray stalk. "Who do you think sent them?"

News from KATU blares from the wall TV in the corner of the room, demanding attention. "The nude body of a woman was found by a couple walking their dogs in the Southwest Hills near the Marquam Nature Park. Police say the body is believed to be 19-year-old Annette Martin, a PSU student who went missing a week ago. Investigators say the woman's throat was slit and that crime has similarities to a body that was found three weeks ago in the Miles Crossing area, outside Astoria. They stopped short of saying the two crimes are connected. As of yet, there are no suspects."

Janet looks over her shoulder toward the television, picks up the remote and clicks off the news before turning her focus back to the flowers and the card.

"Hey, Mom, I'm watching that." Her petulant response yields no reprieve from her mother.

"You don't need all that negativity. Hmmm, that's odd," Janet says. "The note just says, 'Here's to a speedy recovery, Emmarie.' Honey, who is this admirer?"

"How would I know?" she snaps. She can blame the pain for making her short-tempered and get away with it for a while at least.

"Well, everyone I know would *sign* the card."

"You got me, Mom. My friends wouldn't spend a couple hundred on an arrangement." Emmarie keeps poking, a little like one might poke a tongue into the crevasse of a broken tooth. You wince at the pain, yet your tongue finds its way into it over and over. Gently teasing, exploring, prodding beyond the boundaries where she knows she should stop. "And the card does not say 'admirer'," Emmarie corrects.

"You love roses. Portland is the City of Roses, you know."

Growing up on the outskirts of Oregon's largest city, of course, she knows. She rolls her eyes.

Her mother's attempt at small talk dwindles to nothing. But soon she tries again. "Honey, the doctor told me this morning that you'll be home by the end of the week if you continue to make such good progress. Wouldn't that be nice? To be home before your birthday? To sleep in your own bed?"

"I guess." What she really wants is 1) her mother's saccharine to dissolve already and 2) to scratch the itch developing under the cast on her right leg.

"Your brother was going to fly out when he heard about your accident. But we told him he didn't need to abandon his studies. You're going to be fine. Just fine," she declares more sternly the second time as if commanding it to be so. "But now that you're coming home, perhaps he can clear it with his professors to steal away for a few days. You'd like that, wouldn't you?"

Emmarie smiles with genuine affection at the thought. Danny always makes her smile, even when he resorts to holding her down and tickling her like she's still six and he, nine. Despite acting as if she resents him by dragging his name into fights with her parents, she adores her big brother. God, she misses him. Favored child or not, he is the cartilage keeping the family's friction at bay.

She imagines him acing his classes and kicking himself that he wasn't there to protect her. If he had been home, who knows? Maybe she wouldn't have fought with her mother. Maybe she wouldn't have tried to see Jack. Maybe she wouldn't be in the hospital, sewn up like Frankenstein's monster.

"You don't think those flowers are from Danny, do you?" Emmarie asks. No, she decides against this when she thinks about it again. Danny would attempt to be witty, saying something like 'Hey, dummy! Find other ways to get attention.' And he would sign the note simply 'Love, Danny.'

Who else could have sent them? She muses and quickly runs out of possibilities. Jack and Marta both brought flowers with them when they visited. Her parents did as well, of course. Aunt Julia, and even her mother's publisher, sent a plant. Sophia and her other girlfriends wouldn't bother. They opted for Teddy bears and other cuddly tokens of affection.

She thinks about calling the name of the local florist on the card to inquire. But she doubts they could tell her anything when she sees the bouquet came through 1-800-Flowers. So, unless he chooses to reveal himself, her benefactor remains a mystery.

Emmarie approaches healing with the same energy she tackles everything. As predicted, the doctor's concerns about spleen damage and the lingering results of a concussion both come to naught.

The days pass slowly, full of tedium. She complains that she has nothing interesting to do in the hospital between visits of friends and family. All she does is sleep, watch a little boring TV, and dwell on her situation, plotting her escape to Juilliard. She enjoys visits because they break the monotony.

But everyone eventually leaves so she can rest. Rest isn't something she wants. She wants to move without restrictions, to move without the sling that forces her to do everything left-handed, and to move without the cast and crutches that make her hobble. She wants a life without restrictions. She wanted that before, and she especially wants that now. Every chance she gets she is out of bed and doing something. *Anything.*

Emmarie holds a mirror up to inspect a line of black sutures on her forehead at her hairline. In the ten days since her accident, most of Emmarie's bruises fade from ugly bluish-purple to an even uglier mottled, greenish yellow with purple highlights. Her emotional bruises take longer. The suture line is still sore to the touch, but she eagerly anticipates the removal of each stitch as the final assault to her flesh. The PA should arrive any minute to remove them.

She returns the mirror to the table and resumes packing 'get well' cards and gifts into a crate her mother brought before hustling off to some appointment of her own. When that's over, she says she'll be back to take Emmarie home. If her parents didn't have great insurance and deep pockets, the girl suspects she would have been discharged already; her room given to a more needy patient.

Her mother parks the Mercedes in the circle driveway instead of the ample garage. Then she hurries ahead of her daughter to open the massive front door. Emmarie negotiates the steps with aplomb, despite her crutches and shoulder sling.

As the door swings open, the first person Emmarie sees is her brother, home from Harvard. "Danny! No one told me you were actually coming!"

"Can't I surprise my little sister?" He moves to carefully hug her before she even gets inside. He stands holding her, and says: "Speaking of surprises, I'm sorry I missed it this year…but I've already entered us into the Run like Hell 5 K next October. Figured you wouldn't want to do the 10K, given your gimpy-ness. We'll wear the pizza costumes from last year, just to keep things simple," he teases.

"You know we won't win the prize for best costume with those cheesy things! And we sure aren't winning the race, not with you looking all soft around the middle." Emmarie frees her left hand from her crutches to poke his stomach. "Too much late-night studying with Sara Lee, huh?"

They laugh and give each other additional squeezes. When he releases her, Emmarie draws back from his embrace to take a good look at her big brother. He's lost all traces of the little boy Emmarie remembers growing up. In truth, Danny looks terrific, well-muscled, and only a little heavier.

"Harvard is treating you well."

"Can't complain. Here, let me help you get settled." Danny's protective arm around her waist makes her crutches obsolete. He helps her into the family room and onto a recliner.

"I'll get your stuff and take it up to your room. Then I'll come back, and you can fill me in." He kisses her cheek then smiles at his mother, who watches them from the kitchen.

"What do you want for dinner, Emmarie?" her mother calls out. "I'm not sure I have everything for manicotti unless I send your brother to the store…"

Manicotti and garlic bread would be delicious, especially after hospital food and Jell-O, she thinks. "No, it's okay, Mom. What about taco salad?" She won't be able to dictate the menu very long, so she might as well take advantage while she can.

43

She usually receives the royal treatment only on her birthday, now only two days away. Maybe she can parlay this doting session until then. *Probably not.* Next, she thinks: "*Where is my real mother, and why isn't she ragging on me about the Caddy?*"

Her smartphone rings. It's in pristine condition again because her dad had the screen fixed during the first part of her hospital stay when all she did was sleep.

"Great timing. I just got home." She loves that about smartphones. Unlike the regular house phone — *seriously, why did they still have one?* — She can dispense with the formalities of 'hello' or 'Emmarie speaking' because she always knows who's calling. And they always know it's her when she picks up.

Jack's familiar voice in her ear says, "Hey babe. How'ya doin'? Should I come over?"

"Danny's home for a few days, so no, not a great time. He flies back to the East Coast Tuesday. Tuesday after your last class would be better. Mom says she's arranged for all my work and books to be sent here. But I want to see my friends at school. I am going absolutely stir crazy!"

She isn't used to dismissing Jack so quickly, but she doesn't want to miss a minute with her brother either. "You understand, don't you?"

"Sure. I'll call tomorrow though, if that's okay." He sounds a little dejected but maybe it's only her imagination.

"I'd be mad if you didn't," she says.

Later, over huge bowls of the requested taco salad, Janet prattles on about how nice it is to have the family together. Roger asks Danny a lot of questions about school. He also seems to be watching his wife closely, setting up lead-ins to topics she never tackles.

None of it matters to Emmarie. She agrees with her mom for the first time in, oh, *forever,* that it is wonderful to have Danny home, even if just for a few days.

Her phone buzzes again.

"Emmarie, no phones at the dinner table. You know that." It's her dad, not her mom, laying down the law this time.

"Sorry, I guess all my friends just want to wish me well now that I'm home. I'll get rid of them." She picks up her iPhone but doesn't recognize the number. "Hello?" She pauses. "Hello? If you're there, speak up." She pauses again before declaring. "Sorry I can't hear you. I'm hanging up now."

"Who was that, honey?" her mother asks.

"Don't know. I think I could hear someone breathing so it isn't like they accidentally butt-dialed me, or cheek-muted themselves. It's probably just a wrong number."

"That happened to you a couple of times in the hospital, too, didn't it?" Her mother asks. "Was it the same number?"

"How would I remember?" *Who knows? Who cares?* "It's nothing," She dismisses it quickly and tries to get the attention back on Danny where it belongs. "Are you planning on going to Harvard next year too? I only ask because I hear local

45

colleges are all the rage now." She shoots a glance toward her mother who deflects it like a true professional.

"Ah, sure am," Danny answers, caught off guard a bit. "But don't worry, little sis. I'm coming home for your graduation, and I'll be here for you to pester me all summer."

After dinner, Roger excuses himself and Janet gives Emmarie a pass on helping with the dishes. "You need to stay off your leg as much as possible. Just go sit down and visit with Danny while you can. Your dad and I will get these."

This is one time her mother tells her to do something that she doesn't bristle and push back. She could get used to it. "I think I'll take you up on that, if you're sure. Dad doesn't mind, does he?"

"No, he doesn't mind," Roger says as he sneaks up behind her. He kisses her on the cheek and dismisses her. Danny helps her maneuver to a recliner again.

When Emmarie and Danny are safely away in the family room, Roger scolds his wife. "Janet, I don't understand. Our children are together, just like you wanted. Yet you still didn't tell them. I gave you every opportunity."

"Shush. They can probably still hear you."

Emmarie's ears perk up, interrupting her focus on Danny when her brain registers what her mother said. She wishes she'd started listening sooner.

Janet picks up some dishes and carries them into the kitchen. Roger does likewise but refuses to stop pressing. "This weekend. Promise me."

CHAPTER 6

Violated Boundaries

Winter passes, and March comes in like a lion and goes out like a kitten, which is a bit unusual for coastal Oregon. With April's slightly warmer weather around the corner, trilliums dot forest floors and wildflowers like Oregon Beach daisies, Ceanothus 'Blue Jeans' and bear-grass begin to spring up in the fields and hills around Clatsop City.

Along with the last evidence of winter, Emmarie sheds the cast on her right leg in favor of a brace. If it weren't for that brace, she'd brave the brisk breeze for a walk with Jack. But no need to rush things, she thinks. She expects Dr. Bajwa will remove her brace tomorrow.

Instead of walking, she and Jack sit in his old blue Dodge pickup looking over the mudflats at low tide. It smells earthy, salty, fishy. She loves it.

Living on the Oregon coast means awesome scenery even if temperatures never warm enough for her liking, especially with the wind-chill factor most of the year. Still, on a beautiful spring day like today, she can't resist being optimistic, taking stock of her life and options at this point.

"We graduate in a month. Can you believe it?" she asks Jack.

"I'll be glad to be done with school."

School. Her mother hasn't budged an inch yet on Juilliard this year. Nor has she explained herself to her daughter's satisfaction. *Infuriating.* But the end of school also means Danny will be home soon. He represents her last opportunity.

"Emmarie, I've been thinking about us." Jack's voice interrupts her ever-present thoughts of Julliard. He leans over to kiss her, and she kisses him back passionately, even if her thoughts are not in the moment yet. The longer they neck, the more relaxed and into him she feels.

He reaches behind her, underneath her warm turtleneck sweater, and deftly unclasps her bra with one hand. All without coming up for air.

She continues tongue-play while he moves his left hand to cup her breast. He gently squeezes her nipple between his thumb and index finger, and she squeals somewhere between pain and pleasure. He lifts her bra and top, exposing her completely. Instantly her nipples contract into sharp points.

He draws back from her lips to move his mouth to her right breast, which he still holds. She knows she smells of her

48

favorite perfume, which Jack gave her for Christmas. Emmarie tilts her head back and moans softly. She feels her body relaxing, wanting, in all the right places.

He doesn't stop there. He suck-tugs her nipple, then brings his mouth back up to hers hard. She returns the kiss, deep, slow, and long.

Jack thumbs open the button of her jeans and guides the zipper down exposing lacy, bright pink panties. He grins and kisses her midriff. He tugs at her jeans to move them past her hips. "Lift a bit" he urges.

"Jack—I, I don't know…" She protests as his mouth returns to give her no quarter. She feels her heart racing along with her butterflies. "Stop. We talked about this. We agreed we'd wait," she manages to say as his mouth fights hers for domination.

Jack withdraws back into his own space for a moment. "I know how you feel about sex before marriage. But hey, we're practically married. We could be soon, anyway." He punctuates his ersatz proposal with a shorter peck to her lips. It is now Jack's turn to protest. "We've been together for over two years now, Emmarie. I'm the laughingstock of the football team. And the track team. We're ready for the next level." He leans in and starts kissing her again. Between beats, he urges her with "I promise, it's safe."

"Well, that's just it. I'm not sure I'm ready." The mood fades slightly, but he succeeds in getting Emmarie to think about how much she loathes restrictions of any kind, even those she gives herself. In his arms, she can shut her mother out. Even punish her. *So maybe just this once...* She lets him start kissing her again—her breasts, her mouth, her neck. He starts nibbling on her earlobes. It gives her gooseflesh, and she feels resolve melting away.

Then come the words Emmarie expects to hear at some point. They anger her anyway.

"I'm not upset your parents won't let you go away to college."

"Geez, Jack. Get off me!" She pushes him away with all her might. "You of all people should support me." She lies. While she believes he'd do anything for her, she knows he isn't thrilled with the prospect of her going away for months at a time. "What the hell am I supposed to do? Rot here in a backwater town with no opportunity?"

"You could go on one of them singing talent shows. Come on, stay here. We can make it work." Jack slips his left hand over to her knee again and tries to pick up where he left off.

She pushes his hand away. Tears well up in her eyes.

"Why doesn't anyone support me? I'm done here. Take me home. Now!"

Jack sets his jaw, sighs, then faces the steering wheel. He turns the key, revs the engine a few times, and peels back out on the main road. He gives a protracted look toward Emmarie then tops it off with a shake of his head.

She doesn't need anything spelled out. She can play the silent game too.

She leans back to zip up her jeans then forward to hook her bra. She steams: *It takes me both hands to secure what I wear daily, but you, Jack, can unhinge it, and me, in a few seconds flat using only one hand. Life isn't fair.*

After she straightens her clothes and buckles her seat belt, she leans forward to turn on the radio.

"…Another woman has gone missing, this time from Seaside on the Oregon Coast. Police aren't saying if they suspect the so-called Coastal Cutthroat Killer or not. They do report that the Cutthroat Killer is wanted in connection with the bodies of four young women found since September on both sides of the Coastal Range, and the disappearance of another five young women who have not yet been found. In other news…" She reaches forward again and punches an FM button. She isn't in the mood for news. When she's sure she has a station playing her music, she stares out the truck's window, mentally counting landmarks until she reaches home.

"Hey, Mom! I'm going out for a bike ride, okay?" Emmarie hasn't lost her 'post-broken leg' exuberance, even though she'd shed the brace as the last vestige of her accident more than a week earlier. Sure, her bones still ache in the morning and ache if she pushes herself too hard, but Emmarie is delighted to have her life back.

The sun shines, warming the air to a decent 70 degrees. *Life is good.*

The DA's office decided not to cite her in the death of Runyan Park after all. Jack's been especially apologetic for pressuring her to have sex. He'll wait for her as long as she wants, he promises. Again.

Plus, Danny will be home in time to see her march to Pomp and Circumstance with the rest of her graduating class. They'll have all summer together to charm their parents into changing their minds before school next Fall.

She refills her sports bottle with water and a few ice chunks and straps her helmet on. Then she puts her phone on silent and stuffs it into her back pocket. She figures she will ignore the vibrations that signal incoming calls or texts. After all, what's the point of 'getting away from it all' if you allow 'it all' to infringe on your ride?

When she's ready, she opens the garage door and takes her Bianchi Infinito CV Disc bike down from the hook in the ceiling. She inserts the water bottle into its holder on the frame.

"Okay, honey." Her mother says, now standing in the doorway watching her. "But don't ride too far. Turn around before you get exhausted. The doctor says you aren't 100% yet so take—"

"I know, Mom. But I feel good. Stop worrying so much. I promise to rest when I need to."

The air smells fresh with the faint ocean scents Emmarie loves so much. She takes the official Oregon Coast Bike Route, also known as Highway 101, over to Ensign Lane that runs along the northern perimeter of Lewis and Clark State Park. She hasn't been out this way by herself for probably two years. Usually, she takes one of the trails around the flatlands and dunes closer to home.

Her body quickly becomes one with her bike again, as though no time has passed. She loves how a good ride clears cobwebs from her brain. It feels amazing to be out by herself! No one hovering over her. No demands other than those she places upon herself. She will ride until she feels like stopping, despite what she told her mother. Right now, she wants to ride all day. She gives her body notice that it is young, fit, capable, and it will act like it. In a word, life is beginning anew.

The lower 70's might be too cool for some outdoor activities, but the unusually warm ocean weather feels perfect as she pedals a good work out. Biking along, she leaves most remnants of civilization behind her, at least in her mind. Sometimes she listens to seagulls and other birds squawk and chirp their way above her head and dogs barking in the distance. Other times she occupies herself by singing. The farther she rides away from Hwy 101, the fewer and fewer cars she meets and even fewer joggers. Just to her liking.

Except a car full of jerks about her age speeds up behind her, honking like hell and shouting unintelligible curse words out the window as they pass. "Jackasses," she mumbles under her breath. What really bothers her is that she did not even know they were there until they started honking.

The fresh air and stunning scenery bid Emmarie to continue her trek. Nevertheless, after riding a while, she thinks it wise to head home. After all, if she starts home now, she can be there well before it turns too brisk. She looks for a good place to turn around easily. A crossroad appears ahead so she stops pedaling and squeezes her handbrakes to slow forward momentum. With one hand, she removes her phone to message her mom not to worry.

In those few moments of distraction, a van comes up behind her and taps her bike, causing her to plow directly into the gravel and weeds lining the ditch. Emmarie curses her fall and the guy that causes it.

She evaluates the damage while a man appears from the driver's side. "I am so sorry! Here, let me help you up." Without waiting for permission, he reaches down with both hands and pulls her toward him.

"Hey, man, watch where you're going! You don't own the road!"

Emmarie is in the middle of scolding him for his carelessness when she feels a sting on her leg. *It's a little early for a honeybee sting.* Then she sees the needle he stabbed through her bike capris into her thigh. "What the hell? Why did you do th…" she manages to say before she feels her body crumple into his arms.

CHAPTER 7

Living in a New World

⌒

"Roger, come home. I'm worried about Emmarie." Janet's voice even on the phone has more of an edge than it usually has. She tries but can't access her professional, 'Let's-all-be-calm-about-this' psychologist voice. "She left for a bike ride after lunch and she's not back yet. She promised she wouldn't go far. Do you think I should call the sheriff?" Her hands tremble.

"The sheriff? For what?" Roger tries to keep things simple and on point. "She is on her bike, so you know she didn't take a lot of stuff with her. That means she hasn't run away. She probably met up with some friends and lost all track of time. You tried calling her?"

"Of course."

"Maybe her battery is dead."

"Is that supposed to make me feel better? I called Sophia and her other friends too. No one has talked to her all afternoon."

"Did you call the hospital?"

"She's not there. Oh my god, Roger, where can she be?"

"If her battery died and she got a flat tire, that would delay her. There's probably nothing to worry about. But I'll finish up here then drive around some places she may have gone. I'll find her."

"I'm going to call the sheriff anyway. I don't know what else to do."

Doing something constructive in this situation makes her feel better, but she's a ball of nerves not knowing how she should otherwise occupy herself. She neither sits nor stands for more than a minute before an uncontrollable urge comes over her to try something else. She can't focus enough to write.

She imagines her husband has left his office at the community college by now and is driving around looking for their only daughter as promised. She's grateful that he keeps her informed of his progress, or lack thereof, by regular phone calls. Still, when she sees him come through their front door without her baby, she bursts into tears.

"The sheriff says they'll keep an eye out for her, but technically, she isn't a missing person yet," she manages to say once she quells her tears enough.

"All right, let's go over this again." Roger ushers his wife to a couch and sits down. "Were you two fighting?"

"No. It isn't like that. We had a good day. I'm telling you something's wrong." Janet considers her words before speaking again: "Perhaps you should call the sheriff too. Get the department to understand Emmarie wouldn't disappear. She's more responsible than that. Get them to take action."

The home phone rings, and Janet jumps to answer. "That's her!"

"Dr. Kelso? This is Corporal Craig down at the Sheriff's Department. We want to make sure you're home because I'm sending a couple of deputies over to your house."

"D-Did you find her? Emmarie's okay?"

"I can't tell you that, ma'am." He states everything matter-of-factly, as though he does this a hundred times a year. "The officers will explain when they arrive."

Janet and Roger cry together while they wait for the deputies. Then they blow their noses and wipe their eyes with tissues to compose themselves for public scrutiny. Fifteen minutes later, the doorbell rings. Janet takes three deep breaths and lets each out slowly to ground herself.

When she opens the door, she finds two plainclothes deputies standing solemnly before her. One, Carol Carlisle, she knows casually as the cousin of a former neighbor. They occasionally played cards together at Barbara Maxwell's house, that is before the Maxwells retired and moved to Phoenix to be nearer to the grandchildren.

"Good evening, Janet." Carol offers, extending her hand.

"Come in, please."

Once in, the burly, balding black man with Carlisle shakes hands with both Roger and Janet. "Hello. I'm Lieutenant Walter Bellows. I'm the lead detective with the Sheriff's Department looking into your daughter's situation. May we sit down?"

"Where are my manners? Please—" She ushers them into a grand formal living room, decorated in a 'Bohemian meets Coastal Chic' style that melds to reflect Janet's cosmopolitan tastes for both elegance and comfort. "May I get you coffee or something?"

"No, Janet, we're fine," Carlisle says. "Let's get started if you don't mind. Lieutenant Bellows has some questions to ask to help us determine what happened to Emmarie." She sits on the edge of a Tommy Bahama tuxedo arm sofa. Lieutenant Bellows selects a leather recliner, while Janet sits straight-backed, alert in a Goldoni wingback chair.

Bellows lets his ample body sink fully into the cushions. He leans back as though he plans to be there a while. *He likes being in charge*, Janet thinks. *I don't care if he finds my baby.*

He methodically takes out a notepad and pen and takes a moment before he addresses the Doctor and Mr. Kelso. "Look, I know you're worried about your daughter. Understandable. But let's not jump to conclusions. Walk me through what happened."

Janet starts. "Emmarie went out for a bike ride about 1:30. She promised she wouldn't over-exert herself and that she'd come right back. After a couple of hours, I started getting nervous. I called her friends, but they hadn't talked with her. I-I called Roger. He left work to look for her." She glances nervously to Roger.

"Over-exert herself?" Bellows asks.

Janet turns her attention back to the detectives. "Yes. She was in a car accident last fall. Broke her leg quite badly. The doctor said it could take up to a year to fully heal. She only just got the brace off. About two weeks ago, right Roger?" She looks to him again for confirmation.

He nods.

"Where was she headed when she left here?" Carlisle asks.

Janet shrugs her shoulders and shakes her head. "I was in my office writing. We only exchanged a few words. If only—"

"We found her bike," the detective cuts in. "Off Fort Clatsop Road. Can you tell me what she was doing out there? Any friends in the area?"

"I called her friends, those I know about anyway."

"Those you know about?" Bellows repeats. "Does your daughter keep secrets? What would you say your relationship with her is like?"

"No good." Janet flusters. "I mean no, she doesn't keep secrets. And we have a good relationship. Normal mother-daughter stuff."

"Babe, you have been fighting with Emmarie a lot. At least lately," Roger says.

"But that's nothing. Really."

"Nothing? Now is not the time to be less than forthright," her husband urges. "These detectives need to know everything, even if you and I don't think it relates. It might."

Janet's eyes implore Roger to stop, but he doesn't.

"Damn it, Janet!" Roger raises his voice. "You're the one keeping secrets. You refuse to tell Danny and Emmarie that your adrenocortical cancer has come back." Janet winces, so he continues, more gently this time. "Emmarie is upset because she knows you're keeping something from her. She thinks you are unreasonable for not letting her go to Juilliard next Fall."

"She needs to stay closer to home because the future is so…undetermined," Janet explains.

"I know. But babe, the problem is *she* doesn't know."

"Excuse me," Detective Bellows interjects. "To be clear: Danny is your son? Where is he now?"

"He attends Harvard," Roger says.

"Okay. So, Dr. Kelso, you have some sort of cancer and neither child knows about it. Is this why you've been fighting with Emmarie?"

"I guess so. But I wouldn't call it fighting exactly. Emmarie is obdurate about Juilliard. She just knows how to press my buttons."

Carlisle speaks up. "Listen, Janet, we understand. No one is saying that you, of all people, are a bad parent. I mean, my god, your books have helped me navigate some rough times with my kids."

"That's right, Dr. Kelso. We are just trying to get the whole picture." Bellows clears his throat before continuing. "I'll take that water now if it wouldn't be any trouble."

Roger jumps up. "Let me get that for you." He leaves and comes back shortly with a tray carrying a pitcher of ice water and glasses for everyone. He sets it on the low coffee table before them and pours Bellows a drink. Janet dabs a tissue to her eyes.

Bellows takes a long swig before continuing. "Thank you. Do you know of anyone who wants to harm Emmarie? Do either of you have any enemies?"

"No, of course not," Janet says. Roger echoes her sentiments.

"Well, as I mentioned, we found Emmarie's bicycle. Ah, her phone too. Both in the ditch. That's not something we'd expect to see if she were off with friends or has run away."

Bellows clears his throat and continues, "We must assume foul play, but just what, we're not sure. Frankly, I've heard nothing tonight that changes my opinion. Given your family's wealth and high profile in the community, I think your daughter may have been kidnapped."

Stunned, Janet and Roger shake their heads as if their denial changes anything.

"I'm calling the FBI to get ahead of this thing."

Sergeant Carlisle asks, "Is there a room where they can set up? It requires tapping the phone, more questions, and more waiting, I'm afraid."

Janet blankly nods at Carol Carlisle then says, "I don't understand. If you think she's been kidnapped for ransom, then that implies they knew who she is when they took her. Do you think someone has been following her?"

"We live in a new world, Dr. Kelso," Detective Bellows says. The same technology that makes our jobs easier also makes it easier for creeps. For example, you may have used the 'track my phone' feature on your smartphone." He takes a quick sip of water. "Well, some enterprising company created a program called MSpy. If Emmarie has an iPhone, all a creep needs to do is hack in to get her Apple ID. With that, he can physically track her through her phone as long as it's turned on."

He looks to Robert and asks, "Does she have an iPhone?"

"Of course, but surely, we'd know if she's been hacked," Roger says, his statement more of a question than not.

"Wish that were true, but it isn't. Right now, it's too early to know anything for certain."

CHAPTER 8

Wake Up and Smell the Coffee

The FBI sets up in Roger's downstairs study in a matter of hours. By morning, they are ready to trace and record any phone call as it comes in. One technology for the house landline, and another if the demand comes to either parent's smartphone number. Every word and every sound will be recorded, sliced, and diced, and analyzed to ferret out clues.

They also use EnCase forensic software to examine Emmarie's laptop, tap the cloud, read her emails. They search her browser history, gathering data and looking for clues to who might have been in contact with her under the radar. They find nothing unexpected.

Detectives Bellows and Carlisle stay on, continuing to dig to see if they can learn anything that will break the case open. If this is a kidnapping, the ransom demand will no doubt be coming soon, Bellows tells them. When the Kelso family hears from whoever has Emmarie, he reminds them not to let on about FBI involvement.

The Kelsoes finally went to bed at Carlisle's urging, but neither sleeps much. Exhausted or not, Janet feels she must be there for Emmarie, in case they hear anything. By 6 a.m., she is up making coffee and breakfast for everyone. "I want to," she tells the officers. "Keeping busy keeps my mind off things."

"Janet?" She looks up to see Carol Carlisle standing in the kitchen archway.

"Yes? Is there news?"

"They want a good, recent photo of Emmarie, one suitable for distributing to law enforcement agencies," says Carlisle.

"Would her graduation picture do? I have it right here," Janet says, pushing past Carol and into her writing office. "I keep this on my credenza. I love how the color of her shirt and her hair frames her eyes in this one."

"Perfect, it will do nicely. Are you sure we can take it?"

"Carol, do what you need to do. But you bring my little girl back, safe and sound."

"These things, Janet," Carol hesitates. "They don't always go the way we want them to. But I promise you, we'll do everything in our power to find her. Know that, okay? I can't

64

imagine being in your shoes, I mean, if this were Charlotte who'd gone missing…"

The sound of a commotion outside interrupts her. Out the window, they see news vans from KATU, KOIN, KGW, and Fox vying for a good broadcast position at the edge of the massive front lawn. Word is out about a possible abduction of the daughter of a nationally renowned author. So, along with cancer and a missing daughter, the doctor feels trapped.

"This could complicate things." Carlisle admits as she notes the carnival atmosphere of initial set up, with horns blaring, production people and reporters greeting one another and ribbing the competition about their last scoop. Carlisle closes the window that had been letting fresh air infiltrate the kitchen. "Best to ignore them for now. Come back into the living room with me, the detectives have other questions for you."

Janet nods consent but lingers a moment longer, staring out the window. *Is this really happening to my family?* Once again, she draws a deep breath and lets it out slowly to ground herself. She reaches for the coffee and refills her cup. With the carafe still in her right hand, she picks up her mug with her left and heads toward the others. *Normalcy and decency, that's how I'll get through this.*

"Ah, there you are, Dr. Kelso," Bellows says as she reenters the room. "And with more coffee too. You'll want to keep it coming." He waits for her to fill his cup to the brim, then takes a small sip in appreciation before setting it down on the coaster before him. He rustles through his notes then asks her again, "Can you think of anyone who would want to hurt your family?"

Janet stares at the floor, taking time to think before shaking her head.

"Okay, let's back up a bit. Was Emmarie acting normal before she went missing, or did she seem nervous about anything?

"As normal as any teenager."

"Can you think of anything unusual happening in the last few weeks? Any strangers in the neighborhood, any odd conversations you had, anything you might have brushed off as insignificant, but now aren't so sure?"

"Not really," she offers, again after taking time to think through the lieutenant's question. "Emmarie received a few calls over the last few months that she didn't recognize. Said no one was there when she answered. One time it happened when we all were around the dinner table, Danny too. He was home for a couple of days when Emmarie was discharged from the hospital.

"She said she thought she could hear someone breathing, but as I said, that was months ago." Janet takes a good sip from her coffee, adds some sugar, and switches the mug to the other hand. "Do think that's connected?"

Carol speaks up. "That's just it. We don't know what's connected and what isn't, Janet. Not yet anyway. But we're pulling her phone records to make sure everything is benign.

If it isn't, we may have a lead. Is there anything else you can think of?"

"She got flowers in the hospital. No one knew who sent them."

"Was there a card?" Bellows asks.

"Yes, but she threw it away. The normal sentiments of 'get well soon' that sort of thing. It wasn't signed."

"And you ruled out her friends?"

"It was an expensive bouquet …"

"We'll check that out too," he said. "Anything else?"

"I, I don't know! I can't think right now."

"It's okay, Janet. You can tell us later if you remember something," Carlisle says.

Mental avoidance is Janet's default way of dealing with her daughter's absence, but she's having trouble focusing. Her mind wanders in surreal fashion to unimportant things like *Carol could pass for a man if she chose not to wear makeup.*

"Right. Let's go over her friends again," Bellows interjects. "I want you to provide us a list of Emmarie's friends and their contact information. While you're at it, include all your friends and acquaintances that you've had any contact with whatsoever in the past six months. You and Roger both. People you work with, dinner engagements, old friends calling from out of the blue. Do you think you can do that for me?"

Carlisle adds some softening words. "Janet, we don't expect one of your friends to be complicit in this, but they may know something. Even if they don't, the people close to you might trigger a new angle that'll help."

"I understand. Roger and I will start on that list for you right away." She stands and excuses herself. She calls to her husband who is talking with another agent. They have work to do.

Two days pass at an excruciatingly slow pace, at least from Janet's perspective. The FBI and law enforcement personnel from Clatsop County canvass neighbors to see if anyone can provide information no matter how insignificant. There are questions to answer, snacks to prepare, and always more coffee to make. Janet is at her wit's end when her physician gives her a sedative to make her sleep.

No ransom call comes.

CHAPTER 9

Stairway to Heaven

⁓

Emmarie wakes disoriented. Did she hit her head when she crashed her bike? All she remembers is this strange, hallucinogenic dream where she is drowning in a river. A friendly white whale saves her, but it morphs into an evil machine that cryogenically freezes her like Han Solo in the Empire Strikes Back, just before swallowing her whole. Strangely conscious, her ears reverberate with Led Zeppelin's Stairway to Heaven…

Your head is humming, and it won't go
In case you don't know
The piper's calling you to join him
Dear lady, can you hear the wind blow

And did you know
Your stairway lies on the whispering wind...

Her first real awareness involves a musty smell coupled with weak urine that invades her nostrils with each breath. The place she now finds herself in is cloaked in darkness, but gradually her eyes adjust. She discovers she is laying on a dirty mattress spread over a metal bed frame. *Is that cardboard or something like it tacked up in a few places around the room?*

Her arms hurt. She tries bringing them down to her sides, but she realizes her wrists are shackled by a chain threading through the rungs of a metal headboard. Panic overwhelms her. Her heart races. It feels like someone sitting on her throat.

Panic clamps down every cell. She's panicked before, like when she was four and got separated from her mother at the mall, and when she darted out into the street to get a ball then heard a car screech its brakes. But not like this. This feels like a black night terror swallowing her whole. Barely able to breathe, she finds herself unable to scream.

She tugs to test her restraints but neither the headboard nor the crudely welded, steel alloy chain yields. She can, however, move one arm down while stretching out the other. This allows her to change positions and ease the pressure on her arms, just not at the same time. She hurts all over, especially her collarbone, but that could be arm pain echoing through her shoulders. If she could maneuver around...

She wills herself to keep her wits about her.

After a quick assessment, she realizes she's missing her athletic shoes, but her shoeless feet are free. She's fully clothed, even if her crotch and bicycle pants are wet. *Damn, I must have peed myself when I was asleep. Well, that's the least of my worries.*

Emmarie uses her feet and shoulders to lift her butt off the bed a few inches at a time, gradually inching herself closer to the head of the bed. She hopes she'll be able to turn herself sideways and sit if only she can get close enough for the chain to allow it. At least then she will be able to lower her arms to her sides to relieve her aching joints. Her bed squeaks with each body shift she makes. Every squeak makes her cringe. She will be heard. She will be found out.

Should she cry out? Would anyone hear her? If they hear her, will they hurt her?

Keep your wits about you, Emmarie. You must summon help. The fear of imprisonment, especially when a possibility of freedom exists, overwhelms any fear of detection. She makes her decision.

"Help! Is there anybody out there?" she yells. After a pause, she yells again. "HELP!!!" she screams as she rattles her chains to break free of the headboard. Solid. *Shit.*

"Someone, help me, PLEASE!" she yells as loudly as she can. She keeps on yelling until she exhausts herself. Tears well up, then freely flow down her flushed cheeks.

"You ever gonna shut up?" a disembodied voice says from somewhere in the darkness. "Nobody hears you."

She jumps as much as the chains allow. "Hello?" Her tentative voice betrays her as she strains to look around. She sees no one.

"Over here." The voice seems to be coming from behind some boxes, on the other side of the room, closer to the stairs.

"Who are you?"

"Best not to talk. If he's here, he's gonna hear you."

"*IF* he's here? Do you mean we may be alone?" Emmarie whispers.

The voice doesn't answer.

"Can't you hear me? My name is Emmarie. What's your name?"

The voice stays quiet for a few minutes then starts humming softly. To her, the voice sounds male, like that of a young teenager. "Are you chained too? Won't you tell me your name?" she pleads.

After a few more stanzas of something that sounds eerily familiar, the voice sings. "The piper's calling you to join him…"

Emmarie stiffens. "That's it! Stairway to Heaven. I thought it was a weird dream, but you heard it too."

"His favorite song," the boy says in hushed tones. "Always plays it. When he's happy or excited about somethun. He calms himself with it."

"How long have you been here? Look, if we put our heads together, we can find a way out."

"No use. You ain't the first to try."

His words startle her. She hasn't let herself dwell on what her captor plans to do or to think about what he's already done. "What do you mean?"

"Are you dumb?" The boy asks. Then he says simply: "He'll get rid of you like the others if you ain't the right one. They never come back."

"Others?" *OH, MY GOD,* her brain screams. Summoning her courage, she wills herself to ask him to tell her about them. "And what do you mean when you said, 'the right one'?"

"I say 'nuff already."

No matter what she says, she cannot get the boy to say anymore so she turns her attention back to her situation. She looks around the room. It is damp, hence the musty smell, and the walls appear to be solid cinderblock except for the cracks in the mortar climbing in stair-step fashion. Chalky white streaks stain the cement floor that slopes ever so gently toward a grate in the middle of the room, presumably marking a floor drain. There are cobwebs and spiders in the corners and around the exposed rafters, but the remainder of the basement appears tidy. No dust, no dirt, no trash. A door is ajar under the cellar steps. Light seeps around the edges of the cardboard. *Those pieces must be covering windows. Good. Because windows open. And if they don't open, they break.*

Emmarie is hungry. But more than food, she aches for an aspirin. For the first time, she notices a small bottle of water and a protein bar on a table near the bed. If she sits up and swings her legs over to the other side, she can reach both. It isn't much, but it's something.

After she eats, she tries again to get the boy to talk.

"Does he beat you?"

"Got no reason."

"What does he call you? Er, I mean, what's your name?"

"Only ever calls me Boy."

"What should I call you?"

He says nothing. In frustration and anger, she yanks at her chains and pulls them against the headboard until the cuffs cut into the fleshy part of her thumbs and the tender wrist area where her veins are close to the surface. All her efforts make no difference in her situation, except now she's exhausted. And bleeding. She stops trying. For now.

With that, he starts humming again. Emmarie prefers answers but finds his tune oddly soothing. It means she isn't alone. She sings the words quietly to herself until she falls asleep again.

She wakes with a start as she hears the bedsprings creak and feels someone sitting down next to her. She opens her eyes and finds herself facing a ham sandwich and a plastic cup of milk. A body shifts its weight, and she instantly recoils. As her wits return, she turns to see an already balding, nondescript man in his mid-thirties dressed in jeans and a t-shirt resting next to her as if passing time on a park bench. The stubble on his face is a few days old. Even at this distance, his breath and body reek.

"Good morning, sleepy-head. How are we today? I see you have not been compliant. You have hurt yourself."

He moves his arm to pat her leg. Instinctively, she shifts away. When he tries again to touch her, she kicks at him. "You do not want to do that. Unless you want to wake up and find those pretty legs of yours shackled too."

"HELP ME, SOMEBODY!" She wrestles with all her might once again at the chain that holds her.

"Hush. No need for that. I am not going to hurt you. Looks like you are doing a good job of that yourself." He inspects her wrists then says, "No worries. Unless those abrasions become infected, you will be fine." He finishes his medical assessment then draws back to look at her from top to bottom. When he returns his gaze to her face, he adds, "Has the boy told you that screaming will not change anything? We are well away from anyone who could hear you. Besides, you will just make yourself hoarse and disturb my sleep. So, stop it." His voice is tender and condescendingly sweet. But she understands he means business.

"Of course, if you would enjoy a gag, I can oblige. I have one in my toy box." He grins. "See? You have options."

She drops her rebel exterior.

"That is better." He pats her leg, this time without her resistance. "I brought you lunch. You want to keep your strength up. Afterward, I will come back and clean you up."

Thoughts race through her mind. *Play the game. Stay alive.* Her eyes follow him as he stands and heads for the steps. He stops behind the boxes and says something to the boy that she can't hear. The boy mumbles something back. Whatever it is, it provokes the man to respond with a fast, backhand slap. "That is enough from you, boy!"

Emmarie wishes she could have heard their total exchange. And she wishes she could reach the boy, who whimpers now, so she can comfort him. She feels helpless -- and is helpless.

The boy stops sniveling. Emmarie turns to her sandwich and takes a bite. She has poor timing.

"Emmee?"

She takes a swig of milk to quickly swallow what she has in her mouth. "Yes? I'm here. Are you okay? Why did he hit you?"

"You was asking stuff before. Whatcha wanna know?"

"Start with your name. How long have you been here?"

"Dunno. Mom died when I was eight. I ain't got nobody 'cept an uncle. I'm Mason."

"Mason, you don't know how long you've been here? Listen to me. We're going to find a way out. Together." She places her sandwich back on the paper plate. "You may not think so, but I bet you know a lot of things that will help us." She tries to reassure him even though she feels no reassurance herself. "Tell me about the others you mentioned. What happened to them?"

He hesitates but slowly shares. "He brings a girl here for a few days. She does somethun stupid. Makes him mad. He gets rid of her. Dunno where."

"What would happen, Mason? What did she do to make him angry?"

"Dunno. He is nice. She stops being nice back, I guess."

Emmarie's imagination fills in missing details. She eats a few more bites of her sandwich, pondering what to do or say next.

"Hey, what did you mean before, when you said he would get rid of me if I'm not the right one?"

Mason keeps silent as before.

Not knowing when the man would be coming back, she opts to finish her lunch while she can. She forces herself to take the last few bites because she isn't hungry.

The boy finally speaks again. "Sorry, Emmee. I dunno more. Bob brings a girl here. Calls her a slut. When I hear that, I know I'm gonna be alone again."

So, his name is Bob. "What do you think Bob will do when he finds the right one, the one he's looking for?"

"Dunno." Then Mason's voice perks up. "She'll stay with us, I guess."

The prospect doesn't please Emmarie one bit. *If being a slut makes me disappear, and being 'the right one' keeps me locked up at the whims of a lunatic, what the hell choice is that? Will I even know what he wants?* She shudders at the thought and cries.

CHAPTER 10

A Piece of the Action

With the office door shut, Cooper stands before a large metal, utilitarian desk at the Clatsop County Sheriff's Department. Its owner, the Walter Bellows he knows, is a no-frills kind of guy, with one exception. He loves his Camacho Corojo cigars.

Cooper waits for Bellows to get off the phone. He knows higher-ups are pressuring the detective to solve the Kelso kidnapping quickly, given Emmarie's famous mother and speculation by some journalists that the Coastal Cutthroat Killer might be involved. Hell, aren't 12 dead or missing young women more than enough pressure?

Bellows wraps up his call and returns the handset to its cradle. "Go ahead," he growls.

"Walt, I'm not asking you to get me reassigned from Enforcement to a criminal investigation of this magnitude."

"Good. Because I won't do it. There's enough frigging nepotism in this organization already."

Bellows has his principles, Cooper knows, even though 'job before family' cost him his first marriage. He's on his second, and possibly frying that one too.

"Does your aunt even know you're talking to me about this?" Bellows growls.

"There's no reason for her to," Cooper answers.

"What if I tell her you're cutting corners to get ahead in your career?"

"You'd have it all wrong. First, no one who matters makes the connection that you're my uncle, since it's by marriage. It's not like we have the same last name. Second, I'm not asking for favors. I'm doing *you* one."

Bellows stiffens. His collar appears to tighten. Cooper continues.

"I was there, Walt. I investigated Emmarie's accident. I debriefed her parents," Cooper says. He looks Bellows straight in the eye as he admits his thoughts out loud. "Walt, my gut tells me this is somehow connected."

The traffic cop isn't giving up. Without waiting for an invitation, he sits in one of the steel chairs facing the desk. If Bellows wants him gone, he'll have to capitulate or throw him out.

"A connection? Hell, I guess anything is possible." The black man picks up his unlit Camacho from the ashtray and chews the end of it, contemplating. "What makes you think so?"

"A feeling. Emmarie was in and out of consciousness after the wreck, but the paramedics I interviewed said she kept talking about someone. Bystanders I interviewed said a guy was milling around, talking to her before we arrived. Then he vanished. Sounds pretty odd to me. Lookie-loos hang around for every last bit of the action. You and I both know it's probably nothing, but we need to check it out. I want to help," Cooper says.

"So, if you aren't asking me to pull strings for you, what are you asking me?" Bellows tilts his large office chair back. It looks to Cooper as if he's already posturing to say 'no' after he makes his pitch.

"Just keep me in the loop with anything you hear. Throw me a few bones. Let me work the case when I'm off duty. Think of me as an extra, part-time gumshoe. I know you need help."

"Sure you can handle it?" The big man doesn't wait for an answer. He launches right in. "Hell, you're in traffic. I know you can handle blood and guts, but accidents are different. Your sense of mankind's goodness isn't challenged when someone drives loaded and plows into a bus, killing innocent children. It sucks. Should never happen, but that's life.

"Murder, on the other hand, represents the worst of us. Yeah, you got your jealous husbands and your girlfriends who dispatch boyfriends 'in self-defense.' But I'm talking about hunting predators who butcher people for thrills, who love slicing slowly into people just to smell their fear, to watch it dance in their eyes. They enjoy seeing life trickle away, knowing they control everything. They savor their kills, thinking of new ways to brutalize their prey, mutilating sex organs, shoving sticks up anuses and vaginas…

"Day in and day out, you got to get inside the heads of these sewer dwellers. Go down whatever road they take you. Their sickness is a darkness that oozes into your own psyche and changes you. Nothing you do will ever feel enough, because you always get there too late to help the stiff. You'll curse yourself because you can't stop the next one either. All you can do is bring these little shits to justice. Given what the victims go through, justice tastes hollow."

Dash stares at Bellows. He acquired his uncle when his father's sister married him ten years ago. Bellows was the one encouraging him to enter the Academy after getting his degree in criminal justice. Now they share the bond of brotherhood. Out of respect, he lets Bellows finish his say without interruption.

"How will you handle it when you're at a body dump, and the stiff turns out to be Miss Kelso? I'm trying to save you some grief, son. You gotta be sure about this. Don't you think I know your talents of observation are wasted in Traffic? But I'm telling you, it's a blessing. You don't want this."

What Dash doesn't want, he thinks, is to consider his uncle's words. Against his selfish interests, he weighs them anyway. He can only imagine what he'd feel if he sees Emmarie's nude body posed by some pervert, with her head almost decapitated by the knife-wielding perp. It sickens and angers him, too. He lets those feelings motivate him even more.

"I need to help," he says again.

"Homicide consumes you. You're going to have to find a way to cope. Me? I drink."

The men lock themselves in a staring match. Cooper knows Bellows is studying him. In return, Cooper plans to stare all day if he must. *He who gives in first shows weakness.*

It's Bellows. "So, you want to help me? Or help Miss Kelso? It's the same thing, but it might feel different to you," he clarifies. "I'm up to my eyeballs in this Coastal Cutthroat Killer case and all those missing women, right along with the regular suicides and murders that need investigating. Jeez, can't anybody die from natural causes anymore? Miss Kelso would be just another number if it weren't for her mother and the increased national attention that she brings our little community."

"Just tell me what you need," Dash says.

Bellows throws two immense files over to him. "Start by reading those." Then he leans forward in his chair and points his cigar at him. "Don't crap out on me. This is your chance to prove yourself. Otherwise, you'll stay in traffic until you rot."

He knows the lieutenant will try to make good the threat, family, or not. If he takes the files, he commits himself to see it through to the end, even if Emmarie magically appears with amnesia in the shallows at Haystack Rock tomorrow. He doesn't hesitate. He plans to stop at nothing to find her. But on the outside, he pauses for his uncle's benefit, to make him think he's considering his sage advice.

The younger man hoists the files from the desk. He thumbs the edge of each, expecting to find Emmarie's name. He doesn't. Both bear headings for CCK. He swallows hard.

"So, it's true? You don't think Emmarie was kidnapped for ransom? You think the Cutthroat Killer has her?"

"You have to follow what the clues tell you. Truth is, we got no ransom demand. This late, I doubt we'll get one. The two cases may or may not be connected. God let's hope not. But we have to work all angles."

Cooper swallows hard. "I'm still in. Give me the Kelso file and I'll read it, too."

CHAPTER 11

Nice is Nice

Bob makes good on his promise and returns later. He makes small talk with them like it's the most natural thing in the world to have two young people chained to beds in your basement. Emmarie wants to keep in Bob's good graces but can't bring herself to talk with Mason and Bob.

To cope, she tries to separate her emotions into neat boxes to keep from feeling overwhelmed. It isn't working. She does not know what she feels beyond repulsion and confusion. She's terrified and angry, of course, but must not show it. What's her next move?

She settles for observing Bob, studying his movements and behaviors as he busies himself moving the boxes out of the way that separate her from Mason and sweeping up. *He's nothing if not tidy,* she thinks. All told though, she appreciates having Mason in her line of sight now. *It makes two-way conversations easier, more natural.* She feels less alone.

When she feels safe enough to take her eyes off her captor, she scans the boy in earnest. Before her, she sees a curly red-haired youth, perhaps her age but she guesses younger, having ears and a nose that he hasn't quite grown into. He is clean, dressed in jeans and a pocket T, just like their captor. He wears slippers, not shoes, and she notices that he's not manacled exactly as she is. He has full use of his arms. Instead, he's secured by a leg iron with considerable chain length, bolted to the cinderblock wall. He is free to move about, to go to the bathroom under the cellar stairs by himself, to try the windows…

"There now, do you not agree this is better?" Bob asks the two. Mason smiles then thanks him.

Play the game. Emmarie nods. She puts her sole attention back on Bob to steel herself against whatever comes next.

"I promised we would get you cleaned up, so sit tight. I will be back with some bandages for those wrists."

As soon as the older man leaves the stark room and reaches the top of the cellar stairs, Mason whispers to her. "See? Bob is nice. You gotta be nice too. Stupid girls don't stay."

Emmarie lets his words repeat in her head. *Stupid girls don't stay. Okay, so don't be stupid. Stay alive.* In a few moments, she finds herself asking Mason what he means by 'nice.'

"Damn, you stupid. Nice is *NICE*. Smile at him. Do what he wants," Mason says.

His simple words evoke the unknown, fueling more terror as if that's possible. How does she navigate that which she doesn't understand? Every cell in her body freezes with thoughts of what Bob wants. He's in control. In contrast, she controls nothing. Nothing but how she responds. Will she be able to control herself when it matters most?

Bob returns in a few minutes carrying a basin of hot water, soap, and a sponge. He has a towel slung over his right shoulder and he brings a tube of antiseptic cream, gauze, tape, and has scissors in his left breast shirt pocket. He smiles awkwardly at her as he sets the water down on the floor beside her bed.

She thinks him of average build. While he has buds for man boobs, his pecs don't stretch his T-shirt as much as his midsection paunch does. *Still, he'll be strong, stronger than I am.*

Emmarie focuses her gaze upon the scissors. *They aren't very big, but if I can get them, I'll stab him in the eye! No, no good. Unless that kills him, he'll kill me. And if it does kill him, then Mason and I die of starvation.*

He sets the bandage supplies down on the floor next to the water basin.

Shit. There's no way I can reach those scissors now.

Her captor reaches into his right front pants pocket and removes a key that he uses to unlock a cuff from one of her wrists. When he undoes the clasp, he snaps the empty band around the bedpost. Emmarie remains chained to the bed by her other arm. He places the key back into his pants pocket.

He leans over her to clean her free wrist of the dried blood with the warm, damp sponge. Emmarie winces in pain. His simple act of bending in, expelling his dead, stinking breath over her, a breath that smells of rancid tuna mingled with ashtray, makes her think she might pass out. He washes her hand and wrist until the wound is completely clean. Then he gently applies the antibiotic cream and wraps her wrist in the gauze to protect it from further irritation from the cuffs. When satisfied with his work, he re-secures her wrist and follows the steps with the other hand.

"See? Your wrists are not so bad. But you must not do that again. Understand?"

Once he restrains her again, he turns his attention to the rest of her.

He places his palms on each of his knees with his fingers extended. "I suppose we should re-introduce ourselves," he says. "My name is Bob. Perhaps you remember me? It is okay if you do not. I do not expect you too. What is important is that you are here now. I am going to take care of you."

Her mind races, jumbling thoughts together. Have they met before? *This pervert seems to think so. How can I use my free arm to my advantage?* Perhaps she can surprise him by overpowering him. Get the key and use it to unlock her other arm. In the end, she thinks better of it. *He'll be expecting it, especially now. He doesn't trust me yet. I don't have the element of surprise. Play the game.*

"Your clothes smell. I think you must have voided on yourself but do not be ashamed. It is totally normal. But you will chafe if we do not take care of that."

Emmarie stiffens. "It's okay, I'm fine," she says. *Fine, except I'm shackled by you with my damn arms stretched over my head.*

"No, no. I know what I am talking about. Besides, bath time can be fun time."

He smiles broadly at her, his upper lip raising to reveal more gums than teeth. One tooth stands out, blackened and dead from the roots. Probably knocked loose during a bare-fisted bar fight, she imagines, and the source of the foul odor that suffocates her with every breath.

"Zippers are so convenient, are they not?" Bob continues to grin. He grasps the top of her bicycling jersey with his left hand to keep it taut and uses his right hand to lower the zipper stalk to the bottom where it disengages. She naturally kicks her legs to try to maneuver away from him. He picks up the scissors again and stands up.

"No!" Emmarie protests. She digs at the old mattress with her feet, trying to gain traction.

After scolding her about moving so much, he places his right knee on the bed, throws the other knee over her and straddles her hips. "Lie still. It would be a shame to accidentally stab you with my scissors," he warns.

Bob starts by cutting through the collar, over to her shoulder, and up the long-sleeve arm of her jersey to her left wrist. "Sorry to ruin such a nice outfit, but you are not going to need it anymore." He does the same on her right arm before placing the scissors on the bed next to his knees. Still straddling her, he raises himself off his hindquarters enough to roll Emmarie gently to one side so he could pull the top out from under her.

"Hmmm. Women and their fancy, lacy bras." He picks up the scissors again and gently taps them on her breastbone above her cleavage. "Are you just like all the others? You tease men by wearing cute, skimpy lingerie then act all surprised and upset when men get excited?"

Emmarie forces herself to simper. "No" she offers. I'm not like other women." She isn't even sure what she is supposed to mean by that, but he seems to like her answer.

"Good. So, no more arguments from you. Do you want to sit up, or do I cut it off?"

"No, don't cut it off! I'll let you unhook me."

He smiles again and returns the scissors to his breast pocket. He gives his pocket a pat as if to provide a little reminder, a little incentive, before he rocks himself off his straddling position over her, allowing her to arch herself up. With the flick of his thumb and index finger, he unclasps her bra. He pushes the straps up her arms, so they rest on her newly wrapped wrists, still looped around the chains that hold her. He keeps smiling in an odd way as he orders her to lie back again.

She is petrified, her body rigid and cold. Goose flesh runs the length of her body, her nipples on high alert. He plucks his scissors out of his pocket again and, just as he did her matching jersey, he begins to cut up each side of her bike capris. When he gets to the top, he cuts through the elastic band around her waist and the bottoms peel off like breakaway pants at a strip club.

Satisfied with himself, he toys with the lace on her underwear. Running his left index finger in loops and twirls over her pubic bone, he says, "It would be a shame to cut those pretty panties."

"Y-you don't have to. I won't fight you." Emmarie tries to keep her voice from revealing the terror she feels.

Bob doesn't smile this time. Darkness forms along his brow. In his perverted game of cat and mouse, has she surrendered too easily? Is she not making this fun enough for him?

What did Mason say? What did he mean? Bob wants a 'nice' girl or one that's nice to him?

Suddenly his mood lifts, and he speaks again. "I will wash them for you. Lift up."

Emmarie wants to squirm but has nowhere to hide. Now stripped of everything, she can only lay there as Bob ogles every inch of her body. A grin reforms on his lips, not too big this time, but totally self-absorbed, aroused like a peeping Tom. He switches gears without a word and picks up the soapy sponge and begins bathing her body lovingly. He takes his time around every curve, studying her as if he is burning a mental image into his mind to last forever. Emmarie responds by sending her mind to a different place, a place where this isn't happening. Let this stranger wash her shell, her outside flesh. He cannot touch the real her.

Satisfied with his job, Bob dabs the moisture left behind on her skin with the towel. Emmarie opens her eyes and catches Mason staring at her too. She wonders if this is the first time the boy has seen a nude female body. But judging by his natural physical reaction, and his hand down his pants, she decides he watches whenever he can.

"Here, take this," Bob says as he drapes the large damp towel over her body. "We do not want you catching cold." He considers her for a moment longer then adds, "I will bring back some clothes and clean sheets for your bed. A blanket too."

"Thank you, Bob." Emmarie manages to say. "I could use the bathroom too."

"Yes, I suppose you could. Okay, I will come back in a bit, and we will do that."

He reenacts the unchaining/re-chaining routine on her arms to remove her bra straps from the fetters that still hold her. He pauses to cup her bra and panties to his face and inhales. Then briskly, he leaves Emmarie clean, yet humiliated. *What did this guy want?*

"You okay, Emmee?" Mason asks.

"He didn't hurt me."

"You did good. I like you. Bob likes you, too."

"Bob didn't try to do anything with me. Is that normal?"

Mason giggles. "You mean like animals?"

"I guess so. I-I assume that's what he wants."

"Silly girl. Bob is nice. He says, 'Look. Do not touch.' He ain't gonna hurt you for no reason. The others were stupid sluts. They make him do bad things."

CHAPTER 12

A *Little* Birdie

Dash Cooper cannot stop thinking about Emmarie, ever since seeing her helpless in the crumpled Escalade. Wherever she is now, she needs his protection.

So, he basically lies to get those files. He promises his uncle he'll work the case on his off-duty time. He doesn't tell him he's taking vacation days and then a leave of absence from the department to find her if he must. And he doesn't tell him that Emmarie is the kind of girl who gets under a man's skin. Being smart, he's sure his uncle already knows that.

He sits up all night drinking coffee, reading case files, and making notes. He tackles Emmarie's file first to learn all he can about her. Then he reads the folders containing the Coastal Cutthroat Killer investigation to date. By the time he finishes, he has drunk a pot of coffee and can't sleep anyway. In a word, he's wired.

He retrieves his phone from the charger and rings Bellows.

"I may have something."

"We do too. Another body. Get yourself out there," the lieutenant growls and promises to have his people text the location.

Cooper takes time to shave and put on a fresh uniform. As the green kid on the block, he figures he should look professional, even if he feels clueless and expects the coroner and the regulars on the CCK case to treat him like the fifth wheel he is.

What if this body is Emmarie? His uncle's warning finds its mark today. Nerves in the pit of his stomach deny him breakfast as they clench and unclench. The thought of food makes him feel like he's ready to toss whatever is left in his stomach of last night's Salisbury steak TV dinner.

When he's ready, he gathers his notes together and double-checks his smartphone to make sure he has the coordinates.

Damn, Saddle Mountain nature area. He knows this terrain outside Seaside. As a kid, his family summered there as often as they could. On his faithful dirt bike, he'd scoured and explored as much of the wilderness area as his legs would take him between breakfast and lunch, and between lunch and dinner.

The compact area features a 2.5-mile hiking trail to the summit through heavily forested areas, breathtaking balds filled with wildflowers, opening to occasional territorial views. Saddle Mountain is where he learned to read maps. Once, his mother packed sandwiches and sodas, and Dash got to play 'ranger' with his dad all day.

Doing something physical like that was a nice change of pace for him, having grown up with academic parents who weaned him on classic literature and the acts of the gods and demi-gods. The freedom and natural rhythm of those summers, his days culminating by falling asleep with his head in his mother's lap, listening to epic poems read around their primitive campfire, instilled more than good memories in him.

It bred a sense of oneness with his surroundings, an appreciation for adventure, a sense of his own capabilities, and a desire—no, need—to be the best at whatever he undertakes. Like anyone else, he figures, he longs to imprint his mark on the world.

Although at 26, he isn't sure CCK is the place to start. As his uncle inferred, it can make him or break him. Hell, that's the problem. None of this is about him. It's about finding Emmarie—and in time to save her. He picks up his pace and hurries to where he knows the others would be waiting.

When he arrives at the base of the mountain, he notes the small dirt parking area filled with official vehicles. He creates a space for his two-year-old burgundy Jeep Wrangler. Out of habit he sets the parking brake and exits. He nods to the deputy standing guard at the shady trail head as he moves around the closed gate. He heads up the path to find the others. Foliage curls green everywhere.

He advances up the trail; his mind abuzz imagining the killer making the same trek. "If you listen," he remembers his uncle telling him years ago, "a crime scene will talk to you." He observes the narrowness of the trail, the changing pitch of the hill, even the dense underbrush or lack thereof.

When he reaches an area of activity. he scans the team for familiar faces. He finds his uncle and strides up as though he belongs. "What have we got?"

The lieutenant doesn't even look up from his notes. He removes the unlit Camacho from his mouth and says, "The body is in the brush over there about four feet off the trail." He gives a faint nod to where others are working. "Hiker found her when he stepped away from his companions to relieve himself. Like before, we've got a nude body of an unidentified young woman, splayed out like the others, face up."

Cooper nods and moves the distance so he can see the body as he listens to the lieutenant finish his report.

Bellows follows him. "Obvious signs of bruising on the wrists. She was restrained before she was split ear to ear. This is intimate. The killer gets up close and personal with his vic, nose to nose, and eye to eye. He doesn't want to kill them; he wants to feel them die." As soon as Bellow finishes, he re-inserts his gnawed cigar between his lips.

The coroner cuts in before Cooper can ask anything else. "Rigor mortis is complete. Judging by decomp and insect activity, the body has been out here no more than 48 hours. Too early to confirm if she was strangled prior to having her throat cut, like the others, but based on petechiae in the whites of her eyes, and classic purple discoloration around her neck, I'd venture to say he used a ligature to strangle her first."

A dozen people move about, doing their slice of assigned work. The coroner's exclusive eye contact tells Cooper that she's speaking to Bellows.

"I'll have more for you after the post-mortem," she says, then quickly adds: "I'm ready to transport as soon as your guys finish their photos and notes."

Bellows acknowledges her by telling his people to wrap it up as soon as they can. He turns back to his nephew. "That rules out a copycat," Bellows says. "We haven't released the manner of death as asphyxiation to the press."

"ID yet?" Cooper says.

"Nope."

"Then by my calculation, that's Desiree Campbell, missing for the last 9 days," Cooper says.

"That so? Did a little birdie tell you that?" Bellows chides. "We've got 11 or 12 young women unaccounted for, including Miss Kelso, who match this guy's M.O., and you've already decided it's Campbell. Not sure how you roll in traffic, but here, facts drive theory." He shoves his Camacho back between his teeth.

Cooper feels his face flush and his stomach tighten. He can see this body isn't Emmarie. He's memorized the face that invades his dreams. But, as the neophyte major crimes investigator here, and an unofficial one at that, he'd told himself to observe the experts who know how to work homicide. *Only ask them questions, providing your questions aren't too dumb.*

Sure, he'd been at the top of his class in criminal justice and again at the police academy. He'd even won awards, but he knows this doesn't garner him respect. Nor should it, he thinks. He's green, wet behind the ears. But no, he doesn't let that stop him. Instead of learning from them, he rushes to plop both feet into knee-high shit by pronouncing that he knows who the vic is. If he's wrong, he'll never live it down.

Besides, his uncle isn't in the mood now to hear why this is Campbell.

He swallows. Yet he doesn't reign in his excitement. He collects his thoughts by talking through them, wondering if he is explaining the obvious. "It wouldn't be easy to dump her here in the daytime. As the weather warms, activity in this area increases. It would be easier to transport her alive and then kill her, rather than haul dead weight this far up the trail and not be seen."

Bellows looks over to the body with its eyes wide open and pupils cloudy. "I don't disagree. Cut a live victim and blood spurts. Here it oozed. So, he strangles her first before slashing her or he kills her elsewhere after he toys with her then brings her here."

The seasoned lieutenant pauses and resurveys the scene. "Even though we think he strangles her first, he'll have blood on him. Harder for him to disappear into a crowd when he leaves. This guy is free to move around. He doesn't leave fingerprints and packs out any rope or tape he packs in. We might get some trace evidence but not much."

Bellows brings his fingers to his face and scratches an irritation on his check before letting his hand move to rub the back of his neck. "I think he has a killing field and ditches his bodies in out-of-the way places unconnected to where he finds his prey or does his handiwork."

Cooper builds on his uncle's thoughts by adding, "Okay, so this guy is strong enough to fireman-carry a dead, 130-pound naked woman at night up an incline. Must have done it at 2 or 3 o'clock in the morning, wearing a headlamp. Or, he has an accomplice. You don't think he leads them out here, violates them, dispatches them, and somehow stays clean while doing it all."

"Nope. He couldn't stay clean."

Since it isn't Emmarie, Cooper observes the display, staying composed and detached, listening to the clues. He squats down, looks long and hard with clinical eyes at the young woman. He examines the body and the killer's workmanship. The woman's bare feet are clean, further confirming she didn't walk here unless CCK took her shoes after the fact. There is bruising around the wrists and ankles indicating the use of restraints that she fought against. A couple of fingernails are broken or bent back. If they're lucky, they could have the killer's DNA at her fingertips.

He doesn't find this investigative process as difficult as Bellows made it sound. She's a victim, like those whose mangled bodies he deals with regularly. Like them, one moment she's living her life and the next moment she isn't. If he can figure out what happened to her in between those two moments, he may be able to contribute something that helps solve the case.

What does he remember about Campbell? Only that her vitals are on a list in the CCK folder because she meets the basic victim profile: Attractive female between the ages of 18 and 23. Big breasts, small breasts, color or style of hair, none of that seems to matter. He's killed white, black, Asian, and Hispanic young ladies. Streetwalkers and college students. If CCK prefers a specific type, it isn't obvious.

Fortunately, or unfortunately, the scope of CCK's terror spree means that several law enforcement departments assign officers and investigators to a single taskforce that shares leads and information with the FBI. But because no one can be sure what belongs in the CCK file, and what doesn't, all the young women have their own files too. Campbell has a file at the records department, with more substantial information, more 'meat' to digest. He makes a mental note to request it when he gets back into town.

A joint taskforce brings needed resources together. It also means important details can be overlooked or missed altogether if information is slow in coming or fails to be submitted altogether.

Is he taking too much onto himself? Is he supposed to do only what Bellows says needs doing? Clearly, he hasn't thought this through. This crime has so many tentacles, he could be wasting his time focusing on any one of them. None may lead to Emmarie. The more he considers these angles, the more finding her feels out of reach.

What does it matter if he has already overstepped his boundary with Bellows?

Cooper thinks he's found something in the files. He was sure of it, except now he isn't. Isn't sure of anything. He second-guesses himself about pushing the matter with his uncle. Besides, Bellows may have seen the pattern, if one exists, and reject it. In any case, the detective seems closed to hearing more.

Fresh eyes are what they need, but that doesn't mean they appreciate them. CCK and Campbell are unfortunate mysteries he needs to solve on his way to finding Emmarie. To help with motivation, he reminds himself that CCK's victims have loved ones too.

He latches on to the little solace he finds. *You can't get fired if you're a volunteer.*

His relief doesn't last. His next thought is: *Yes, but stupid can still get you kicked off the case.*

CHAPTER 13

Poking Bears

Bob returns with her underwear, dryer warm and neatly folded, along with well-used dark green hospital scrubs for Emmarie to wear. He leaves them in the bathroom under the cellar stairs, along with a toothbrush, Crest toothpaste, and a plastic cup. He unchains her from the bed and re-attaches her to an exposed pipe in the middle of the wall opposite the bathroom door. She can have her privacy while she does her business. The little room smells faintly of sewer, as though the old flange under the toilet needs replacing.

The bare-bones room contains the toilet, an old rusty mirrored medicine cabinet, a chipped, white pedestal sink with Mason's blue plastic cup and toothbrush already resting upon it, and a single bare light bulb with a short pull chain, screwed into a fixture above the sink. The ceiling slants so a tall occupant would have to bend to access the sink or mirror. It strikes Emmarie that her captor may have pre-measured the chain. Without her arms being fully stretched, she can alternately use both the commode and the sink. She washes her free hand by flexing her fingers around a bar of soap while letting water flow over them, then bringing her soapy hand to the shackled one that she moistened with a cupped palm of water. She repeats the process to rinse the soap away from her cuffed hand.

After she finishes, Bob leads Emmarie back to her bed prison. The dirty mattress now sports fresh-smelling, blue and white striped sheets, a pillow, and a decent quilt to warm her against the damp chill. She thinks his attempt at making her comfortable is absurd given his culpability in her captivity, but she's grateful.

Before he leaves again to go upstairs, he apologizes to Emmarie for re-securing her to the bed. "It is necessary, for now at least," he says, as if that both explains and excuses his behavior. "I will get you something more suitable to wear when I can," he says. He reaches down to wipe her auburn hair to the side and away from her eyes. She tenses again, but she lets him smooth her hair.

"With the pure I wilt show myself pure; and with the perverse I wilt show myself froward," Bob quotes.

She tries not to show her anger or fear, lest she provoke him, not knowing of course, what 'nice' means or what will set him off. She tries to calm herself, at least enough to not let fear obscure her thoughts. Bob hasn't tried anything yet. Mason does not make it sound like he thinks he will, either.

She observes everything. She counts the number of steps leading out of the cellar, based on the sounds of Bob's footfalls. When she detects the sounds of rattling pots and pans above her, she imagines cooking. Most of the time she's right. He'll shortly appear with food for them to eat. Most of all, she listens to when he's quiet and when he's active, looking for patterns.

She learns when Bob allows the single bare light bulb in the middle of the room to be on. She judges by the way the glow comes and goes around the cardboard that another day passed. To fill time, she talks with Mason as much as possible. Sometimes she gets him to tell her things. Other times he's a closed book that refuses to be read. She envies his ability to move about more freely.

Emmarie learns the routine of how and when she can use the bathroom. She has several minutes combined throughout each day, that she sings and lets the water run to mask the sounds she makes while scraping the butt end of her plastic toothbrush against the rough cinderblocks behind the commode. She does it there so her scuff marks are not easily seen. When she feels she's pushed it as far as she should, she returns the brush, pointy side down and bristles up, into her pink plastic cup, and emerges still singing her song.

The dampness of the walls eats at her bones, and she cannot move enough to increase warm blood flow through her limbs. In her mind, she hears her mother say, "Nothing ventured, nothing gained," but to ask for anything feels risky. *Only stupid people poke bears.* Regardless, she makes up her mind to appeal to Bob for warmer clothes or something to improve her situation, the next time she sees him.

"He won't come for hours," Mason tells her.

"Why? Where did he go? And how can you be sure?"

"I know. He works a lot at night."

"When I first got here, he brought me scrubs to wear. Does he work in a hospital?"

Mason giggles.

Emmarie realizes why the boy giggles. *He must think we're playing the 20 Questions game again.* She switches gears.

"Honey, instead of talking about Bob, why don't you tell me about your family? I've told you about mine." She cares about the boy, but she calculates her moves. Mason, she believes, is the key to escaping. When the day comes to try, she hopes to take him with her. He must trust her.

"I ain't got nobody else," Mason says slowly. "Mama's boyfriend beat my big sister and me. He put his smokes out on my arm and laughed. He beat Mama too, 'cause she let the medicine run out. Once a dirty guy came by and Mama let him take Missy into another room. When they came out, he gave Mama the medicine. Missy wouldn't stop crying, so Mama slapped her. Then she made her leave with him. It all right, Mama told me, 'cause Missy's old enough to know how the world works." He drops his voice. "She was ten." He rocks himself back and forth as he tells his story. "I know how the world works too."

After a few moments, Mason shifts his weight upon his bed, still rocking, and continues talking. "One night, Mama's boyfriend hit her bad. I hid. Cops came. Dragged me out from under my bed." He paws at the floor with his free foot. "They tell me I gotta live with new people 'cause Mama's dead. But them people hate me. Locked me in a barn for days with no food. They tell me to lie to caseworkers when they come 'round. But no one comes. Then Bob took me, and I like it here better."

He falls silent. Stunned, Emmarie wonders if it's true. By his admission, he's been here for several years. That must skew his version of reality, she thinks. *Nevertheless, it could be true.* "I am so sorry," she finally manages to say.

"It's okay." His face brightens. "Bob's nice. He feeds me. I got clothes anna warm bed. He talks to me and buys me things." He drops his voice a few decibels when he admits, shamefully she thinks, that Bob sometimes hits him. "But only when I deserves it," he adds.

"Has Bob ever touched you?"

"He touches me all the time."

"No, honey, I mean, has he ever tried to touch your private parts?"

"Silly girl," he giggles again. "Only slutty animals and married people do that."

Emmarie falls asleep fitfully that night. She is running, running frantically through the woods with a bear hot on her heels. No matter which way she turns, she finds herself face to face with snarling ugly teeth and paws with claws the size of daggers, readying to swipe at her. Her legs become leaden, and she can't run anymore. The bear morphs too. It transforms into a growling coyote, who encircles her, drooling, nipping at her legs. Even in her dreams, she has the cold, hard stare of hungry eyes on her. She feels about to be devoured. Still sleeping, beads of sweat pour off her brow; she tosses from side to side. Trapped.

She bolts awake to find a form standing over her.

CHAPTER 14

Recycling

⌣⟶

When Cooper returns to his apartment after the body dump, he allows himself a few minutes to de-stress. He saunters to the tank to feed his albino. "Hey, Casper, did you miss me?" After all these months, he's still fascinated by the snake unhinging its jaws to swallow a thawed mouse. Dash watches for a few moments before turning his attention back to the files of the dead and missing women.

He re-reads his notes and chronicles his observations. Not officially, of course. Let those who know what they're doing do that in their regular reports. These are his thoughts and perceptions. Like the pattern he sees when he studies the CCK files.

Reported missing 9/18: Rebecca Sue Stanley, aged 20, from Sauvie Island. Found dead 9/25 in a field outside Mills Crossing. Coroner estimated date of death to be 9/25.

Reported missing 9/20: Kaitlyn Marie Anderson, aged 20, from Lincoln City.

Reported missing 10/4: Allison Renee Delacroix, aged 18, from Astoria.

Reported missing 10/6: Annette Rose Martin, aged 19, PSU student from Portland. Found dead 10/15 near Marquam Nature Park. Coroner estimated date of death to be 10/13.

Reported missing 10/30: Cynthia Jane Ochenski, aged 19, from Tillamook.

Reported missing 11/9: Monique Sheppard, aged 22, from Astoria.

Reported missing 1/6: Rashona Macy Gilbert, aged 20, from Portland. Found dead 1/14 in hills outside McMinnville. Coroner estimated date of death to be 1/13.

Reported missing 1/19: Brianna Olivia Chastain, aged 20, from Hillsboro.

Reported missing 2/9: Kaiko Suzuki, aged 18, PSU student from Portland. Found dead 2/21 in a remote area of Tillamook State Forest. Coroner estimated date of death to be 2/16.

Reported missing 4/13: Desiree Ann Campbell, aged 21, from Seaside.

Reported missing 4/29: Emmarie Lynn Kelso, aged 18, from Clatsop City.

Reported missing 4/29: Kylee Roberta Roberts, AKA "Sunshine," aged 18, known prostitute from Portland.

Cooper uses a pencil to enter opposite Desiree Ann Campbell's name: Found dead 4/22 at Saddle Mountain. Coroner estimates date of death to be 4/20.

He checks and rechecks his figures. If he's right about the body being Desiree, his theory will have solid footing. He sighs deeply, believing he will know much more should May 6th come and go without another body. Of course, this is not an exact science. Bodies aren't always found immediately. Coroners determine the date of death by the state of rigor mortis and by evaluating decomposition and insect activity. Weather affects the latter two greatly.

The bottom line, no matter how good the coroner's estimate is, it's still an educated guess. Nonetheless, it appears to him that the Coastal Cutthroat Killer does not act all that random. He may grab his victims after stalking them, or by chance, but he kills them one week later. Why a week?

With his theory advanced as much as possible until the coroner determines the vic's identity, Dash calls the records department and uses Bellows' name to order a copy of Campbell's file. He plans to make good on his internal promise to learn more about her, to figure out how she spent her last moments on earth. Who does she see? Who does she talk to? Where does she go?

The records clerk tells him he can pick up the file by late afternoon, so he returns to Emmarie's case. He wants to focus on finding Emmarie but what can he do on her file that he hasn't already done? Do nothing and wait for his imagined May 6th CCK deadline to pass? Both as a cop and a man, that's not an option, nor would that relieve his compulsion to find her.

He told Bellows he believes Emmarie's disappearance is tied to her accident. Sure, he'd bullshitted his way into her investigation, but he's right about the lookie-loos. They stand around gawking until action stops feeding their hunger for excitement. By leaving, this mystery man of hers doesn't fit the mold.

He decides to recontact each bystander he interviewed earlier. Months later they aren't likely to remember anything new, but if he can uncover a breadcrumb that helps him find her, that's exactly what he'll do. At least, he'd know. Knowing is better than not knowing. *Doing something is better than doing nothing.*

First, Dash drives by the intersection of Tillamook and Iredale again. It no longer bears the scars of the accident that almost took Emmarie's life. A new light pole's up and the pavement bears no more burned rubber ribbons. All glass shards, bits of fragmented metal, and broken plastic had been swept up months ago, just as the rain had washed away all traces of blood.

He parks to scour the area on foot. Cooper doesn't know what he expects to find, given he's driven this intersection in his squad car many times since October.

He reruns that night over again in his head. The rain, the jaws of life, Runyan Park. *What am I missing?* Is he missing anything? The event could be exactly as determined six months ago. Nothing but a tragic accident. He begs under his breath, "Speak to me!"

Frustrated with himself, he retreats to his Jeep. He'll start on those witness calls as soon as he arrives at the Sheriff's Department's conference room where he's basing his workstation.

He checks with Records again and the Campbell file won't be ready for him until 5 p.m. He fills his wait time dialing for answers. At least he feels back in his element as a traffic cop instead of feeling like an imposter with Major Crimes.

The Jones couple repeat their recollections, matching their previous statements. She called 911 immediately while her husband checked on Mr. Park, who was clearly deceased. Obermeyer, Jackson, and Culpepper each admit to looking up only after hearing the crash. They hadn't seen the impact or what led to it. Each stayed after the ambulances dispersed and tow trucks dragged off the wreckages.

Cooper doesn't care about the crash itself. He needs to hear what they saw before and after the impact. The witnesses reiterate the usual stuff: Mr. Jones checked on Park. No one checks on Emmarie because a man is already with her. Obermeyer, Culpepper, and the Joneses describe the man as nearing middle age, roughly 5 feet 8, wearing a coat, hat, and

gloves. Jackson can't describe him at all. The light is poor; it'
raining. The mystery man is unremarkable. Nothing new
here.

It's getting close to 5 p.m. and he has only Silas Newsome
still to call. Should he bother? He punches in the telephone
number anyway.

"Mr. Newsome? This is Deputy Cooper. I investigated an
automobile accident you witnessed in October."

"Sure, sure. I remember you." Newsome suddenly sounds
nervously alert. But cops are used to people being nervous
around them. They certainly drive differently as soon as they
realize a patrol car is behind them.

"What can I do for you, sir?" Newsome asks.

"I want you to go over the events of that night again." He
hopes the authority of his law enforcement position will be
enough for the man to volunteer his time. Cooper does not
divulge why he is asking. He doesn't want to taint any
information he gets.

"That's a good many months ago, Officer. I'm not sure
what I can tell you now," Newsome hedges.

"Just tell me what you remember," Cooper says, as though
his request is simple and routine.

"Well, I was getting money out of an ATM when I heard
a loud crash and screaming, but I think the screaming came
from a woman on the street."

"That would have been Mrs. Jones."

"Okay, she starts screaming and I turn around. I think the screaming lady excitedly called 911. People were shouting. I expected a gas tank to explode and kill us all, so I stayed put. No use getting closer. The cars were pretty smashed, and the people were dead anyway. Nothing I could do," he repeats.

"Did you see who checked on the driver of the Escalade?"

"It was a man."

"Yes. Can you remember anything about him? Can you describe him for me?"

"Not really. I believe he wore dark clothes, definitely a coat. It was cold. I didn't notice him until I saw him at the Escalade, and I didn't see him talking to anyone but the young lady, so I guess she wasn't dead after all."

"Could you overhear anything he said?"

"Sorry."

"How about distinguishing features? Did he wear glasses, have long hair, anything?"

"If he did, I don't remember. I was watching the commotion. He didn't talk to me, and he didn't wait for the authorities to get there."

"Really? You saw him leave?"

"Yes, er, well, no. He was on the driver's side talking to that girl and then at some point, he moved to the other side of the Escalade. I saw him there for a moment, looking into the car. Then, I was distracted by the sirens, so I looked away to watch the emergency vehicles roll-up. When I looked back, he wasn't there. He must have headed west because that's the only direction I didn't have a good view.

"Thank you, Mr. Newsome. That's all for now. I appreciate your time." When the deputy ends the call, he feels right back where he started. No new revelations.

Or is there?

Hold your horses!

Silas Newsome says he'd stopped at an ATM to make a withdrawal. Of course! On the corner of Peter Iredale Avenue is a bank. Bank ATMs have surveillance cameras. *If I'm lucky, the camera may have captured a shot of Emmarie's elusive friend.*

Unfortunately, he doesn't remember seeing reference to that ATM video in the official file, even though it should have pulled it last October. He checks. *Says here they did pull it, but the file has gone missing.* One of the insurance companies – either Park's or Kelsoes' should have it, but Cooper thinks it'd be easier to get it again. *If I leave now, I might be able to get to the bank before they close. The Campbell file can wait.*

With seconds to spare, he enters the Reliant National Bank, flashes his credentials, and asks to speak to the manager. She appears before him within two minutes to usher him into her smartly styled office. "Deputy Cooper, I'm Stella Granger. How may I help you today?"

"I'm here to inquire about your ATM camera. May I see your footage from October 12th?"

"No, I'm sorry that isn't possible."

"Look, I can get a warrant," he bluffs. He isn't at all sure he could get a warrant, at least not based on this crazy assumption alone.

"That's not necessary," she says. "I'm afraid we don't keep the footage after three months. Haven't seen the need for it. What's the date again?"

"October 12th."

"I can check with security, but most likely they'll have deleted the digital file by now."

"All the same, I'd appreciate you checking."

"Of course. It'll take some time. Give me your contact info and I'll let you know."

Cooper keeps his professional facial expression pasted on, slips her his card, and thanks her for her time. Inside, however, his hopes are as crushed as Kelso's crumpled Cadillac. Disheartened, he isn't sure what his next step should be. Ask Liberty Mutual and Allstate insurance companies, he figures, but that takes time Emmarie doesn't have. Nothing he can do now but work the Campbell file.

His phone buzzes on his utility belt. Bellows requests, or rather demands, to see him.

"I can be in your office in 15," Cooper says.

From the bank, it would only take him ten minutes to be in front of Detective Bellows. Liking his five-minute margin, Dash Cooper uses the time to mentally prepare.

"How in the hell did you know that was Desiree Campbell?" Bellows presses.

"I told you I thought I'd found something in the CCK files. It's not obvious because we don't always find the bodies right away. But to date, it's clockwork. The Cutthroat Killer kills his victims seven days after he takes them."

Cooper offers to get his notes to show his uncle. Being waved off by Bellow's side-to-side head shake, the younger man explains, "For that pattern to be true, it couldn't have been anyone but Campbell, even if we didn't find her until 48 hours later. He keeps them a week before killing and dumping them. We need to figure out what is so significant about that week."

"Torture sex, I'd venture. Why a week? Hell, a psychopathic deviant doesn't need a reason," Bellows says.

"It's a gamble, but the takeaway here, Walt, is that the other missing women may not be the work of CCK. I think it's worth putting a small task force on each file to hunt for similarities between the victims. Once we assume CCK is not involved in those cases, we're examining their files with fresh eyes. Who knows what we'll find?"

Bellows furrows his ample brows and chews on his ever-present unlit Camacho. He pushes himself away from his desk and stands up. "Not prepared to do that, son. Clatsop County doesn't have the manpower. And I don't have jurisdiction over many of these cases. Nor do I call the shots on the Task Force. But I do have you. Consider yourself assigned."

That's more files you got dumped in your lap, buddy. Bellows didn't say it, but he doesn't need to. *You may be on the fringe of the Portland Task Force, but you'd find the manpower if you believed me.*

CHAPTER 15

A Little Surprise

⟳

Emmarie screams. Mason, not Bob, towers over her, almost able to touch her. Through the sweatpants he now wears, she sees every inch of his engorged manhood.

It had never occurred to her that Mason's leg chain allows him to get so close to her.

In her relief, she focuses on calming her heart and the rush of adrenaline coursing through her veins. *Mason is just a boy*, familiar with deviance to be sure, but a simple boy, lacking any semblance of normalcy in his life. *Probably the result of malnutrition or too many beatings.* She pities him.

"Mason, go back to your bed, please," she urges as soon as she regains her wits. He doesn't budge.

She summons all the authority she can and tries again. "Mason, I said, 'Go back to your bed.' Now." Their eyes deadlock, but Emmarie speaks again softer this time. "I forgive you, Mason, but it isn't nice to invade someone else's personal space."

"Not nice?"

"BOY!" Bob flips the light switch on. The solitary bulb fills the space with harsh, artificial daybreak, a good hour before dawn should appear she thinks.

Emmarie blinks her eyes first to shield them, then to adjust her vision. The expression on her captor's face scares her. Immediately, Mason withdraws to his bed. Bob smacks him hard across his face and the boy cowers, whimpering like a scolded dog.

"Well, well, I see you two have not wasted much time. And here I have been planning a little surprise for you, my dear. Something every girl wants because I thought you were the right one." Bob walks to her bed and lowers himself to one knee. His breath smells of old cigarettes, stale beer, and necrotized gums.

He strokes her hair with his hand. "To think I was going to have you as my wife, to take care of you forever. I was prepared to treat you like a queen! You would not have a worry in the world. A man protects what is his."

When he stands, Emmarie recoils. The odd tone of his voice and the words he says horrifies her. *Marry her? Only married people do that. Isn't that what Mason said?*

Her mind explodes into overdrive. "No, Bob. Nothing happened. I was sleeping. It wasn't my fault. Whatever you're thinking, I beg you to reconsider."

"I thought you were pure, undefiled by men, special." He spits on the cellar floor in disgust. "But I guess I am wrong. You are a slut like the others!" He slaps her hard, causing a big welt to swell on her reddened cheek.

She lets out a soft cry then in defiance returns her gaze directly at him. Mason's warnings flood over her. *Stupid sluts force him to do bad things. Bob makes them disappear...*

Emmarie remembers and softens her edge. She begins to grasp at anything she thinks might soothe him. "I haven't been with a man. But you're also wrong about the one I want. I don't want Mason..." She tries her best to sound open, receptive, sorrowful, even seductive. "I want you. Please, Bob, forgive me. I-I didn't mean to upset you. Please, let me stay here with you. I'll be nice! I swear it. PLEASE!"

Bob scrutinizes her.

In her mind, this is good. The longer he takes to act, the less likely he'll strike her again. The less likely he'll beat her to a pulp, strangle her, or drag her off to God-knows-where to slit her throat. She closes her eyes and begins singing *Stairway to Heaven* to herself, yet well within his hearing.

She senses him sit down on the bed next to her. She peeks to see him cradling his head in his hands. Five minutes, ten minutes pass. She keeps singing. Finally, he lifts his chin and murmurs to her. "Emmarie, do not make me hurt you again.

I forgive you. And if you want me, you shall have me." He smiles at her while moving to pat her lower belly. "Right away. We will have the ceremony today."

Emmarie manages to smile. "Thank you." Testing the waters, she ventures farther out. "Bob, you're right about something else too. Every girl dreams of her wedding day. It would be nice, a token of your love, if you'd let me wear something nicer than these clothes. Would you do that for me?"

"I suppose you want a wedding dress. I do not have one yet."

"I'll wait…"

"No," he flares. "We will be married today, all pure and official."

"Okay, okay. Then at least let me clean up and prepare myself for you. Would you bring me a washcloth and shampoo? And I'd love to shave my legs. Do you think I could do that? For you?" She doesn't want him focusing on her request for a razor so she quickly adds, "Oh, and do you have any perfume I can wear?"

She watches him physically soften his demeanor at her suggestions. He leans in to kiss her. She arches up to meet him and allows his tongue to thrust into her mouth, probing and exploring. She prays the kiss won't last longer than she can hold her breath. Everything in her wants to vomit but she wills herself not to. She must not gag, must not vomit, *MUST NOT*. She even manages a pretend little purr for him, a slight little adoring 'coo,' as if to communicate she's happy at last. *Maybe I do have what it takes to win an Oscar.*

Bob pulls back. "I have something a little nicer you can wear. I have it in a trunk upstairs. It was my grandmother's," he explains.

Emmarie wonders what any grandmother of Bob's would have worn. In truth, she can't imagine him having relatives at all. Instead, she's sure he was hatched somewhere. If not hatched, then surely, he was reared by a warped mother, who abandoned or indulged him in her distorted world in which only animals make love outside marriage, yet it is perfectly acceptable to kidnap, terrorize, and kill people.

"I may have little cologne left, too, that you can wear."

"Wonderful,' Emmarie squeals in fake delight. She wills herself to smile at him. "May I have extra time in the bathroom? It's bad luck for you to see me until I'm ready…"

Bob agrees. He kisses her forehead and promises to cook a big breakfast for such a big day. First, he'll bring her some ice to put on her face to reduce the unfortunate swelling. Then they'll eat. He'll bring her the clothes and the perfume she wants. He tells her she'll have at least an hour, maybe two, in the bathroom to herself because he needs time to find a Bible and locate the words for the traditional ceremony. He would also make up his queen-sized bed with fresh, silk sheets.

He reaches back with his left hand and squeezes her leg. "We will move to my room so we will have privacy to consummate our union. Afterward, you will wear restraints like these only during playtime." He kisses the tip of his left middle finger, places it on her nose then traces an imaginary line downward over her lips to her chin, down her neck, over her cleavage, and ultimately reaching her navel where he uses his index finger to draw circles. While he traces and retraces the outline of her belly button, he finishes telling her his surprise.

"I have other toys you may like too. You will find adult activities can be quite varied. But, no rush. Wedding night first. Most of the time, once you are my wife, you will wear a single leg shackle, like Mason, so you will have more freedom to move about."

"Thank you, my love. What a wonderful wedding present," Emmarie's acting skills not going to waste.

CHAPTER 16

Leaping the Grand Canyon

As soon as he could, Cooper picks up files for all the missing women on the Task Force's list except the known CCK victims. His interest lay in the unaccounted ones. Kylee Roberta Roberts is too new to affect his theory and he refuses to believe that Emmarie and the others met the same fate as Campbell.

That is, at least until he's proven wrong, or his calculated May 6th deadline delivers another body. If it does, it could be Emmarie. He must work fast. For now, at least, she is alive. He knows it. He feels it. He insists on it.

He brews a pot of fresh coffee, enjoying the heady Colombian aroma, while he organizes the individual files based on the date of disappearance. Then he grabs his laptop and opens a spreadsheet. He makes column headers of each woman's name. Then he starts adding rows for the details he wants to track. As he thinks of these things, such as hometown, occupation, location last seen, he adds additional rows. With enough details, a pattern might emerge.

He knows the professionals have such software but he, being in traffic, has no access to it unless he asks for favors. It isn't as though he's officially on the Task Force. His way is better, he thinks, because it forces him to think about every detail as he enters it, to filter and churn everything over until he's sure he misses nothing.

As he works from the breakfast bar separating his small kitchen from the rest of his living space, he takes the top file from the stack he arranged on his left, enters all the information he can, then places it on his right. By 7 p.m., he's moved all the files from the left to his right, into the 'DONE' pile.

A growl from his stomach reminds him that he hasn't eaten all day. He decides to order Chinese from Lao Lee's Kitchen. He favors mom and pop establishments over the chain varieties and adores Lao Lee. *Kung Pao Chicken? Maybe not on an empty stomach laced with nerves and caffeine. Better choose the snow pea pod chicken combo dinner.* His order comes with soup, fried rice, fried wonton, fried shrimp appetizer, and an egg roll. *That's a lot of fried food; I better not eat it all.* Besides, he rationalizes, it will make tomorrow morning's breakfast easy.

He unplugs his laptop, looks in on Casper, then settles onto the couch with the laptop on his legs while he waits for the food to arrive. He sorts and resorts the spreadsheet looking for patterns and clues. A few of the young women are students, some employed, some not; some runaways, some prostitutes, and all loved by someone. All missing.

Why? Is this the work of a single perpetrator? Or any perpetrator at all? Perhaps these girls ran away. Some ran a little farther off-grid and may show up later in Chicago, Omaha, or Miami. But not Emmarie. She hasn't run away. *And if not Emmarie, then probably not the others either.*

In his gut, he believes most, if not all, these women are linked. He focuses on Emmarie's data column. Who else shares ANY data characteristics? To his amazement, he notices that three others, besides Emmarie, disappear while riding a bicycle. Bicycles are as common as air in Oregon, even when it rains. But four bike disappearances out of 7 seems out of proportion. He hides those columns and looks at the remaining three women. Two missing women were last seen talking to someone in a white van or someone reported seeing a white van in the area. *That's not much to work on, but it's something.*

He hustles over to the hard files and rummages through the 'bike' files belonging to Emmarie, Kaitlyn Anderson, Allison Delacroix, and Cynthia Ochenski. All are from Oregon's coastal areas, this side of the Pacific Coast Range.

Scouring through them he finds buried forensic reports that mention white paint transfer somewhere on the bike frames.

The doorbell rings as Dash has an 'ah-ha' moment.

He runs to the door and throws it open without even verifying that it is Lao Lee's regular delivery boy, a high-school kid named Jimmy, on the other side. A risky breach of protocol like that is stupid for any law enforcement officer who makes his living making enemies.

When he sees Jimmy holding out his sack of food, he could have kissed him. He fishes in his wallet, dispenses a $15 tip on a $15 meal, then closes the door abruptly.

"Thank you, Officer Cooper!" he hears the young man yell through the door.

White paint equals white van. Six out of seven missing women have the white van as the common denominator! He's sure of it.

What type of white van? His work in traffic taught him there are box vans, crew vans, conversion vans, minivans, panel vans, and more. In between bites of fried rice, he devours the two files where witnesses mention a white van. He re-reads their descriptions. Nothing remarkable, again, but both seem to reference a panel van, one that is at least a few years old, one that lacks a good shine and has a few dents, scrapes, and abrasions in the paint. *Makes perfect sense.*

He imagines a panel van converted into a carpeted hippie bedroom on wheels, or a stark mobile box in which the perp tosses his victims to transport them to God-knows-where,

132

probably a world foreign to them, far away. All these women would be shuttled and harbored together in small groups otherwise… Otherwise, he doesn't know. The economics are wrong. If he's right, it's too large of an operation for one man. He loves Lao Lee's food, but suddenly he loses his appetite.

He removes his phone from its case on his belt. It's approaching the time of night he hates to make phone calls, but this one isn't social. He scrolls through his contacts and punches the name. While it rings, he imagines his aunt and uncle finally relaxing after a long day. She with her pinot noir and he with a scotch and a lit stogie, sitting on padded, rattan rocking chairs in their screened-in back porch, feet up, discussing how they should retire into the house because of the cold night air, but neither moving a muscle to do so.

He hates to ruin a nice evening, but his uncle gets calls at all hours of the night. Comes with the job.

"Walt, sorry, this can't wait," he says, his excitement barely in check. "Have you heard of a sex trafficking ring operating out of Portland?"

"That's a leap the size of the Grand Canyon, isn't it, kid?"

"Maybe. I don't know yet. It's one possibility I want to check out. Do you know who I should ask for at Portland PD?"

"I'll find a contact for you in the morning. See? Everything short of a new, dead body can wait." He ends his call with a click.

Cooper kicks himself. Again. His uncle is a pragmatist. *Of course, Walter cares about solving these cases.* But, unlike

133

himself, the grizzled detective has seen everything. Through it all, he's learned to pace himself.

Pacing is something that Cooper has limited skill with and Emmarie has no time for.

CHAPTER 17

Parting Gifts from Trunk Granny

⟿

Emmarie sits on her bed, one arm resting near the headboard while the other hand holds the ice pack against her throbbing cheekbone. This is nothing she tells herself. Painful to the touch, it doesn't feel like 'nothing,' but it is, compared to what will happen next, she figures. She lives or he does. Either way, the welt's nothing.

She thinks of her mom and her pre-packaged advice. What would she say now? What advice would she offer her daughter in this situation? Emmarie remembers 'buck up, little Buckeroo' her mother repeated often when she was little. She thinks of hundreds of pointless platitudes and sees them bouncing off the real metal that holds her in this hellhole. Her anger boils. The situation exceeds her mother's ability to fix. It far exceeds hers too. Somehow, she must find a way.

She thinks of being with Jack in his pickup before he pushes things farther than she wanted. Pleasant thoughts of intimacy turn dour, as she begins to dwell on Bob's plans for her. What should be the normal, special, and cherished part of sharing her life and her body will be lost. She will die inside.

Bob's rancid breath alone will kill me. Between his stench, and his violating her, she will not stomach it. She *will* vomit on him. She knows she will. Then he'll hit her over and over until her lifeless body submits to his exploration and games. When he's had her, he'll reach for the pillow and snuff the life out of her. That is more efficient and handier, cleaner, and what a neat freak would do. He will enjoy carving her up with a butcher knife too, but to have a knife so near while she is alive isn't smart.

Bob won't do that because Bob is smart. He'll know that I'd grab it and use it on him. Instead, she reasons, he'll settle for slitting her throat and carving 'Bob was here' into her abdomen later if it suits him. He'll relish watching her rebellious blood ooze, not pump, from her dead, mangled body.

Mason giggles as he sits on his bed. He rocks himself back and forth singing the childhood nursery taunt over and over, "Bob and Emmarie, sitting in a tree. K-I-S-S-I-N-G."

NO. She'll find a way to escape, or she'll die trying, the alternative too dreadful. Unfortunately, she doubts her ability to free Mason and take him with her unless she first kills Bob. She does not hate the idea. They are in this together. She'd promised him.

Bob enters the cellar, whistling Stairway to Heaven. He gives a tray of scrambled eggs, fried bacon, buttered whole-wheat toast with a dollop of strawberry jam, a small bowl of fruit cocktail, and a cup of orange juice to Mason.

"I will be right back with our breakfast," he shouts over his shoulder to Emmarie as he bounds back up the steps. Soon he returns with a tray loaded with enough food to put them both into a coma. He sets the tray on the end table beside her bed. He pauses to look at her and withdraws the key from his pants' pocket. He leans over, unlocks her right arm so she can sit up and eat. The loose cuff he re-clasps around a vertical rung of the headboard. He kisses her on the forehead before pulling up a chair to join her.

Another day in paradise. My wedding day, no less. Too bad she can barely get down a few bites of egg and toast, and a nibble of bacon, which she would have scarfed at home. She needs the energy. Plus, if she is going to vomit on him later, she wants plenty of it, chunky and vile from stomach bile and undigested globs of unrecognized goo. Bob, on the other hand, seems to be wolfing down his portion, and hers too.

"Emmarie, my love, you are not eating much."

Does nothing escape his notice? Her inner actress reappears. "I'm too excited, I guess. You're a good cook, Bob. It's delicious," she manages. "Although I can't wait to cook for

137

you, as a wife should." Partially true, she thinks. *At least I long to get my hands on a heavy skillet of yours.*

"Finish up," he pats her free arm. "I will wash these and clean up the kitchen, then come back so you can start your beauty ritual. As promised," he says almost magnanimously. "By noon today, you will be in my arms as my wife."

Ceremony or no ceremony, Bob, I'll never be your wife. By noon today, one of us will be negotiating with St. Peter.

Bob returns sooner than Emmarie hopes. Through the open bathroom door, she watches him while he hangs a dress, still in dry cleaner's sheathing, on a bare nail jutting from the door. He places a blue reusable bag made from standard recycled RPET materials on the pedestal sink. She assumes he's filled it with soap, shampoo, washcloth, towel, hairbrush, razor, and perfume. A separate bucket already sits on the floor, next to the sink.

When he finishes setting up her supplies, he returns to the bed and sits down next to her. "I hope you understand I did what I could to make this special for you on such short notice. You have your dress and your perfume. The boy will serve as our witness. Of course, we cannot have a real preacher because we are private people. But it is the words you say before God that matters anyway. He will hear you repeat them, and we will be married, the same as anybody else. You will be mine. The marriage bed undefiled."

Emmarie isn't all that familiar with Bible passages, but she thinks he twists his way through, deciding for himself what to highlight and what to ignore. The bits and pieces she remembers from going with her aunt to Sunday School bear no resemblance to Bob's doctrine. *Even that which he chooses to honor, he warps.* She realizes that while she hadn't thought much about it before, she now hopes Hell exists with all her heart. *God, let Hell have a reservation for Bob today.*

Having said his peace, Bob removes the precious key and unlocks the shackle from the headboard. He unthreads the chain from the headboard and walks her like a dog on a leash over to the cellar bathroom. Like before, he clasps the cuff around the pipe and tugs at it to make sure it remains secure. This is the normal bathroom routine with her left wrist secured at the end of a chain attached to the pipe. She has quite a bit of free movement available to her if she preplans her actions. Bob kisses her cheek and excuses himself, closing the door behind him.

Emmarie has no idea how long she has. She rifles through the sack, evaluating each item as she removes it. She's right about the soap, shampoo, hairbrush, perfume, and towel. She's wrong about the razor. Instead of an inexpensive disposable razor like a Lady Schick or Gillette Venus, or better yet, a good quality safety razor she can use to fashion a weapon, Bob brought her a charged electric razor. *I doubt this is heavy enough to club him.* Unless she can figure out a way to shock him with it, he may as well have brought her a paperweight.

At the bottom of the bag, she finds four items she hadn't requested. The first, a small bottle of liquid foundation. She doesn't tend to wear make-up. Had Bob provided it to conceal the bruise he gave her that morning? She winces as she tries to apply it. Partly from the discomfort, but mostly from her desire to not hide what he did to her, she replaces the lid on the bottle after one dab.

The second surprise in the bag is a box containing an expensive-looking set of pearls to wear with his grandmother's dress. She guesses the necklace comes from his mother or grandmother, too. *Perhaps trunk granny.* Emmarie would play his dress-up game to bring a tear to his eye, right before she finds a way to make him cry in agony.

The third surprise is a 1950's style black garter belt with the Pour Moi label still attached and black silk stockings. Either this guy has a fetish, or he lives in a different world. Both, most likely. Finally, she retrieves from the bag a pair of saucy black lace panties and matching bra. Black, not white as more fitting for a wedding, but more to Bob's inclinations, she thinks. The panties and bra are clean, but not new, so she assumes they belonged to another girl, one who no longer needs them because she forced Bob to do bad things. *Damn stupid girl*, she can hear Mason repeating.

Emmarie draws as much warm water in the bucket as she can. Between the bucket and the sink, she hopes to wash her hair. She'll skip all the other primping she promised. She determines that he isn't going to enjoy her clean, or dirty, for that matter unless she's dead. Nevertheless, she must give him the illusion of pampering, so he suspects nothing.

Toweling up her hair, she turns on the shaver and lets it hum. In the meantime, she inverts her toothbrush shiv from her drinking cup, brushes her teeth, then goes to work rubbing the handle ferociously back and forth against the rough cinderblock.

When an appropriate amount of time passes, Emmarie turns off the razor and sets about getting dressed in all the trappings. Black bra and panties, garter belt, black stockings. She sits on the commode and works them up her toes, calves, and knees to her thighs, careful not to put a run in either stocking. It isn't easy, the fine mesh weave catches on her humid skin. Everything needs to be perfect, as Bob fantasizes. She needs him to drop his guard.

She takes the towel from her hair and lets her hair finish air drying. *Bob said he didn't have a wedding dress so what did he bring me?*

She removes the hanger from the nail and strips away the garment's protective wrapping to reveal a 1950's style, off-the-shoulder swing dress with black lace and a scalloped black velvet bodice, gathered at the waist. The skirt pouf is emerald-green taffeta overlaid with black lace of black and green butterflies, underlaid with a white tulle petticoat. A black patent-leather belt completes the ensemble. She slips the dress over her head and zips the side zipper. It fits perfectly. It doesn't really need the belt, but she cinches it up anyway.

The gorgeous pearls she clasps around her neck. The classic 18-inch strand lays loosely. She dabs the perfume, Chanel No. 5, probably also his grandmother's she thinks, behind her ears, on her pulse points well away from her healing wrists, and at the top of her cleavage. She even places a dollop under her nose on the dip above her lip, where she hopes it'll help cover the odor wafting from Bob's breath.

When she feels ready, she works on her shiv a bit more as she sings loudly to mask the sounds of grinding and scraping. Then she rinses off the shavings and dries the tool on her towel before she tucks it into her bra where she can access it quickly. She might as well stick a sign on her breasts advertising 'Danger: Shiv enclosed.' The lump is unmistakable.

Bob knocks on the door. "Are you ready? It is time."

She must think of something else. Fast.

CHAPTER 18

Backing Up and Inching Forward

As Bellows had promised, Cooper receives contact information for the Portland precinct the following morning. He recopies the number from his text onto a piece of scrap paper and fondles it between thumb and forefinger, trying to decide whether to dial.

In the light of day, his theory sounds more than a little crazy. It sounds ludicrous. What in the world will he say to this guy? *"Hey, dude, I think you professionals are looking in all the wrong places for seven missing women. I think they're right under your nose, caught up in some sex trafficking ring…"* *CLICK.*

Emmarie. Damn. Okay, I won't say that, I'll just ask questions.

He dials the number and expects the inevitable transfer from the department to the Head of Vice, Lieutenant Randall. He's caught off-guard when Randall answers directly.

"Ah, Lt. Randall, this is Deputy Cooper, in Clatsop County. Lt. Bellows thought you might be able to help me."

"Shoot. What do you need?"

Lt. Randall is stoic and as direct as his uncle. The personality must come with the job, Cooper guesses.

"I understand you know sex offenses in Portland," he blurts out.

"Well, not personally, if that's what you mean." Randall chuckles.

So, okay, not as stoic and humorless as my uncle when it comes to work.

"We got our share of prostitutes and johns."

"Anything organized?"

"Not exactly. We've not detected links to any known crime family, drug cartel, pornography gang or syndicate. A white slavery ring, perhaps, but that's not even accurate."

Cooper perks up. "Tell me more."

"There's been an uptick in missing girls for the past year, year and a half. We believe they're sold overseas to wealthy men. Some end up working the streets in major international cities, Dubai, Berlin, Shanghai. No papers, no contacts, no options. Hell, no language skills to communicate."

Year and a half? "What's the profile?"

"White, mostly, but not always. Age 16 to 22 but again, not always. We've got missing girls as young as 12 and 13. They are often run-aways that young, but again, not always."

Cooper hasn't considered that others might be missing on this scale, not just those fitting the CCK profile, and not before CCK started his cutting spree. "How does it work?" he asks next.

"Not sure. We think he takes them, houses them somewhere local, then moves them as soon as he can to New Orleans. They're sequestered in New Orleans for false paperwork. Our understanding of the system gets really sketchy after that."

"Any ideas on who 'he' is?"

"Cooper, I don't believe in one-way streets. Why don't you back up a bit and tell me why you're so interested?"

Cooper blanches, grateful to be on the phone with him, not in front of him in his office right now. Facing Bellows is hard enough, but he can always play the family card. Here, Randall finding out he is a traffic cop, masquerading as a Major Crimes investigator, is the last thing he needs. He briefly clears his throat and launches in.

"Some of your missing young women, and others on our side of the state, have been flagged as fitting the CCK profile. I'm helping Lt. Bellows out with the CCK taskforce. But I'll tell you, Lt. Randall, I don't think most of these women are CCK at all."

"Your turn, Cooper. Tell me more."

"It's not the prevailing theory, of course. In fact, it's not even a theory of the taskforce. It's my personal theory, that um, Bellows has yet to support," he admits. "But I see evidence suggesting these women meet a fate totally different than CCK. A sex trafficking ring fits better than anything else."

Cooper pauses, unsure what else to say. If what Randall says is happening, Emmarie could be someplace between here and New Orleans, maybe overseas already. He has no time for tiptoeing. "Lt. Randall, I realize this is out of my jurisdiction, but if I come to Portland, would you let me see everything you have on this? Quid pro quo, of course. I'll show you what I have."

"No time like the present, I guess."

"Great. I can be there tomorrow." They settle on a time window and Cooper ends the call quickly without giving Randall a chance to change his mind. He determines to leave bright and early to be there by nine, depending on the commuter traffic entering Portland.

Excited about his appointment and a sense of making progress, Cooper opens the Campbell file. He sees she was reported missing by her parents on the morning of 4/13 when she didn't return home from work. She is last seen leaving the Seaside Burger King where she is the manager. The restaurant closes at 10 p.m. The drive-in window stays open until midnight.

He reads and rereads the information, yet nothing sticks. His head is 2,600 miles away in New Orleans. He does not want to imagine Emmarie there, nor what she's gone through already.

Surely, the New Orleans police force are cooperating with Randall. But he fears they could be just going through the motions. He's heard that corruption runs deep in the history and politics of the Big Easy. *Could that be how this ring operates? The Feds must be involved, so they'd have to cooperate...*

He makes notes on what he wants to ask Randall when they meet and closes the ignored file before him when his phone rings.

"Deputy Cooper? Stella Granger, Reliant National Bank, getting back to you about that security camera footage."

"Great."

"I don't know about great, but I have good news. Security deleted the digital record as I suspected. But one of our new security guys knows quite a bit about computers. He found the file still on our hard drive. Most of it has not been written over. I'm not sure you'll be able to get much from it though.

"I'll take what I can get."

"Okay, I'll have security send it over."

Cooper feels energized. Finally, two things are going his way.

He pulls out Emmarie's file and sees his accident report and statements from the people Bellows' team interviewed

147

when she went missing: Parents, neighbors, girlfriends, boyfriend, friends of friends, co-workers, and co-workers of her parents. Anybody who'd ever written hate mail to Dr. Brooks Kelso, or anyone carrying a grudge against the community college's Director for Dispute Resolution. It's all in there.

None of it is going to be helpful, though, if she's been kidnapped by a sex trafficking ring. Nothing in her file will apply, except maybe his accident report, the forensics report on her bike, and the ATM camera footage, if even that, he reminds himself.

Nothing like starting an investigation over when time is of the essence.

CHAPTER 19

To Have and To Hold/Til Death Do Us Part

Emmarie unlatches the door and waits for Bob to enter and unlock her wrist. He doesn't. Instead, he unlocks the cuff from the pipe and leads her out. She welds a demur smile onto her face and looks around. For the first time, she does not see Mason. Of course, she remembers, he is their witness. *Bob's fake ceremony must be planned for upstairs. Good. Upstairs is 14 steep steps closer to freedom.*

"One, two, three, four," she counts to herself as he proceeds up the steps. *You shouldn't turn your back on me, lover boy.* "Five, six, seven, eight." Emmarie gives a little cry as she slips and falls onto a knee. Bob whips around and reaches down to help her, as she hopes he would. By bending over to assist her, he puts himself off balance.

"Big mistake," she says under her breath as she lunges upward. With a quick flip of her arm, she has the chain around his neck. He claws at it, trying to keep her from squeezing it tighter. He tumbles back down a few stairs into her. Emmarie continues squeezing the chain until he stops struggling. She relaxes her grip, using her free hand to fish into his pants pocket where she saw him drop the key. As soon as she finds it, she withdraws it quickly. Her fingers tremble as she tries to insert it into the small lock. Flowing adrenaline is not her friend right now. In the relative darkness of the cellar stairwell, she can't see what she's doing, and she can't do it by feel alone. More light beckons her from the top of the stairs. She maneuvers around Bob, and with seven more steps finishes her ascent.

As soon as she emerges from the darkened stairwell, she forgets the key in her fist and quickly surveys the little house to get her bearings. The blinds and curtains are drawn, keeping at bay any natural sunlight. However, Bob has sprinkled lit candles on tables and countertops. *Either the power is out, or he fancies himself a romantic.* She notices Mason, unshackled, standing in the doorjamb of a room in front of her.

"Mason! Honey, this is our chance. We can get out of here." She starts for the door, holding her hand out toward him.

"And go where? This is home." He looks around her, past her to the stairwell. "Did you hurt Bob?" he asks.

"No, honey, this is not your home." She stops to plead with Mason to leave. "You belong somewhere safe, where Bob can't hit you anymore. We've got to leave, now."

Mason smiles broadly for the first time since she caught him watching her sleep. *Is he's beginning to understand?*

As Emmarie focuses on Mason, urging him to join her, Bob grabs her from behind. She screams in surprise, turns, and kicks at him. She tries desperately to extract herself from his pawing, grasping hands that mean to send her to oblivion. It's to no avail; Bob has regained both balance and breath, energized by fury.

"Run, Mason!" She screams. Bob knocks her down, and the small key she holds so tightly in her fist drops and scoots across the floor somewhere. Bob hits her hard, bare-knuckled on the cheek where he slapped so hard her earlier. She cries out in pain and tries to knee him in the groin. But with him on top of her, pinning her shoulders with his forearm and the rest of her body with his own, she can't move her knee with any momentum. Her attempt to put him in the fetal position falls disastrously flat. She squirms underneath and slaps wildly at him.

Bob seems to relish her protests.

"You bitch! You are a slut after all," he seethes at her between coughs. "I will see you get what a slut deserves!" His black eyes burn with a different, cruel intensity that tells

151

Emmarie that he intends to overpower her and take her right there on the floor. He doesn't need marriage or shackles. Bob executes a lightning-fast pushup maneuver with his legs, bringing his shoe tips back down between her shins. In one sweeping motion, he widens his feet and spread-eagles her. Laughing, he reaches down and unzips himself.

Emmarie flails her feet, trying to dig in her heels for traction against the bare floor. Her stockings make her feet slip and she gets nowhere. "Bastard!"

He slips his right hand up her dress, trying to yank down the panties he'd given her. The garter belt that secures her stockings keeps her underwear stationary as well. He can't slide her panties past the top of her hosiery where the garters hold them. As adeptly as he removed her bra earlier, he flicks open with thumb and index finger the clasps that secure the garter to the silk stockings. One, two, three. She feels each garter around her left leg release with a little snap.

She sees he's enjoying the process and wonders how many women he's raped like this. *If you try to kiss me, I'll bite your damned, dirty tongue off!* He grins broadly at her, blackened tooth, gums, and all. He communicates without using any words. She knows he is saying: 'I am in control. I am one maneuver away from taking everything from you but life itself. I'll do that later.'

Emmarie reaches down to her right thigh and retrieves the shiv she slid into the top of her stocking. With all her might she slams it into the back of his left leg hoping to hit his femoral artery. She misses the artery, driving it only into his muscle, but he gasps out in surprise and pain all the same. He stiffens momentarily, rolling off her slightly. She withdraws the shiv and rams it into his side. He clutches at himself, allowing her to flip over and start scrambling away on all fours. But the adrenaline that flows through her courses through his body as well. He is on his knees in no time, trying to wrestle her to the ground again.

She turns around and whips the chain and empty manacle at him, catching him on the chin, splitting it open.

"Damn you, bitch!" he yells, barely pausing to bring his hand up to his face to feel the damage. He comes at her again.

With the element of surprise now gone, she calculates that the toothbrush shiv in one hand and the de facto medieval mace in the other isn't enough to stop him. *He just needs to grab the chain and loop it around my neck. He'll squeeze until my eyeballs pop out…exactly what I should have done to him.* Emmarie locks her eyes on him and scrambles to her feet, stepping backward, arms touching anything and everything they can, searching for a better weapon to use. "Mason?" she calls out.

"He is not going to save you, bitch." Bob says, still coughing some. "You spoiled, rich tramp, you are going to get everything that is coming to you. And then some."

With every step toward her he makes, she takes a step back. *Candles. I'll burn your damned house down around you.*

Blood oozes down his leg and from the wounds to his chin and side. Still, he comes toward her. He laughs and lunges again as her right-hand finds a heavy, square glass ashtray. She whacks the pointed corner into his head, letting butts and ashes scatter. He stumbles forward, grasping at her body, smearing his blood on her and his grandmother's beautiful swing dress as he falls. She uses the shiv again for good measure, plunging it between his ribs.

Mason cries.

"Mason, you're free," she whispers. "Why didn't you run?" Emmarie moves to comfort him. He pushes her away and kneels over Bob.

"Is he dead?" Mason asks between gasping sobs.

"I don't know. I'm not sure. But we've got to go.

"I won't leave."

"Mason. Honey let's go. NOW. Look, we'll run and get him help. Okay?" Emmarie pleads with him, but he seems frozen in place.

Stockholm syndrome, she remembers her mother telling her, is when hostages or kidnap victims display affection for their captors and refuse to testify against them. Emmarie did not care at all about the fancy diagnosis her mother used. As an eight-year-old, all she wanted to know was 'Would the hostages she saw on TV be okay?'

"All right," she tells Mason. "I'm going without you. I'll send someone back. Please help me find the key to this thing," she says, pointing to the shackle.

Bob lets out a deep groan.

He isn't dead. Emmarie stops caring about the key. She runs to the door and throws back the security chain and deadbolt that separates her from final freedom. As soon as she is outside, she scans her surroundings for her bearings and options. She is in the middle of a mature, second-growth forest, standing on the porch of an old house, at least 100 feet or so from an old logging road. Her heart beats so loudly in her chest, she thinks it'll burst.

To her right, she sees a newer gray Chevrolet Colorado truck and runs to it. She can't find the keys under the seat or resting on the sun visor, or anywhere else she thinks to look. She doesn't know how to hotwire a vehicle either, even though she's seen it done in countless movies. Discouraged, she abandons the truck. She gathers the four feet of chain hanging from her left wrist and starts to run as fast as she can toward civilization.

Except she doesn't know in where civilization is. The wrong way down the road, one way or the other, and she could be moving farther away from help, not closer. She second-guesses herself and changes directions, wishing in vain that it was dark instead of mid-day. If it were dark, she might be able to see lights in the distance, but now she sees nothing but trees. If it were dark, the darkness would help conceal her. As it is, the noon-day sun obscures all clues regarding east or west.

Her second problem is that she is shoeless. The silk stockings do nothing to protect her tender feet from the little rocks that cut into the softened pads and arches of her feet as she runs, nor do they bar twigs and burs that snag on them and prick her. *Run anyway!* She wills her legs.

She needs to get off the road. True, the road would be faster, but Bob can jump in his Chevy and come after her. She wouldn't put it past him. She must hide in the woods, deep enough off-road that he can't see her. Traveling this way will be much slower because she will have to pick her way barefooted through heavy underbrush. Still, it's safer from the biggest predator out here. Bob.

Her side aches as she gulps for air. Lactic acid builds up in her legs. She can't run much longer so she leaves the road clearing and cuts into the woods, hoping against hope that he hasn't already made it to his truck and is following far enough behind that she doesn't hear the engine, but close enough to see the point at which she veers off the road.

CHAPTER 20

All Dressed Up Going Nowhere

Emmarie runs or walks for what seems like hours over bracken, sword and deer ferns, through tangled underbrush, past wild blackberry bushes, and around saplings and mature oaks, alder, maple and vine maple, but mostly Douglas firs. She identifies these by their dark, short needles and an inch or more light new growth at the ends, making the trees look almost frosted. These are the trees planted after a hundred years of clearcutting practices in the area.

Traversing over rises and miniature valleys, she tries to keep the old logging road on her left, about a football field's distance away, making her less noticeable to anyone on the road looking for her. She isn't a lost hiker who failed to show up at a pre-determined gathering site. Certainly, no park ranger is looking for an escaped kidnapping victim. No, the only one who would be searching, she must avoid at all costs.

Following the road had been her only plan since roads lead to places, or come from places, where people are. Away from the road, she would be lost. But with all the dips and turns, she isn't sure the distance between her and the road now.

She cuts back to reassure herself that the rocky dirt road is still there. Except it isn't. When no road appears, she sits down upon a stump and the fallacy of her plan strikes her.

Roads curve. It must have veered away at some point, or I did. Hell, I could have been walking in circles for hours.

Exhausted, she realizes that she might be closer now to her prison cellar than when she first left the road. She begins to weep.

She cries until she laughs, imagining the sight she must be. Dirty, sweaty, bloody. Her bare feet swollen from the cuts and pricks, yet decked out in a party dress and pearls, with huge runs in her black stockings, out in the middle of nowhere, a manacle and chain at her side.

When she regains a little energy and clearer mental functioning, she tries to judge 'North' by reading the moss on the trees, the way they taught her in elementary school. Teachers said that moss grows on the north-facing sides of trees. Turns out, that isn't 100 percent accurate. Depending on sunlight, moss might grow better or fuller on the north side, but it grows all around these trees and even rests on the branches of snags and live trees alike. Not so much like the Spanish moss she'd seen dripping from trees while visiting Savannah one summer, but like a thick mat caressing the tops of boughs. *Good thing I don't care so much about heading North.* Still, recognizing North would help her avoid the disorientation that jeopardizes her forward momentum.

No matter. The green moss is becoming more difficult to see altogether now as daylight slips away. In the deep forest, where sunlight struggles to penetrate the tangled limbs and foliage above, it might be only 4 p.m., but still getting dark. She doesn't have a plan for darkness.

True, she'd wished for darkness when she first left the old house, but now she realizes that darkness hides inevitable tripping hazards. She might fall and break her leg again, especially the one that's not 100 percent yet. Darkness also means temperatures will plummet. *Springtime or not, this means freezing my butt off.*

Should she make a bed of leaves here? Cover herself with whatever she can find, and hunker down until morning? Is it too risky to continue without being able to see the subtle changes in the ground? Is it riskier to stay in one place, waiting for Bob to catch up to her? She finally decides she would pick a direction and walk until the risk of walking further proves too high. Only then will she consider stopping.

Another half-hour passes, she guesses, before she reaches a flowing stream, flush with snow run-off from higher up.

Based on its size, it looks to be perennial, meaning it flows throughout the year, rather than being seasonal. A couple of hundred years ago explorers and Indians would drink freely without thinking; its life source refreshing and renewing every cell within them with fresh, ice-cold water. Now, her thoughts fell to a biology lecture on giardia and cryptosporidium, both parasites from animal feces that live in streams and run-off like this and cause watery diarrhea.

I don't need THAT out here, but without water, I'll not survive the days it may take to reach safety. She lays down and cups handfuls of the icy liquid to her lips until she feels she can drink no more.

Emmarie has another decision to make. Should she follow the creek and hope it leads somewhere? Or should she cross over and continue the heading she selected while sitting on the stump? If she follows the stream, she'll have continued access to water and maybe fish or crawdads. She could use her tulle underskirt as ersatz fish netting.

On the other hand, the very idea of changing directions makes her feel like the hours she's invested so far would be wasted. Like she would be quitting right before a big payoff. It is the same illogical mentality of upside-down gamblers who believe one more toss of the dice or one more hand of poker will restore their fortune.

Okay, the stream might be better, but what if the stream snakes back in the direction from which she's come? What if bears and wildcats hunt along the stream?

Under the Influence

She looks around as best she can in the dim remnants of sunlight, evaluating her options and staring at the creek. The rushing stream stirs up a distant childhood memory, one she'd thought she'd forgotten, from well before her mother hit the bestseller list and stayed there. The longer she stares at the creek, the stronger the memory grows.

At best guess, she was only four or five. A knock at their door came late one night. It was a neighbor who'd come to ask her father to help search for his teen-aged son who'd run away. Pitch black outside, her father and other neighbors searched with deputies from the sheriff's department for hours. The next day, her mother made sandwiches and coffee on a camp stove for the volunteers. She remembers seeing funny flippers on men dressed in tight black, watery suits. Her mother told her these were scuba divers searching nearby Salmon Creek. She doesn't know the details her parents hid from her, except that the divers ultimately found the boy submerged, tangled in tree roots. Funny how water both sustains life and takes it away.

From her own driver's education, she knows well enough never to drive a car across a flooded roadway because six inches of rushing water can dislodge and carry away vehicles weighing several thousand pounds. *What am I, compared to a car?*

She has no idea how deep this stream is, nor can she pick a route over slimy, slippery rocks without seeing them. Water plays tricks, refracting light so objects underwater appear different than they are, closer to the surface or even a few inches to the side. The last thing she needs, if not death by drowning, is death by hypothermia as night falls after getting drenched.

She makes up her mind then, without too much mental effort after all. She will sleep and decide her direction in the morning. If she crosses over, the dawn will be critical for choosing a safe place anyway.

Emmarie spies a fir tree not far from the creek bank, whose broad, heavy limbs hang down almost to the ground. Its canopy will be her shelter, providing some break from wind and rain, and hiding her from unwanted eyes. She finds she can sit under it, upright with her head between the branches if she chooses. But sitting up holds no appeal.

She climbs out from under the tree to find a rock she can use as a pillow and to gather some moss and leaves she hopes will cover her legs for a little extra warmth. The last thing she does is remove her tulle slip so she can use it as a blanket to cover her exposed arms, upper chest, and core. Her legs and feet will be cold, but they would be anyway. *The tulle will keep my core warmer.*

She curls up, says a brief prayer, and remembers tent camping with Danny as kids. Danny taught her what the nighttime sounds were and how not to be afraid. She isn't afraid now either, of the sounds that crickets and other insects make, or of the owl hooting in the canopy somewhere nearby. She's afraid only of the footsteps she thinks she hears.

CHAPTER 21

If a Tree Falls in the Woods

After a fitful sleep, Emmarie awakes to the crisp, cold air of the morning. She climbs out from under her tree and pulls her tulle skirt over her head like a poncho. She feels eyes on her but sees no one. Still, she self-consciously pees behind a rock. Every muscle in her body aches and screams at her. She's hungry too.

It doesn't matter. She hurries to fill her belly with more refreshing water which dulls her hunger at least temporarily.

The road was on her left when she left the house. Now, she could turn left or right to follow the creek, upstream or down. She remembers that most streams and rivers in the area flow either north to the Columbia River or west to the Pacific

Ocean unless of course, she is on the east side of the Coastal Range. There gravity pulls the water from rainfall and snow runoff down the hills into the creeks, sloughs, and drainage basins of the Willamette Valley.

Wherever it flows, people will be there. Her choice feels like a crapshoot, but it isn't.

The icy water shakes the cobwebs from her head. Judging by the water's gentle current, as well as the moss and lichen on the trees, she is on the east side of the Range. The road may be somewhere to her left, but she decides to follow the stream to her right, which by her calculations, means down the terrain. *Down should be easier and lead to homesteads eventually.*

She doesn't walk next to the water as the ground is spongy there. She also picks her path to avoid the distinctive, three-leaf pattern of poison oak. Deftly, she moves around boulders and rocks and past trees in her line of sight. A twig snaps behind her.

Immediately she freezes. *I knew it! I'm not alone after all.* Should she run?

Slowly, she pivots to see an elk cow lumber down to the creek for its morning drink. *If a cow is here, its mate must be nearby.* After a moment of watching her and waiting to see if the larger elk would show himself, she continues tracing the creek to its expected intersection with civilization.

It starts to rain. Emmarie enjoys both the smell of rain and rain itself; it washes the air clean and makes brown areas green. And at first, it makes her feel cleaner. Until it rains so much that instead of the air smelling fresh, her nose fills with the earthy, musty odor of composted soils with layers upon layers of rotting leaves, death, and decay.

Incessant raindrops make her shiver as she becomes wet and wetter. Droplets dribble into her eyes, making it harder to see, and easier to slip on old, wet leaves and mud. She considers finding another tree she can crawl under, but why? Oregon rain can last for hours, even days. She's hungry, cold, and must find help. "After what you've been through, you won't melt," she tells herself out loud.

Emmarie has no real choice. *Staying in one place may be what you do when rescuers are searching for you, but it's the opposite when the only one looking wants to kill you.*

She decides to follow her creek while daylight lasts. The one concession she makes to herself, if she hasn't found help by then, is to stop earlier than total nightfall to see if she can catch a fish. *There's no way to cook it with everything being drenched; but a little sushi is starting to sound good.*

The morning morphs into afternoon with occasional breaks in the cloud cover.

As she approaches a small clearing in the trees, she catches a glimpse of two men. With rifles. She halts immediately in her tracks.

They haven't seen her yet, she's sure of it. Part of her wants to cry out, to jump up and down and wave her arms above her head like a maniac. But they have guns. Too early, she thinks, for regular hunting season, which comes in the fall. She can think of no reason for them to be here except that they are up to no good. No good at best. At worst, Bob has his friends hunting her down like an animal.

Emmarie slinks back into the woods and finds a newly fallen tree that she can hide behind, nestling herself within its branches. Provided the men stay roughly where they are, she can see if they spot her. What she'd do then, she doesn't know. All she knows for certain as she hides, is that her visions of sushi die somewhere in the boughs around her while the rain comes down.

"Hey, Bruce! Do you see any sign of her?"

"Naw, lost her in the trees. She's probably gone."

"Come on, then, let's call it quits. I'm soaked."

"Yeah, me too. Let me take a leak then we'll leave." The elder of the two walks away from his buddy, directly toward Emmarie.

Every instinct demands she freeze. Or run. She doesn't know what to do. She tries to melt into the tree, become a limb herself. She thinks of extracting herself from the fir but wouldn't be able to without announcing herself. *Can I? Will it be worth it?* How far and how fast can she run? *It won't matter.*

She can't outrun their guns. She's trapped. The black velvet bodice with its green and black taffeta skirt may serve to camouflage her among the boughs, but that damn, white slip poncho spotlights her. It may as well be a white flag, the universal sign of surrender.

No. I do not surrender.

"Well, lookey what we have here," Bruce says, as he spies her through the heavy branches. "Hey, Jon, get your ass over here!"

CHAPTER 22

Carpe Momentum

⟿

Dash finds it difficult to sleep much past 4 a.m., in part because he's used to shift work in Traffic but mostly because he's feeling one step closer to finding Emmarie. He rises, shaves and showers by 4:30 a.m., which is too early to leave for Portland. Instead of his uniform, he opts for the dark blue Ted Baker London suit he'd purchased for almost half-price at Nordstrom's last year. Add a light blue shirt and a Paul Frederick striped tie, he's good to go he thinks. But leaving at 5 a.m. for what is a two-hour drive still puts him in the city too early to meet with Randall. He grabs a box for his files and notes, then gathers everything he'd spread out the night before to examine. He opens his laptop and plays yet again the footage Reliant National Bank sent over the previous afternoon.

Ms. Granger is right. He isn't sure how much good the surveillance footage will do him. Most the time, the camera films Silas Newsome's back as he moves in and out of frame. Beyond his ample body, you occasionally see the driver's side of the Escalade, but bank cameras are meant to capture images up to a couple of feet away, not thirty.

All the anticipated footage did for Cooper is confirm what he already knows: An unidentified man talks with Emmarie. He shows up almost immediately, which means that he, too, had been a bystander. As Newsome said, he moves to the other side of the Escalade, the passenger side, before disappearing out of camera range altogether. Presumably, he heads west to a vehicle. But all Dash sees is Newsome's back again.

Dash finishes last night's Italian sub sandwich for breakfast, along with his black coffee, then fills a tall travel mug. As a cop, he can drink a lot of joe without feeling caffeine jitters. The buzz he feels this morning centers on meeting Lt. Randall.

When it finally makes sense to leave, he takes the Sunset Highway into the city. He knows commuter traffic will get worse the closer he is to Portland, but he hadn't figured on the snail's pace all the way in. Now he kicks himself for not leaving as soon as he could.

Good thing no cop guarantees his availability at a specific time. That's the nature of the job for him, and especially for Randall as the head of Vice in a no-holds-barred city like Portland.

170

Portland has always been that way, Cooper thinks. He knows enough history and local lore from growing up there to know it's no San Francisco, Chicago, or New York. Like those cities though, Portland's infrastructure and morals lag behind its population booms. Portland is a progressive city where anything can be secured at a price if you have connections.

Stumptown, a.k.a. Mudtown, outgrew the bergs that derided it with those nicknames, becoming the largest, most prosperous commercial center and port in Oregon. But not without hiccups along the way. 'The Forbidden City of the West' stayed a dangerous frontier town, reported by the local Oregonian newspaper to be "the most filthy city in the Northern States," long before it blossomed into the beautiful, independent-minded City of Roses today.

When he lived here, he was too young to notice. But now, as a small-town resident, Portland reminds Cooper of an ant-hive. Industrious and eclectic on top with teeming layers of complexity making up the substrata. Big money. Liberal interests. Political favors. Power mongers and cogs. Secrets. Fetishes. Survival.

Remnants of its rough and tumble beginnings still exist in attitudes and structure. Underneath the pleasant, laid-back parks and rose gardens, underneath the steel skyscrapers, bustling art museums, and avant-garde statues, lies the notorious Portland of old, where Shanghai tunnels connect the basements of most taverns and hotels from the Old

Town/Chinatown neighborhood through the business district, to the Willamette River waterfront.

Seattle advertises its infamous underground, but many don't know Portland has one too. Little is now known of the labyrinth of interconnected basements, low ceilings, and makeshift rooms, purportedly facilitating sneaking illegal goods in both directions between ship and shore. Other tunnels connected underground gambling houses, opium dens, and brothels, even holding cells for kidnapped labor awaiting transport to Asia as crewmembers or 'entertainment.' Most passageways in the catacomb system have succumbed to disrepair, except for those along the tourist routes.

Cooper misses the entrance to underground parking for the 2nd Street Precinct and circles the block. "The unofficial motto, 'Keep Portland Weird' fits," he mumbles to himself. *Not that downtown is weird, but the vibe sure can be.*

It's still raining 'liquid sunshine' as the locals call it. He'd been prepared to carry his file box on his head to keep his suit dry but now he doesn't have to because he finally locates a spot in the parking garage. Once in the lobby of the precinct, he confirms his appointment, gets his security pass then asks directions to Lt. Randall's office.

"Happy to meet you, Deputy Cooper," Randall says as he stands at his desk. "Close the door behind you, if you would."

Cooper presses the box against his chest to steady it with one hand while he uses his free arm to pull the door shut. He sets his box down on an empty chair in front of him. "I appreciate you meeting me, especially on such short notice," he says as he grabs the lieutenant's hand for an obligatory, two-pump shake.

"As I indicated on the phone, my work on the Coastal Cutthroat Killer case has made me aware of a dozen young ladies that have gone missing since September. You mentioned others have gone missing long before September. I don't think most of my missing girls have anything to do with CCK, just as yours probably don't."

"I see," Randall says, as he sits back down behind his desk, and gestures to the remaining vacant chair next to Cooper's file box. "Please, take a seat."

As Cooper does, he feels Randall sizing him up. An older cop checking out a younger one is not unusual, but this wasn't regular testosterone posturing.

Randall steeples his fingers. "You should know after we talked yesterday, I called Lt. Bellows. Professional courtesy, of course. I understand you've gone a bit off trail. But to your credit, you as much as told me that yesterday. Bellows doesn't share your conclusions. Thinks you're running ahead without much supporting your suppositions."

Cooper takes it on the chin. "That's exactly why I'm here, Sir, to see if there's any basis for my hunches." *What did Walt tell this guy? Did he expose me as a run-of-the-mill traffic cop?*

"Bellows tells me you're sharp. But, hell, you're not on the official CCK taskforce. You're not included in his man-hour reports. I don't know what you have on him. But I guess you've got something, which is why he's giving you head to run with this."

"Right on all counts," the young officer admits. Already caught bending the truth about his role with the CCK investigation, Cooper knows he must stand up for himself or he won't get access to Randall's information. His 5-hour round-trip to Portland flashes before his eyes as a potential waste of precious time.

"The Coastal Cutthroat Killer — for whatever reason — kills his victims after he keeps them one week. At least thus far. We don't always find the bodies right away, so it wasn't obvious at first. But unless he changes his pattern, any women missing longer than about a week or two probably aren't his."

"Interesting." Randall pauses then appears to change the subject. "Are you familiar with the Green River Killer up in the Seattle area?"

"Sure, somewhat familiar at least. Gary Ridgeway, right? Confessed to 71 murders in Washington and Oregon over a 20-year spree I think."

"That's correct," Randall smiles. "My point is that Bellows is right." He pauses like any cop would, to let that sink in. "Even if you're correct about keeping them alive for a week, I'm afraid it means little." Randall draws out his pronunciation of those last three words.

'It means nothing,' you mean.

"Most of Ridgeway's victims were skeletons when authorities discovered them. In fact, three known victims have yet to be identified after all this time." Randall stands and walks to a Keurig on his credenza. "Black?" He continues speaking as it brews. "Just because you've found some CCK victims a couple of days after he kept them alive for a week, doesn't mean the ones you haven't found aren't out there right now becoming compost."

Randall has him. And he's right. The pattern he thinks he's found means squat. For sure it doesn't mean there aren't CCK victims **punctuating the terrain** somewhere, yet to be found.

Cooper slowly nods as he processes Randall's comments. Finally, he admits, "I'll grant you that. However, given the other nuances of his M.O., CCK wants his bodies found. He leaves them in out-of-the-way places, sure, but he displays them. Going off the beaten path is more a component of CCK not wanting to get caught, rather than not wanting the bodies to be seen."

"So, you're a profiler now?"

"There's more." Cooper remembers Randall's dislike of one-way streets. He hopes by sharing his information first, Randall will capitulate. "None of our known CCK files mention this, but six files of the remaining missing women do. Witnesses report seeing a white van in the neighborhoods where these women went missing. Well, not all of them. When a white van isn't mentioned, forensics say there's white paint transfer onto the bicycles some of these women were riding."

"Again, interesting," Randall parries. "But that doesn't rule out CCK."

"Your missing women matching CCK's profile of 18 to 23 years of age may already be included in the taskforce list I have. But the others, the younger ones you mentioned… How many are known prostitutes or come from the street, and how many would be considered 'fresh meat,' if you'll pardon that vulgarity."

Randall takes a sip of his own coffee while he thinks. "I can't answer that off the top of my head, but I can tell you that most of our missing young ladies would not be characterized as working girls, not obviously anyway. From my memory, none have records or street names. Parents and friends attest to them having nothing but the usual problems."

Cooper feels the momentum turn. "Look, it's a theory, one with obvious holes in it that you've graciously pointed out. But I'm not costing either department extra payroll. And contrary to what Bellows may think, I'm not hunting facts to match my pet theory. I'm following all the leads to see where they take me. I think we can help each other."

Let me try at least.

CHAPTER 23

Tick Tock Tick Tock

Lt. Randall stares at the file box Cooper lugged in, while he scratches his neck. "All right, Cooper. Quid pro quo. I'll give you Officer Lupe Díaz for the day. She'll get you up to speed on what we know, and you'll do likewise for her. Got that?"

"Absolutely," he agrees with confidence, hiding the fact that for the most part, he's already offered all his fresh insights and information. He doubts if he can add to Portland's resources, but he sure wants access to theirs.

"Good. Let me introduce you." Rather than getting up, he punches an intercom button on his desk and instantly connects to Díaz. "Díaz, my office, please."

In a New York minute, she opens the door and leans in. "Yes, boss?"

"I want to introduce you to Dashiell Cooper, he's on a field trip from Clatsop County. I told him you'd swap information on our human trafficking investigation. So, give him whatever he needs today, okay?"

"If you say so," she nods to Randall before turning her attention to Cooper. "Lupe Díaz, at your service. Why don't you bring your box of goodies to our conference room? You can work in there. Here, I'll show you. Follow me."

Something about being ordered about by a strong, confidant woman, Dash rather likes it.

When she has him settled in the conference room, Díaz excuses herself to get her laptop and a legal pad. While she's gone, Cooper plugs in his PC and loads the email with the ATM footage. He uses his personal hotspot to do it. Díaz returns shortly.

"Before we get started, look at this. It's a long shot, but have you ever seen this guy before?"

"Seen him before? I can barely see him now," she says, scrunching her face up. "I'm not sure what resources Clatsop has, but the state's forensic department can clean that up if Randall authorizes it."

Her light-hearted dig against his department does not go unnoticed, but he chooses not to spar with her. Not that he wouldn't enjoy the banter, but it doesn't feel appropriate now, not when both Randall's and Emmarie's clocks tick away. He does, however, automatically drop his eyes to look at her left hand when she pulls out a chair next to him and sits down. No ring.

"Yeah, they could, I mean, they will, but I only got this late yesterday. I think this guy is somehow linked to one of our missing women."

"Why?"

"Granted, it's one of my hunches, but it's the way he behaves. See here? He leaves before the authorities come. None of the other witnesses did. They usually don't unless they have something to hide."

"This girl went missing right after her accident?"

"No, about six months later. I haven't figured that part out. Her parents report some strange occurrences over those months though. More to the point, she's one of six missing women we can link to a white van."

"I don't see a white van in the clip."

She is stating facts, but it reminds Cooper of how little rational basis or quantifiable reasons he has for his hunches. "I know."

"So, okay," she takes her eyes away from the video and refocuses on him. "Besides wanting to know who this guy is, what else do you want to know?" She opens her laptop then doesn't wait for his answer. "I've been working on human trafficking after we noticed a pattern developing. But I suppose Randall told you, in a year and a half, we have a barebones understanding of how this works. It's not a white slavery ring, but many of our missing women are white, WASP white."

She pours herself a glass of water from the pitcher that an underling brought in when Cooper first arrived. "We aren't sure if the girls are victims of chance encounters or if they're stalked first, making their disappearances more of a concerted effort. I say 'girls' because we have some in puberty that have disappeared.

"We also don't know how many people are involved," she continues, "but we do believe that the network involves New Orleans. It may be that Portland is a feeder city, like an Atlanta or Houston, with the national hub in New Orleans. If that's so, it'd be nice if they were a whole lot more cooperative.

"Anyway, we think that international buyers end up with most of the girls. Those that don't fetch a baseline price might get shipped off to stateside brothels that specialize in innocence over technique. By the time they get used up there, they're usually hooked on drugs and resold to street pimps, all happening on the opposite ends of the country from where they're nabbed."

"Keeps the girls dependent." Cooper adds. "Sounds like you know quite a lot." He pulls out his own legal pad with his on-going list of questions. His pen speeds across the paper as she speaks, making notes only he will be able to read if he can read them at all later.

"If they stalk their victims, maybe that's where ATM man comes in to play," Díaz says. "Maybe that's where he meets her and takes a shining to her. But that doesn't make a lot of sense if the goal is to shuttle these women off to New Orleans. There'd be nothing personal about it. It'd make sense to select females according to type, to need, even to the ease of taking them, not to whether you like them or not."

Díaz muses out loud. Cooper likes her willingness to brainstorm openly instead of playing her cards tightly.

"What if it's both?" Cooper asks. "Maybe several guys are responsible for grabbing girls and putting them somewhere until someone orders paperwork from a counterfeiter and hauls them to the Big Easy. The counterfeiter doesn't have to be in New Orleans; he could be here, there, or anywhere, provided he can get his documents to the international shipper. Maybe there's no one way these women rise to the attention of this group."

"Okay," she speculates. "The Feds should have a shortlist of the guys with the skillset to pull off the counterfeiting well enough. International terrorism tightened everything up. The docs they use now must be spot-on. If we can find the printer and apply pressure, he can lead us to his contact in Louisiana. The feeders aren't the big boys. They may not be privy to the others. They get paid when they deliver. So, unless we can catch them red-handed, the Feds will have to break the case in New Orleans first, then get leverage to identify the others."

"In the meantime, damn-it, their machine keeps gobbling up innocents and spitting out money. Can we track them via bank transfers?" Cooper asks.

"Not likely, not at the local level anyway. It'll be a cash business," Díaz says. "For New Orleans and international buyers, it'll involve off-shore accounts. The Feds are working on human trafficking, of course. We aren't sure the role of the players here."

Cooper thinks of Emmarie and loses his professional veneer. He lets disappointment register across his face.

"Sorry to let you down, Cooper. But I like your style. Who's your personal interest in this case?"

"Call me Dash. My friends do."

"We're friends now?" She smiles. "Okay, Dash, friends don't withhold information. I'm a detective and I detect a personal interest. Obsessed with ATM man, volunteering your time. Randall told me. Spill it."

Cooper is about to tell Díaz about the young woman in the ATM clip when the cell phone on his waist buzzes.

It's Bellows. "One week since the last report of a missing woman, Mr. Psychic, and we have another body. Are you still in Portland?"

CHAPTER 24

Deadline Drops

———

"By your reckoning, the victim is either Kelso or Roberts," Bellows says. "That's fair because there's no decomp reported by the ranger who found her."

Cooper doesn't feel like gloating. All he manages to push out his dry throat is 'Where?' Then he turns to Officer Díaz to say, "Excuse me."

"A ranger found her. Clatsop State Forest, near a creek, off-road outside Neverstill," Bellows continues. "A team is on its way there now, but it will take more than an hour to get out there. So, sit tight. I'll have them text you a photo."

Bellows pauses and softens his voice. "Look, Dash, I'm sorry. Based on what the ranger said about rigor mortis, it isn't one of the other ladies on the list. Not unless he kept her alive for a lot longer than a week."

Cooper knows what his uncle is trying to say. *Damn it.* He wishes he's wrong, but his own theory is playing out. Cooper no longer hears anything but his thoughts screaming at him until he manages to refocus his attention on Bellows.

"…just because there's no decomp. Hey, it might not be either of these women. We can't jump to conclusions, Dash. It might be a woman who wasn't reported missing, or at least not reported missing from this area. Doesn't rule out a body dump from Washington state either. That happens too. Might not be CCK at all." Bellows adds.

It sounds to Dash like his uncle is trying to backtrack from the snarky comment he opened with, but more likely it's his pragmatism coming through.

"No," Cooper agrees, finally able to talk. "It doesn't." Thanks for letting me know, and yes, please have your people text me a photo. I'll recognize Emmarie if it's her." He swallows hard. A beat passes before he adds, "I'm wrapping it up here. Do you want me to head out to see the ranger? If I leave now, I can meet the forensics team.

"Suit yourself," Bellows offers. "Depends on what you want to do. You'll have her photo outside the hour."

Cooper ends the call and slowly puts his phone back on his belt.

"I think you answered my question, Dash," Díaz says.

After he thanks Díaz and Randall for their time and assistance, he promises to keep in touch and let them know if

184

he learns anything that can help with their investigation. He means every word when he says it, but his promise tastes hollow in his mouth.

Portland needs to play in the big leagues with the Feds and New Orleans. He is a small-town traffic cop pulling on a lifeline thrown by his uncle. That is all. If this new body turns out to be Emmarie, then his quest is over. He'll use his last few vacation days for a world-class bender. If this isn't Emmarie, a bender might still be in order. The bottom line is that he should promise Randall and Díaz nothing. Nothing is what you give when that's what you've got.

Standing around waiting for a photo to arrive does nothing but churn his breakfast and the quick burger he'd grabbed with Díaz. His senses tell him he's penned in, blocked, useless. *Might as well be trapped in a cage with a lion. At least then I could vent this... this...what-ever it is I'm feeling.*

He weighs his options. He can find a motel room now and start throwing back the bourbons as soon as the photo comes, or he can head to Clatsop City along the Columbia River. Take the I-5 freeway across the bridge to Vancouver, then up to Longview, Washington, before cutting back into Oregon via the Lewis and Clark Bridge. That route's faster than taking the road out of Portland past Sauvie Island and St. Helens. The Washington route brings him back into Oregon in position to take the 202 over to the body dump, if he ultimately chooses to go.

But if he can stomach this one at all, why hurry? He elects to run up the 405 freeway to scenic Highway 30, up the Oregon side. He wants time to think.

He's paralleling St. Johns when his phone buzzes. It's Bellows again. He doesn't want to answer but he finds a place to pull his Jeep off the road to safely take the call.

"Dash, they found Emmarie Kelso. The body dump—"

The young deputy vomits acidic bile into his mouth.

"It isn't her." Bellows says. "Columbia County just notified us that a couple of hunters reported finding her in the woods. She's exhausted, suffering from hypothermia, bruised and hungry, but otherwise all right. They are transporting her via helicopter to a hospital in Portland now. Portland PD is involved."

"I'm turning around. Which hospital?"

"Oregon Health Sciences University."

Dash ends the call, not sure what he feels. Relieved? Obviously. His body shakes, and his eyes mist over so he can't see. Screaming doesn't make sense considering such good news, but he needs to vent the pressure of the emotional roller coaster he's been riding. So, there at the entrance to the U.S. Army Corps of Engineers facility, short of the St. Johns Bridge and the Ridge Trail Trailhead, with his Wrangler windows sealed tight, Dashiell H. Cooper lets out a primal scream.

Then he draws more fresh air deep into his lungs and lets out another one. He's certain the other drivers can hear him, even above the din of their own passing cars, but he doesn't care. He doesn't care if they can hear, and he doesn't care what they think.

Emmarie is not only alive; she's SAFE at OHSU. He sits there several minutes, wrapping his head around the news. Finally, as stomach cramps and racing pulse begins to subside, his eyesight clears. He feels composed, or at least more so than before.

He turns some music on and waits for a gap in traffic large enough to pull out, working his way over into the open median. Once there, he makes a left turn to merge into the oncoming lane of busy Hwy 30 traffic headed back to Portland, only a few horn blasts and middle fingers worse for wear.

CHAPTER 25

Up and Down

Dr. Janet Brooks Kelso, for all the free advice she gives others, after they plunk down $29.95 for one of her books of course, has not done well in Emmarie's absence. Her leading advice — forgive yourself — she hasn't yet taken. She means to, but she cannot find the right combination that will allow self-clemency, or even permission for such forgiveness, to flow from her heart. *Good thing my readers don't know, or they'll think me a fraud.*

She sits at her desk trying to focus enough to put final touches on her 'farewell' book. In it, she dispenses the honest reflections and cutting-edge psychology and advice that makes her this generation's Dr. Phil. In this particular book, she details her personal struggle with cancer and the choices she makes, all woven into standard advice fare. Focusing on the manuscript to the degree she needs to, is out of the question.

So many things she wants to tell her daughter but never has. Sure, she often tells Emmarie that she loves her, but isn't saying 'I love you' just what people say now? Like saying 'Chao' to friends dispersing after a light brunch. Words can't convey the depth of love Janet feels for her children. And not just for her children, but for Emmarie, specifically.

Emmarie is a carbon copy of herself. Inquisitive, strong-willed, intelligent, stubborn. Stubborn to a fault, she thinks. Then there's her firstborn son, Danny. She doesn't think her daughter lives in Danny's shadow, but she believes Emmarie believes that. And how many times has she contributed to that lie with 'Danny this' and 'Danny that'?

Her mind travels to that bleak time when Emmarie was five -- the loss of a baby, a baby boy, broke her heart beyond any feeling that it could ever be repaired. Yet through the love of her children and husband, it somehow was. It took months. During those days, Emmarie drew her momma crayon pictures trying to cheer her up, not understanding days of crashing hormones and disappointments. Emmarie had been far too young to understand that nothing was her fault. *Nothing is Emmarie's fault now either.*

This feels like unfinished business, like painful heartbreak beyond repair, just as it did then.

Wherever Emmarie is, does she know I love her, more than I can possibly communicate?

Precisely because she loves her children so much, she didn't want to tell them her cancer had returned with a vengeance. More to the point, she did not want her children to know that she is refusing the extraordinary measures to extend her life, against the will of her husband and her doctors. She didn't want them acting differently toward her.

God, how she and Roger had argued over her decision. But it was her decision, wasn't it?

All she wanted then, and now, is to finish her final book and exit with all the grace she can muster. Of course, Roger doesn't agree. *But he doesn't have to go through the invasive chemo and radiation treatments that suck me dry, making me sick all the time, not able to enjoy my family. And for what? Almost no odds of defeating cancer this time? No thank you.*

"I'm not a victim, and I'm not giving up!" she'd screamed at him. "All I'm doing is not prolonging the inevitable. Can't you see I'm embracing the circle of life? I'm going to live on my terms even if it means going out on my terms!"

That is the message of the manuscript before her. But she can't corral her thoughts. They bounce between Emmarie, Danny, Roger, and her unfinished bucket list. She tries to protect her children, a little too much, perhaps. The news would make Emmarie sad, causing her to tiptoe around her during their remaining time together. Janet doesn't want to put that kind of pressure on her, nor does she want her daughter making sacrifices either. It is enough to tell Emmarie to put off Juilliard just for a year. *Am I being unreasonable keeping Emmarie closer to home for a few months?* None of that matters now anyway.

She would give anything for her daughter's safe return. More than a week missing feels like an eternity apart. Will she have opportunity to tell Emmarie how much she loves her? And that she is sorry?

Her doorbell rings, jarring her loose from the obsessions that engulf her.

It's Lieutenant Bellows.

"Oh, God! NO!" she says as soon as she sees him on her front steps.

"Don't be alarmed, Dr. Kelso. I have good news. May I come in?"

"Yes, yes, of course. Please." She ushers him into the living room, where they'd sat before. His team and the FBI left only a few days ago when it became apparent that this was not a kidnap for ransom situation. With her house quiet once again, she hadn't quite known what to do with herself, except stare at her book, trying to keep busy, trying to finish.

"You say you have good news? But I- I heard they found a body..."

"Is Mr. Kelso home?"

Roger rounds the corner as the detective asks. "I'm here. I'm afraid Danny's not. We sent him to the hardware store." They love having their son there. He helps fill the void, the dreaded silence that came after the FBI left and the casseroles from neighbors and friends slowed. Janet can't imagine a world without her children.

"Mr. Kelso," Bellows extends his hand before turning back to Janet. "Yes, unfortunately, there is another body, but that's not why I'm here. I don't usually get to deliver good news in my line of work. Some hunters came upon Emmarie earlier today, lost in the woods. She's safe. She's being treated at OHSU for exposure and some injuries, but she's okay. It's my understanding that they may keep her for a few days for observation. Columbia County Sheriff's department and Portland police will debrief her, but I have a deputy on his way there now. Dashiell Cooper, you may remember him from her accident."

"Can we see her?"

"That's a medical question for her doctors, but from my perspective, I don't see why not."

As soon as Bellows leaves, Janet calls the hospital for a status report and learns that her daughter is sleeping well. She doesn't want to wake her.

It's late in the day, yet she and Roger make plans to leave immediately for Portland. Janet packs a bag for herself and one for Roger with all the essentials: Toothbrushes, razor, Roger's Lipitor, and her thyroid medication and pain pills. She throws in one change of clothes for each of them, plus one for Emmarie. If they need more, it will be a great excuse to go shopping.

Roger busies himself by calling the Port of Astoria Regional Airport to let them know he'll be taking his Beechcraft Bonanza V-tail. Next, he calls a rental car company to have a luxury sedan waiting for them at the Hillsboro Airport, the airport closest to OHSU that can handle the requirements of his powerful airplane.

They drive to Astoria's small airport and Roger begins his pre-flight planning. The weather on the coast and in the coastal range can change on a dime; however, the early morning rains that showed no signs of breaking cleared with bands of weather to the north and south of them. He files a visual flight plan.

"Nothing that should affect the flight," he tells Janet. "But I wish now I hadn't kept the plane's instrument panel vintage."

Janet cannot stop chatting about Emmarie being safe while Roger runs through his preflight checklist. Then she catches herself and apologizes for distracting him. He performs the checklist routine like a machine. Indeed, he's done it a hundred times. Janet knows how important this is, yet she cannot contain her excitement and desire to talk.

Roger gets both magnetos to ignite and the engine roars to life. Everything looks good.

The Bonanza is ready to take off. With a pat on his wife's knee, he pulls back on the yoke, releases the brakes that hold the craft in check, and opens it up. They speed down the tarmac and feel the tires bounce once then take to the air for good. They climb the first ten feet then gradually gain altitude. When they are high enough, he retracts the landing gear.

Flying over land at 160 miles an hour, they'll be on the other side of the Coastal Range in a matter of minutes by following the coast toward Seaside then cutting due East over the mountains to follow Hwy 26 below. His preflight preparations and getting to and from the airstrips will take longer than the flight itself, Roger informs his wife.

Janet loves flying, especially along the coastline, seeing the open expanse before her, feeling invincible, and now, elated with the news about Emmarie. She can only imagine the horrors her daughter experienced, but it's over. *I'll not think about that now. Emmarie did whatever she needed to do to survive. She's safe.* We will arrange whatever help is necessary to get her through this, she decides. *We will get through this together.*

Roger banks his sweeping turn roughly over Seaside as planned. With an airplane this fast, every maneuver takes more distance to accomplish. They'd put the coast behind them when Janet asks, "Roger, do you think they'll let us bring her home with us? I don't imagine she'll want to talk to me professionally, but she might be willing to see a colleague of mine. Dr. Abrams, perhaps. She's good."

"We don't know anything yet, Janet. Let's not speculate on how to help her until we know what help she needs."

"I know but…"

"Hold up. We're headed into a fast-moving thunderstorm. The weather cells must have merged, and I don't see a gap in the clouds anymore. We're going to get our plane washed."

"Can we go around it?"

"Just let me focus," he snaps. "No. I'm turning back." He attempts a climbing left hand turn as Janet's knuckles turn white.

She tries to keep silent, watching nervously as Roger moves his hands and eyesight quickly back and forth between the controls. The fast-flying Bonanza hits turbulence and drops and tilts. Janet screams, "Are we okay?"

"Wind-shear." Beyond that, he doesn't answer.

Turbulence continues to bounce the small craft as Roger tries to correct, not sure which correction would counter the sudden down drafts. "Hang on, you son of a bitch! CLIMB!

Those are the last words his wife of 24 years hears as their Bonanza makes a spiral dive, clips the top of a tall fir, slams into Saddle Mountain, and shatters as it rolls.

CHAPTER 26

Breaking News

⌇⟶

Dash passes news reporters from all the major stations gathering with their production and camera vans in front of the Oregon Health Sciences University to announce that the daughter of Dr. Janet Brooks Kelso is indeed safe after being abducted a little over one week ago.

He enters the hospital, flashes his badge at the information attendant desk, and obtains her room number. He flashes his badge again to the Portland police officer finishing up with Emmarie. She's in a hospital bed, face swollen and bruised, and an I.V. in her left arm, not unlike he saw her in October. "Emmarie, I don't like seeing you this way," he mutters to himself.

"Officer Brown, may I speak to you outside for a few minutes?" They step out into the hallway, out of earshot before Cooper says, "What can you tell me?"

"Her name is Emmarie Lynn Kelso of Clatsop City, missing since the 20th. She's had quite an ordeal. A couple of cougar hunters found her barefoot, outside of Keasey, wearing a wrist manacle and chain."

"Cougar hunters?"

"Yeah, that's about the only creature you can legally hunt year-round in Oregon. Need a license, but these guys did things by the book. They had been tracking a female cat when they decided to give up. One guy was taking a leak when he noticed the woman hiding. He approached her and she freaked out. Put up a good fight I hear. Clipped one in the lip. It's a good thing they got her calmed down because if she'd wrestled a gun away, she might be facing murder charges."

"Is Columbia County or Portland PD in receipt of the manacle?" His phone buzzes with an incoming text that includes a photo of a young Caucasian woman, spread eagle face up. He glances, figures the body is Kylee Roberta Roberts based on the obvious similarities to the way CCK displays his victims and returns his attention to Officer Brown.

"Portland PD. Just got the contraption off her. They collected trace including fingerprints before they decided how to cut it off. Wanted to keep it intact as much as possible. The technician told me he collected smudges. Probably won't do us any good. We bagged everything she was wearing as evidence too."

"Okay, thanks." Cooper turns to enter the hospital room but stops with his hand on the door handle. "Hey, do me a favor, would you? Call Officer Lupe Díaz in Vice and notify her that Emmarie is here. She may be a witness in the investigation Díaz is working on."

When he enters the room, Cooper takes another moment to look at the face that's enchanted him ever since she waited on him in the pet store. Battered, for sure, but still lovely. *And she's awake.* "Hi, how are you feeling?"

"I've been better, obviously. Hey, I've already told the officers what I know. I don't know what else I can tell you."

"I'm not with Portland police. I'm with Clatsop County. I can get a copy of your statement with their report. I'm here to check on you."

The quizzical look on her face prompts him to explain further. "I work with Lt. Bellows, the lead investigator on your missing person case. I happened to be collaborating with Portland PD today when I heard they'd found you."

"Do you carry any sway?"

"I'm sorry. What?"

"Do you have any authority? I can't get them to let me out of here so I can help find this guy. I wounded him. I don't know if I killed him. But he has another captive, a boy named Mason. We've got to help him."

"Emmarie, listen to me. The doctors and the police know what they're doing. Your feet are bandaged. Your soles must be shredded after walking through the underbrush without boots on. If you're here, it's because you need medical attention and rest. You can help get this guy later."

She turns her bruised face away from him.

Disappointment? Frustration? Rejection? He doesn't know. He thinks he should take a different approach. "Look, I was the deputy who investigated your accident in October. Perhaps you remember me?"

She moves her face to realign with his again. "Why does every man assume I remember him? No offense, I hope."

"What do you mean?"

"Bob, the pervert who took me, said the same thing. Said I might remember him, but I don't."

"What else did he say? Did he say where you'd met before?"

"No. But he was preparing to cut off my clothes so forgive me if I was a little preoccupied."

Cooper melts. He'd guessed she'd been through hell, and he doesn't want to push her. He wants to hold her, to rock her, to make it all better.

"I'm sorry," she says. "I don't mean to be a jerk. I know you're trying to do your job. It's just that I was literally chained to a bed, dreaming of freedom. I got free. Now I'm back in a bed, chained by monitors and needles. I can't leave when I want to. So, no, it doesn't feel like too much has changed. But at least Nurse Ratched doesn't stink."

"Did you include this in your statement?"

"What? That Nurse Ratched doesn't stink?" She grins lightly at him. "I didn't provide a play by play if that's what you mean."

Cooper smiles back. He catches her reference to the late Ken Kesey's *One Flew Over the Cuckoo's Nest*. Dash is himself a bibliophile, aware of the book and movie's cult status. Almost everyone in Oregon knows the Nurse Ratched character by the University of Oregon's alum.

"Emmarie, I know you won't enjoy reliving the details. But there may be things you haven't told us that would help. Or things you remember later that are important. If you don't mind, I want to help you get him off the streets so he can't hurt anyone else."

"Why would I mind?" She pushes her dinner tray away from her after eating only the orange Jell-O.

"What I meant was, I'd like you to go over everything again with me. Then call me, personally, if you remember anything else."

"Will you see that I get out of here tomorrow?"

"If I can. I planned on staying in Portland." *Liar.* "I'll talk to your doctors and see what I can arrange, provided you do your best to get some rest after you walk me through what happened."

"Deal."

About an hour into Emmarie telling her story again, with Cooper stopping her to ask for details, his phone rings. It's Bellows again. He excuses himself and leaves the room to take the call.

"Yeah, Walt. What's up?"

"Are you with Miss Kelso?"

"Yes, I am. Why? Do you need me at the body dump?"

"No, son, got that covered. Although I would appreciate you following up with the team when you get back. Seems like our guy is getting sloppy. He left some evidence behind that he doesn't usually leave."

"I'm intrigued. Tell me—"

"That's not why I'm calling, son. Miss Kelso can't get a break. A small plane went down in the Coastal Range and the tail number identifies the V-tail Beechcraft Bonanza as Roger Kelso's plane. Both onboard were killed instantly."

"You're kidding me! Shit."

"I was just at their house to tell them we'd found their daughter. Now I'm going out again to notify her brother. Damn shame. Anyway, some uniforms are on their way to the hospital to notify Kelso now. You might want to stay there with her. This isn't going to be easy."

"Understood. Thanks for the heads up."

Instead of returning to Emmarie's room immediately, Cooper walks to the nurses' station to let them know. He asks them to temporarily disable her television set for a day or two so she wouldn't be hounded by 24/7 news reports showing grim footage. He asks the nurses to give her a couple of sleeping pills or a sedative, if necessary, but he knows they'd need a doctor's order first. He's still at the nurses' desk when uniformed officers appear. He introduces himself, then escorts them to her room. He stands on the opposite side of the bed while they speak.

"Hi, Miss Kelso?" one of them begins.

"Enough already. I surrender. What's with you cops?"

"We're sorry to disturb you, but I'm afraid we have bad news," the older one says.

"You found him and he's dead? That isn't bad news."

"No, ma'am. Your parents' plane went down over the Coastal Range on their way here. We have several eyewitnesses to the crash, but we aren't sure what happened yet. I'm sorry to inform you that your parents are deceased."

"Oh, God! No. No! Please, God, NO!" She begins to cry. "What about Danny? Is my brother all right?"

"As far as we know, only your parents were onboard. Your brother is fine. He's being notified now," the other officer pipes up. "Miss Kelso, we are truly sorry for your loss. The accident will be investigated by the NTSB, the National Transportation Safety Board, and you'll get more information when they learn more."

"Are you sure it was my dad's plane?"

"Yes, ma'am. Tail number confirms it."

They ask if she is okay or if they should call the nurse or something, but Emmarie shakes her head. She turns away and lets her tears fall silently. With nothing else they can do, the notification team tip toes out of the room, whispering about the Bonanza's notoriety as "The Doctor Killer" in bad weather.

Dash moves forward, closer to Emmarie and takes her hand. "I am so sorry."

She pulls her hand away and tells him, "If you don't mind, I think I'd prefer to be alone." She begins to rock almost imperceptibly, arms tucked against her stomach.

"Of course," Dash says dolefully before he tries again. "I'm going to the cafeteria for a bite to eat. Hospital food is notoriously bad. Want some?"

She shakes her head without smiling at his humor.

"Okay, well, I'll come back to check on you before I leave."

"Thanks," she mumbles.

Forty minutes later when he returns, he finds her sleeping, aided by Lunesta or something stronger he figures. He looks around the room to a chair in the corner. It doesn't look very comfy, and it doesn't come with the bourbon he expected to be sipping by now.

Still, if the choice is a strange bed in a random hotel room or staying close to Emmarie in case she needs a familiar face, he has no choice. No choice at all. He makes his way to the nurse's station to ask for a pillow and a blanket.

CHAPTER 27

Moving Violations

Cooper wakes early. The aging leather upright chair in Emmarie's hospital room is not conducive to rolling over and sleeping in, like his own cozy bed or even his sofa. He notices her awake, eyeing him.

"Good morning. How did you sleep?" he asks her.

"I slept."

"Are you okay? Do you feel like talking?"

"Do you mean, as newly orphaned, do I want to talk about it? No. But if you mean how do I *feel*, I *feel* like you should keep your part of the deal. Get me out of here."

She has every right to be angry, he reminds himself.

"Sure, but breakfast first. I think I can find my way back to the cafeteria. Perhaps we should start by asking the nurses if you can join me."

"Maybe I'm not hungry."

"But you should try to eat. Take a little juice or something," he encourages. "Either way, it's a good ruse to show them you can handle being up and around, right?" He smiles gently at her and waits for her to agree.

She nods. "Is this IV pole mobile, or do you think we can get them to take the needle out of my hand? And what about clothes? This blue hospital isn't fashionable outside this room."

"You handle breakfast first. I'll see about clothes then try to get your doctors to sign off on your discharge. Deal?"

"Deal." Emmarie pushes her nurse call button. While she waits, she asks, "Hey, Deputy Cooper…Why did you sleep here last night?"

"Would you believe I'm too cheap to spring for a hotel? Reminded me of my college days, crashing at a friend's pad." He rises, comes over to her bed, and pats her free hand. "You should call me Dash. After all, we spent the night together."

She rolls her eyes and Dash thinks he sees a brief smile form, then flee her lips.

The nurse appears and tells Emmarie that she would check with the doctor about removing the IV, but if Emmarie feels like it, she has permission to walk to the cafeteria, dragging the pole along with her. The only problem, the nurse states, is rigging up better coverage for her derriere than the two ties the gown provides. Since the police took her clothes as evidence, she doesn't even have the benefit of underwear between her and the waiting world.

"On second thought, Dash, could you move clothes forward on the agenda? Size 6 to 8. I'm done hanging my ass out before strangers. You can bring me breakfast along with clothes if you insist. I promise I'll eat."

He clicks his heels like a German officer taking orders from a superior. "Of course," he says. As much as Dash, the man, wants to flirt with her after she places the image of her ass in his mind, Cooper, the law enforcement officer, maintains decorum. Now is not the place or the time for flirting any more than he already has.

"In the meantime," he says as he excuses himself, "Work your magic on the doctors but don't go anywhere. I'm coming right back."

When he returns 90 minutes later, Dash carries a Nordstrom shopping bag containing everything she might need. Underwear, a spaghetti-strap camisole, a pair of Levi 501's, a mint green V-neck top with raglan sleeves, socks, and two pairs of black Adidas, one size 7 and one 8, just in case.

"The sales lady helped me," he admits. "I hope you like them. They should fit well enough to get you out of here. Oh, and I didn't know what you wanted to eat. But you can't go wrong with McDonald's, right? I got you a sausage burrito and a Fruit-N-Yogurt Parfait. And coffee." He extends the hand that holds a carrier with two coffees, cream and sugar, and a sack with her food.

"You're not eating?"

"Just the coffee," he says as he lifts his from the carrier.

"You tricked me." She takes a bite from her parfait. "Are you sure you don't want the burrito?"

"I'm good. What's the word here?"

"I talked the doctor into giving me the 'all clear' signal. He prefers I stay. But he'll release me if I insist on it, which I do… except I don't want to go home. I've already talked to Danny and reassured him I'm fine." She eagerly takes another bite of yogurt. "Last night we agreed I could help you find Mason and the house where Bob kept us. Are you still game, or do I need to find another cop to help me?"

"I have no jurisdiction outside Clatsop County. Based on where they found you, we need to involve the Columbia County Sheriff Department. I don't know anyone there. But I'm connected to a lieutenant who has connections. I'll make the call."

Later, after Dash arranges everything, the nurse removes Emmarie's I.V. and secures a square of sterile cotton gauze to the spot with cohesive wrap bandage tape. Now that she's able to move more freely, she asks Dash to leave the room while she dresses. When he returns, she is working on getting her swollen feet into her new shoes.

She winces but continues undeterred. Then she allows Dash to help her stand and take a few steps.

So far so good.

Wrapping things up at OSHU and driving to meet the sheriff in Vernonia takes three hours. First, they had to enlist hospital staff to help her sneak out the back way to avoid the horde of reporters, who in feeding frenzy style, all hoped to scoop each other. The loss of Dr. Brooks Kelso and her husband, sans happy reunion with their missing daughter, is the national tragedy du jour.

When they meet up with Sheriff Dunham in Vernonia, he has a map spread on his desk detailing every back road and creek in the area. "The hunters say they found you right about here," he points to a nondescript section of the map. "With that said, you say you followed this creek for a while. Sound right?" He looks first to Emmarie then to Cooper and back to Emmarie.

She moves her eyes from studying the map to studying the sheriff. His green uniform sports coffee stains and he needs a haircut to match her pre-conceived idea of what a rural sheriff should look like. Most of all, he needs to clean his glasses, she thinks, wondering how in the world he can see out of them. He might confuse a dot on his glasses for a dot on the map. Is she really putting her chances of finding Bob in his hands?

"Well, assuming I'm right," Dunham continues, "We got two options. Based on where you think you walked, you can show us on the map where this house of yours is. We'll identify some roads in the area and start knocking on doors. Not much out there but old logging roads and a few cabins."

"And the other alternative?" Cooper asks.

"Well, that requires a lot of walking and has its own risks. Requires Miss Kelso to retrace her steps. She says she followed this creek here. The danger is her not recognizing the point at which she reached the stream. She wouldn't know when to lead you and me south."

He's talking to Cooper as though I'm not here.

"The other risk," he continues, "is that she didn't travel a northernly route to get to the creek. Retracing her route to find the house could take as long as us running down every road and every house in the area."

Cooper considers the map then asks, "What do you think, Emmarie? Do you think you could retrace your route to find the house? Would you recognize the house if you saw it again?"

Her zeal and impatience are now tempered by the sheer magnitude of the search area. But she promised Mason. And she needs to see Bob in the grave or at least behind bars. She is afraid of being wrong and of leading them in circles. In circles is exactly how she may have traveled since leaving the porch, that is until she remembered to pay attention to the moss. *The house could be anywhere.*

She turns the map in her direction to face it with North at the top. "You say they found me here. I don't see a road anywhere in this vicinity that I can swear is the one I ran down before I cut into the woods." She makes a large sweeping motion with her index finger southwest of her extraction point, and continues, "But I do think I can find the place where I slept by the creek. I walked as much as I could due North to get there as I could from a stump. I think I can get you to the area of that stump. It's getting from the stump to his house that I'm not sure about."

"It will be quite a walk," Dunham points out. "But if you're up to it, and can get us to your stump, we'll send up a drone from that point to scout for roads in the area. That should narrow things down a bit." Sheriff Dunham gets on his phone and arranges for the drone, an expert pilot, and a follow-up car to be on standby, tracking their coordinates as they search. He also arranges for deputies to descend upon the house as soon as they find it.

In the meantime, Cooper changes out of his rumpled suit into jeans and a jacket and better hiking boots that he picked up for himself at Nordstrom's at the same time he purchased clothes for Emmarie.

"You look nice," she says as he exits the men's room. "Much more comfortable. Are you sure you want to do this?"

"Shouldn't I be asking you that?" Dash says.

"I have a vested interest. And apparently, I am the key to finding this place. You, on the other hand, have no jurisdiction in Columbia County, as you've stated. You have no need to be here if you don't want to tag along."

"You make 'tagging along' sound like a bad thing, like I'm a third wheel. You still need me."

"I do?"

"Yes. You think since I fulfilled my obligation to spring you from the hospital that you don't need me anymore. That's wrong. I'm your ride to Clatsop City. Besides, I could use the exercise."

Emmarie looks off into space and nods without smiling. She's letting him off the hook, but he isn't biting. "Okay then, no complaining when you want to rest, but I push on."

"I've been talking to the drone pilot," Dunham says, as he re-enters his office. "He thinks there's a better way of doing this and I agree." He sits behind his desk with a fresh cup of coffee in his hand. "Look, starting out now, we only have a few hours before you're back in the same position you were in the other day. Running out of daylight in the woods and stranded. Instead, we use basic math. We know about how far you could have walked along that creek between daybreak and when the hunters found you. The pilot thinks he can plot that out to find the general spot where you would have intersected the stream. He thinks he can start the drone there and work back in a southerly direction as far as you are likely to have come between noon and nightfall your first day.

"He'll shoot us overhead footage of the area. There are so few structures off those old logging roads, he thinks he can narrow it down for us significantly. Maybe to a couple of potential locations that we'll drive to tomorrow."

212

"That's settled then. We will reconvene here in the morning," Dash says. "Can you make any recommendations where we can stay?"

"Talk to Brenda over at the Caden Motel. If she has room, she'll take good care of you. Tell her I sent you," Dunham suggests.

Dash turns to Emmarie. "Is this okay with you? I suppose a late lunch or early dinner is in order too."

The Caden Motel is a two-story, light yellow house with wrap around porch both downstairs and up, with double front doors painted bright red, a block off Nehalem Highway, the main drag. The proprietor laughs when they drop Sheriff Dunham's name, saying that she'll charge them double for their acquaintance. "If he's a close friend of yours, it'll be triple!" she cackles.

Emmarie and Dash take her last two rooms before heading off for a meal at the Black Iron Grill. She orders a Cobb salad and he the Berry Good Turkey sandwich. Both pick at their food when it arrives.

"I would have thought you'd be hungrier, skipping breakfast," she says as she pushes her own salad around with her fork. This is the first opportunity she has had, while doing nothing else important, to evaluate her new friend up close and personal. He sits directly across from her.

He is taller than she is by at least 6 inches she guesses, with dark wavy hair and inviting, intense grey eyes. *Or are his eyes blue?* She swears in different light his gorgeous eyes change colors. He has a straight, white smile. So unlike Bob. Dash's smile is so striking, she resists the temptation to ask if his father was an orthodontist.

After a reasonable silence, Dash breaks in. "Not unlike you, I have a lot on my mind. I volunteered to help Lt. Bellows. Other than seeing you turn up safe, I haven't done anything with his cases recently." He takes a bite of the potato salad that rests beside his sandwich. "This is good. Do you want some?"

"No, thanks. Yesterday was a full day," Emmarie says, her eyes tearing up. "I appreciate you coming to the hospital. And for staying." She drops her voice and her glance, allowing herself only the briefest moment to collect herself after thinking about her parents.

"I shouldn't talk about it," Dash continues, "especially while we're eating, but a ranger found a body northwest of here yesterday. I have a responsibility with that investigation."

"Are you talking about the Cascade Cutthroat Killer?"

He looks at her quizzically.

"Are you surprised I know about it? I watch the news, or at least I did up until a week ago. Does the taskforce have any leads?"

"No. I mean, we're working the leads we have, but we could use a big break. Lt. Bellows told me our killer got sloppy and left evidence behind not too far from here. Since I'm stalled on your case until tomorrow, I was wondering why this guy changed his M.O." Dash looks directly at her, smiles, then adds, "but I prefer thinking about you. I mean your case."

"Sounds like law enforcement officers never get a day off."

"On the contrary. I'm on vacation."

CHAPTER 28

Dashed Hopes

The day breaks clear and sunny. After serving her B & B guests breakfast, the proprietor of the Caden Motel gives Dash and Emmarie two large paper cups with lids for their expedition. They both select strong, black coffee, no milk, before climbing into Dash's Jeep Wrangler and heading out to meet Sheriff Dunham. By the time they get there, the sheriff's crew have all but devoured a box of assorted donuts. Emmarie declines when offered one of the leftover pastries.

Sheriff Dunham briefs them on the tactics of their search approach. Remnants of glazed apple fritter crumbs cling to the corners of his mouth and stick to his shirt. He takes a swig of his coffee then says, "We got these aerial shots yesterday from our drone pilot." He points to his laptop resting on the hood of his patrol vehicle. "You two ride with me. My deputies will take the other vehicle. We will head down this road here from which we can check out a couple of properties. You can see the road forks here, so we can drive by that one too to see if Miss Kelso here recognizes the place."

Dunham and Cooper hop into the front seat of his sheriff's SUV so Emmarie dutifully climbs into the back. She doesn't mind. Let law enforcement swap stories while she contents herself with her own thoughts. Occasionally one of them directs a comment or question to her but largely they leave her alone. Her own thoughts vie for attention like eager preschoolers.

Soon paved roads give way to gravel then to dirt. Houses that break the tree line become scarcer and more remote until the scenery becomes nothing but a montage of trees, sunlight cutting through like a strobe light.

"Most of the places out this way," she hears Dunham explain, "belong to retirees or are second homes, used in the summer and maybe on a handful of weekends throughout the year. Absentee landlords make the mistake of renting out these older houses without thoroughly vetting their tenants. Used to be a big problem before marijuana was legal. They cut down trees and grow plants right under everybody's noses. Just with a little aerial camouflage. That's largely changed, but every so often we come upon a meth house. Same deal. Poor owners never even know what's happening on their property."

"It's remote," Cooper agrees.

The jostling of the rutted dirt road combines with blinking sunlight and the rancid smell of body grease emanates from the seat cushions. It stirs Emmarie's stomach like a boiling cauldron. She tries to lower her window for some fresh air, but it doesn't budge. She realizes most people transported in the back of the sheriff's vehicle are criminals. Like them, she is at the sheriff's mercy.

"I'm feeling a little sick. Would you please open my window?" Perhaps the fresh air will help keep her breakfast down.

"Why don't we stop for a few minutes?" Cooper suggests. "You can fill me in on where we are on the map."

"Sure, we are about to turn onto that road that forks, so I figure we got another ten minutes to the first house. But we can stop if the little lady needs to regroup."

Emmarie's brow furrows and her eyes narrow. She glares at the back of Dunham's head while she waits for Cooper to let her out of the vehicle. *The little lady.*

"Would you prefer sitting in the front seat, Emmarie?" Cooper asks.

"It's okay. I'll be fine." Emmarie continues to glare at the sheriff who walks over to a tree to take a piss. "I have a stronger constitution than you men realize."

Cooper pipes up, "Don't lump me in with him, Emmarie. I stand amazed by what you're handling." He puts a hand on her shoulder and smiles at her. "You're like that watch. You take a licking and keep on ticking."

"I don't think I need any more of this coffee." She reaches into the back seat, grabs her cup, pulls off the lid, and pours it out. "Too acidic for my stomach right now."

"You can sit up front," Cooper says again.

"No. I said I'm fine," she says with finality. "I don't like being told what to do."

"I can see that, which is why I offered, instead of ordering you."

"You think you can order me to do anything?" Emmarie challenges.

"Just trying to help." Cooper returns to the front seat and abruptly closes the car door.

"If you're ready, Sheriff," Emmarie says as he jumps over a small drainage ditch at the side of the road on his way back to the car. "Let's get on with it."

The sheriff pulls back out onto the dirt road, still wet from yesterday's rains, and turns left at his first opportunity. They come upon an A-frame house and slow.

"No," Emmarie says. The place looks like an old farmhouse with a porch."

In another ten minutes or so they slow as they approach another house fitting her description. Emmarie stares at the blue house, then finally says she thinks the house they are looking for is brown but in need of fresh paint.

"Well, we got one more abandoned house out this way then we'll double back and take the fork that goes up the other way," Dunham says. "The house and land were seized by the

DEA and auctioned off a few years back. As far as I know, nobody lives there."

They pull into the driveway that breaks through the trees to either check it out or turn around, based on Emmarie's input.

"Here. This looks right." Emmarie speaks slowly.

Dunham lowers her window more. He gives orders to the other SUV over his radio. Both cars park and the officers draw their weapons. "You'll be safer here, Miss. Wait for us."

Unless Cooper lets her out, she has no choice.

She watches the men approach the house, guns at the ready. The porch creaks under their footfalls before the sheriff knocks on the door. No response. He tries the door and finds it locked. He signals with his service pistol to the other officers to branch out to peer into the windows. They see nothing. No furniture but a few faded curtains and drapes over broken plastic blinds.

Dunham and Cooper return to the patrol car and pull up ownership information on the dashboard computer. "Purchased at auction by a company in Baton Rouge. Okay, let's break it down."

Dash opens the rear car door for Emmarie.

They enter the building, guns still out, with Emmarie following close behind Dash. "This is it," she declares from the doorway.

Surveying the place, she sees the large open room ending with a kitchen, with vestibules to each side, which are either bedrooms, bathrooms, or closets. Not a stick of furniture or a piece of packing paper remains.

"This is where Mason stood when Bob brought me upstairs…" Her eyes search the floor for blood, but she sees none. "I stabbed Bob here. Over there are the stairs leading to the cellar."

The deputies head down the stairs first, with Emmarie behind them. The narrow stairwell opens to the basement, which is as previously described except now it is flooded with sunlight from the windows that have no cardboard coverings. The room is spotless, swept, and sterilized with bleach. In fact, the whole house smells of bleach. The only visual evidence of her ordeal is a sturdy metal eye hook embedded in the cinderblock near where Mason's bed had been.

"Can't say I'm surprised," Sheriff Dunham says. "We won't likely find much evidence here. The guy had more than 24 hours to clear out. Just the same, we'll call a forensics team. Perhaps they can find a fingerprint or something."

"Safe to say you didn't kill him. But Portland has the dress you were wearing, Emmarie," Dash says. "You stabbed him, so they'll be able to lift blood off it. We'll find him."

She knows he is trying to comfort her, but it isn't working. She walks past him to sit outside on the porch steps. She cradles her face in her hands and sobs.

CHAPTER 29

Grounds for Dismissal

Back in Clatsop City, Dash delivers Emmarie to her home on Sea Breeze. He turns onto the hedge-lined drive, past manicured gardens, and trees to the massive house. Danny rushes to help his sister out of the Jeep Wrangler and Cooper watches as they stand in the driveway, hugging and refusing to release one another. The reunion arouses no small feeling of satisfaction within him.

"Aunt Julia's here. We've been waiting for you," he says to her, before turning to Cooper. "Thank you for bringing her home, Deputy. We'll take it from here."

Dash doesn't like being dismissed. He has so much more he wants to ask Emmarie, to hear the soft lilt in her voice. But he understands. With visible wounds marring her face and everything that's happened, she will want her privacy. *Emmarie deserves the opportunity to relax and decompress.*

He also needs to catch up on the latest body dump and report back to his uncle, as promised.

"Emmarie, try to get some rest. I'll likely need to run things by you, but I'll call first, okay?"

"Sure, anytime Dash. Thanks." Emmarie turns her back on him and looks toward her brother.

Cooper hears her brother ask, "Dash, is it now?" Then he watches Danny poke his sister in the ribs as he helps her into the house.

In short order, 20 minutes or so, Cooper finds himself back at home, sitting alone with Casper in his apartment, knee-deep in the CCK files scattered about his living room floor. Details about the known CCK victims surround him, plus the files on other missing women. Each file contains hundreds of police notes, transcripts of interviews with suspects and with witnesses, plus timelines, diagrams, and sketches. *Where to start?*

He likes to keep his apartment neat, but today not so much. He ignores the dishes in the sink, a used shot glass, a bag of potato chips spilled on the coffee table, and his shoes and dirty socks scattered around the living room, right where he removed them days before. So much work to do, yet he drowns in his thoughts.

Forensic reports take longer in real life than they do on episodic TV. If only they weren't still waiting for reports on the trace found on Roberts. He has reports on the small amount of trace evidence found on Stanley and Samamoto. The coroner found a fiber on each, consistent with parachute cordage. This cordage has almost imperceptible orange paint spray droplets only six microns in size. The department found it by using a scanning electron microscope that breaks down the individual components in the paint to ten elements common in such paint plus two contaminates. The Samamoto and Stanley cases are linked, he thinks, although he didn't need forensic information to tell them that the same guy killed both women.

On the bodies of Martin and Gilbert, they found a few fungal spore particulates, not native to the areas where the women were found. This would be unintentional transfer from somewhere CCK has taken both or from something he used with both.

This scant trace evidence is what signals that something is off with how they found Kylee Roberta Roberts.

That last body dump doesn't make sense. Maybe it's a copycat effort. He wishes he'd been there in person to see for himself, instead of relying on the photographs and notes taken by others. But he wasn't there for obvious reasons. Nor would he change things with Emmarie, even if he could. Seeing her safe in the hospital and being there when the news came of her parents, satisfies him more than looking at another CCK victim. Walt Bellows' words about cursing yourself because you can't do enough rings true.

225

He studies the photos taken by the taskforce. A footprint. Same irreverent display, same ear to ear slash. The coroner's report should say if she was first strangled before he opened her up. He bets she was. *This guy likes routine. Yet he breaks his pattern. This guy never leaves chewed gum wadded up in a wrapper at his scenes.*

Nor does he leave an empty beer can next to the body. Sure, these items could have been deposited before the body and have nothing to do with the victim or her killer. That seems more reasonable to him than CCK suddenly leaving evidence behind.

What had Randall told him about the Green River Killer? Oh, yes, Ridgeway occasionally contaminated his scenes with cigarettes, gum, or papers belonging to others to confuse the police. *Is that what you did, CCK?*

He expects the forensic report to show DNA on the lip of the beer can and any fingerprints on the can itself to be unrelated to the case. He knows they'll use the lot number to track where the can was sold. Knowing this could add one more puzzle piece to the picture if CCK purchased and drank the beer. However, he suspects a decoy.

Likewise, with the chewing gum. Forensics may get DNA from saliva or bite impressions from the sample, but probably not. *That's what CCK wants. For us to spin our wheels getting nowhere.* DNA in the gum might not even match the beer can, but it makes a better decoy for CCK, creating a stronger illusion if it does, he thinks.

If this is CCK contaminating the scene, he must be nervous that we're close. Maybe we already know who he is.

With fresh vigor, Dash re-reads the known CCK files, digging through countless interviews and interrogations, moving the puzzle pieces around, looking for patterns. Based on what he sees, he determines the best suspects include truck driver Martin K. Sparks with a rap sheet for petty theft, assault, and attempted rape; Adrik Volkov, a legal Russian immigrant turned felon turned Internet business owner; and Robert Gearhart, an insurance salesman with a criminal record including solicitation, whose tastes gravitate toward sadomasochism.

Identifying CCK from these investigative files might make his career, but identification would only be a solid hit to the outfield, letting the runner take third base. Alone, no score. They still need evidence to prove their case against CCK in a court of law. Juries like indisputable science over circumstantial evidence, favoring science they understand. Now common-place, juries understand DNA. The public's love affair with it has only grown. If they can't get DNA from CCK off his victims, a sharp defense attorney might be able to shred the DA's case.

If the aluminum can and the gum belong to CCK, why leave them behind? Has he gotten careless? If they don't belong to him, why plant this DNA evidence? All he can figure is that CCK wins by sidetracking the police, or by giving future defense lawyers something to establish reasonable doubt.

Another problem in winning justice for CCK's victims cannot be ignored, he thinks. Oregon recognizes capital punishment. It's on the books at least. However, the State hasn't carried out lethal injection since 2011, when then-governor John Kitzhaber announced a moratorium on executions pending review. The prosecution needs a strong case against a murder suspect to reach the unanimous guilty vote required, let alone set aside the ban and kick start the State's willingness to apply the death penalty. *CCK has the notoriety to be such a case, to be sure.* The prosecution needs flawless evidence and lots of it. They need laser focus.

In his heart of hearts, he doubts Martin Sparks has the intelligence to outwit the police but maybe it doesn't take a high IQ. He googles Gary Ridgeway's intelligence quotient. No rocket scientist that one. Experts estimate his IQ to be in the low 80's yet his spree continued for 20 years. On the face of it, that doesn't exactly exclude Sparks.

He likes Volkov for the murders. The man is single. He operates an Internet business, and the Internet is the great equalizer. He does not need to interact with people. After serving time in Utah for the brutal rape of an 18-year-old nursing student, he reinvented himself and now sells survival gear and self-help resources for living off-grid. He has no time clock to punch, no one to whom he is accountable. He has the means to travel about the state as he likes and the know-how to survive under the radar.

He also likes Gearhart. Gearhart is a married man who likes things rough. As an insurance salesman, he has opportunity to set his hours and travel as necessary. But if he is honest, Cooper simply likes Robert Gearhart because of nickname possibilities. He doubts very much if Gearhart is Emmarie's Bob because she remained unmolested. Of course, that doesn't mean Gearhart isn't CCK.

Robert Gearhart is bad news and Emmarie's Bob is an odd nut, but that is likely the extent of things, he thinks. Dash can almost warp his imagination enough to understand the likes of a Gary Ridgeway or a CCK. They enact their hatred of women while rejecting society's mores. Dash thinks Bob holds himself to a moral code of sorts, and by doing so, feels justified in his actions, as if he alone takes the high road. Psychopathic to be sure, but unlike any psychopath he's studied.

Cooper's base problem, he knows, is keeping the CCK cases, the missing girls, and Bob separate in his mind. Blending histories, details, and motives behind all the dead and missing women is too easy. All he wants to think about is Emmarie. If the cases aren't linked, Bob certainly enjoys perfect cover working on the sidelines of CCK.

It makes Dash's head spin. One problem at a time. That is his preferred pace, like in traffic, when lives are no longer on the line. He wonders if he's cut out for this.

He picks up Emmarie's file. He studies the police department's rendition of her attacker, based on Emmarie's best recollection. Other than a gummy smile and a blackened tooth, which would only show should he smile, the face on the paper resembles a middle-aged man from Anywhere, USA. Someone who is there one minute and forgotten the next. Nothing remarkable. His mind wanders to how often he may have even passed him on the street, never suspecting what lurks underneath.

He reads Emmarie's official statement, again, and pours over the photographs of the manacle and chain dangling from her wrist, and of her in the blood-stained black and green party dress. Even then, with a bruised cheek and no cosmetics, her natural beauty can't be denied. He contemplates her face, particularly the shape of her eyebrows and eyelashes, framing the pools of inviting honey that others call eyes. *No, she isn't pretty. She's gorgeous.*

Paternal feelings stir inside him, revealing themselves now for what they are. Not paternal at all. He can't concentrate. Just as file details run together, so do his feelings for Emmarie, stunting his ability to be clear-headed. He understands why the medical profession frowns on its physicians treating family members. They are too close to make tough decisions. He feels that way now.

After he found Emmarie, or more accurately, after she escaped without his help, everything changed within him. He feels no pressure to continue except for the promises he made his uncle.

Having no one else to talk to, he calls out to Casper. "Do you think 'ole boy, I can simply return to Traffic after vacation and Walt won't notice? I gotta admit, my friend, that's the only place I feel competent." *If I could end this masquerade as a major crime detective without my uncle thinking I'm a flake, I would. But I can't bail now.*

If he can't stop Bob, perhaps he can help place CCK behind bars or on a slab.

He picks up the phone to call Bellows but accidentally dials Emmarie's home phone instead.

Danny answers the ring quickly, too quickly, catching Dash off guard before he realizes what he's done. It isn't Bellows' voice. He scrambles.

"Hi, is your sister there?"

Danny hands the phone to Emmarie.

"I-I was calling to check on you. How are you?"

"I'm okay." Gone is a hint of playful parlay she showed before.

To be expected. Her escape bolstered her in every way. But the loss of her parents must have gutted her. "Do you need anything?"

"No. But thank you." Her answers are short and specific. She doesn't throw him a lifeline or a bone.

"Okay, well, if you think of anything you need. Or you remember something, you've got my number," Dash says.

"That reminds me. Danny got me a new phone. I'll text you my new number in case you need to reach me." She ends the call abruptly.

His next call finds Bellows. "Walt, do you think you could arrange for us to have another chat with the three suspects I like for CCK? I'm seeing some inconsistencies here." Bellows agrees and keeps the call short, as Cooper expects. Having finished his law enforcement business, Dash pours himself a bourbon and thinks about his accidental call to Emmarie. *That's a Freudian slip if I ever saw one.*

Idiot. You sounded like a needy junior high kid calling the prom queen.

Yes—but at least you got the prom queen's new phone number.

CHAPTER 30

I Will Remember You

"Numb."

"What?"

"Numb. I feel numb," Emmarie tells Aunt Julia, her mother's sister, up from New Mexico for the funeral. She takes a sip from the mug of hot, jasmine tea that Danny made for her, and gazes out the window. The sky looks as if Uranus, the Greek god of the firmament, has fused thick strokes of Manatee and Timberwolf-colored Crayolas, with large areas of Eggplant for effect. If raindrops don't start falling soon, the churning clouds could be signaling the start of an apocalypse instead of a coastal storm. Still, Emmarie feels numb.

"Of course, you do. You've been through so much in just a couple weeks. It's enough to give you emotional whiplash. Don't be surprised if you feel a bevy of emotions - even contradictory ones - in rapid-fire succession," Julia says, sounding very much like Mom, Emmarie thinks.

"That's just it. I feel nothing."

Danny puts his arm around his sister as they sit on the couch together. He has no words.

"Whatever you're feeling makes sense and serves a purpose," Aunt Julia says. "But I also believe that right now, you haven't processed all that's happened. Being held captive by that awful man, your parents' plane crash, having your hopes dashed when you found that house empty. Experts say it's quite normal to feel angry one moment then apathetic the next. Be prepared for an emotional tornado to slam you like a trailer park in Kansas. Allow yourself to feel it, then release it."

"By 'experts,' you're talking about Mom?" Emmarie puffs a miniature raspberry. *Still telling me what I should and shouldn't feel.* A week ago, Emmarie wished, and prayed, and bargained with a God she isn't sure she believes in for her life to return to 'normal.' Normal with Jack. Normal with her mother. Even normal fighting over irrelevant things like going away to college. *So, this is my new normal.*

"Why don't you stay with me in Roswell for a while, until you figure out what you want to do. Danny, you too, if you don't have to rush right back to Harvard," she says to him.

"No, I'm here for Emmarie, for the summer or longer, if necessary," he says. "We'll have the house to close up and affairs to settle."

"There's time for that. No need to rush things," Julia says. "Well, the offer stands if you change your minds."

Aunt Julia is so much like her mother, trying to fix things when no fix exists, Emmarie thinks.

"You both have a lot of decisions facing you, and if I can help in any way, let me know," Julia says. "For now, I suppose, we should decide what we should do for your parents. It would be easier for us all if we have the funeral and memorial service here. Everyone from the community college could come. Your mom will draw a respectful crowd anywhere. That's the problem. I know of nowhere here, except the college's auditorium, where there'd be room for such a service. But on such short notice, I don't know. I'm sure they're preparing for graduation too. Honey, when is your graduation?"

After a brief pause, Julia continues, as if silence is deadly in and of itself. "I know your mother was clear about what she wants. No fuss. And your father hates funerals. But funerals are not for those who've passed, they are for the living to help us move forward. Years ago, when Janet had her battle with cancer, she told me that she wanted to be buried, not cremated. Do you know if that's still true? And your father, of course, I imagine he wants whatever your mother wants. Wanted. I mean. Honey?"

Emmarie isn't paying attention. It falls to the three of them, Julia, Danny, and Emmarie to weigh their options for a memorial service for her parents, but this is turning out to be an organized-by-aunt event.

"Whatever you think best, Aunt Julia," Danny says. "I think this is too much for Emmarie to focus on right now. Would you mind deciding the details?"

"Yes," Emmarie says. "I'm fine with whatever you want. I-I'm sorry to drop this on you, I-I can't right now. I'd like to lie down if you don't mind." Tears well up in her eyes.

"Of course, dear. Danny, would you help her up to her room and make sure she has everything she needs? I'll jot some basic ideas down for you to review this evening."

The memorial service is tasteful and lovely if you discount the media outside. Aunt Julia arranges for a public memorial service at the Kridel Grand Ballroom at the Portland Art Museum, which turns out to be a stroke of genius, she claims, given Dr. Kelso's love and patronage of the Arts. The facility holds 1000 adoring fans from all over the nation, but Emmarie does not attend.

She reserves her energy for the local funeral and private, graveside ceremony in Clatsop City's own Oceanview Memorial Park. Aunt Julia, working in conjunction with Danny and the funeral director, arranges everything as their parents would have liked, or at least would have appreciated, if such affairs could be either liked or appreciated by the deceased.

Two closed caskets of solid dark mahogany, ornate and glossy, rest in front of family and friends, who are ostensibly there to honor and remember Janet and Roger, and arguably, to support the Kelso family during their time of greatest need. Framed, almost life-sized photographs, befitting the White House, stand beside the closed caskets. Multi-colored wreaths and standing bouquets of every color of spring blossom dot the chapel too, augmenting the ample white and purple arrangements Julia ordered.

Roger always felt people came to funerals out of obligation, not wanting to appear callous or shallow, Emmarie remembers her aunt telling her. "But your mom knew the importance of closure."

This is one reason Emmarie does not argue with any suggestion her aunt makes. The other reason, of course, is her inability to accept what is going on around her. People offering their condolences and making promises to 'help you in any way' all seems surreal. She pastes her now familiar, 'all is okay with the world' smile upon her face and shakes every hand extended to her.

Inside, she feels suspended in molasses, going through the motions. Survival mode. Admittedly, it's nice to get hugs from her closest friends and family, as there has been no time, nor energy, nor normalcy, to see them right after she escaped. It is also nice, she supposes, to see others she hasn't seen in a while, too, all happy and relieved to see her home.

Emmarie sits with Aunt Julia, Danny, and family from their father's side. Jack comes and sits with the family and holds her hand. He doesn't say much, although he tells her he wants to talk to her about something… It will wait.

Emmarie's best friend, Sophia, is there, and Marta. So is Lt. Bellows and his wife, still quite attractive in her early 50's. Danny explains that Bellows has been pivotal in the department's efforts to find her. Carol Carlisle, whom she vaguely remembers having some tie-in with an old neighbor, sits with them. Cooper comes too, hanging back, watchful, and ill-at-ease. *I guess funerals do that to some people.*

Aunt Julia found a non-denominational minister to say a few words after which she reads a poem she's written for Janet and Roger. Emmarie is on the program to sing Sarah McLachlan's *I Will Remember You* and Simon and Garfunkel's *Bridge Over Troubled Water,* which she accomplishes faultlessly. Several other family members and friends offer kind words and memories in typical eulogy fashion.

Emmarie breezes through the funeral because none of this is real. Surely, she will wake up to the smell of her mother making a big Denver omelet and crispy fried potatoes. Surely, this nightmare will end soon.

The minister says a final prayer and asks the family and guests to remain seated while the pallbearers, twelve in all, hoist each casket and file out carrying their charges to waiting hearses. Danny elects to be a pallbearer. Then the minister invites everyone to the graveside service to follow. The skies cooperate and withhold their drizzle.

Marta approaches Emmarie after the service and hugs her, then she uses her fingers to brush back some errant hair from the girl's face like her mother would have done. "I'm so sorry, honey. Are you okay?"

For the first time ever, Emmarie finds small talk difficult even with Marta. She nods 'yes' instead.

Marta rushes to fill the awkward silence. "I know you've got plenty of things to think about now, between your accident and recovery, and now this. But I thought you'd want to know your rescued kitten is still getting along famously as the mascot of the store. Of course, she isn't a kitten anymore to look at her. But she's healthy and happy. I call her Opal."

"Thanks, Marta. It was irresponsible of me to dump her on you."

"Not at all! That's what I do, so don't spend another moment worrying about that. But if you do need anything, Honey, anything at all, please let me know. Okay?"

Again, Emmarie manages to nod her head in assent.

Marta kisses her cheek, hugs her again and then leaves her so that others can offer their condolences and organize 'who is going with whom' to the cemetery. As the family files out to their cars for the funeral procession, Jack holds back.

"Aren't you coming to the cemetery?" Emmarie asks him.

"No, I don't think so. This is enough for me."

"Oh, I thought you would then come back to the house with me."

"I know." His voice low and soft.

Amy, in a tight, scoop neck black dress, along with another friend comes up and hugs Emmarie, saying how sorry they are. With that, Amy turns to Jack and asks if he is ready to go.

"Go?" Emmarie asks.

"Yeah, her car is in the shop, so I brought her," Jack explains.

Amy smiles sheepishly and inches closer to Jack. She slips her hand in the small of his back and places the other playfully on his chest. "I guess we should get moving."

"Emmarie, I'll call you, okay?" Jack says.

She does not feel what Aunt Julia forecasted. No tornado of emotions slamming her around like an empty can in the street. She feels just one emotion. The feeling of being totally and utterly alone.

CHAPTER 31

Business Disputes

⟞⟶

"This is harassment. You can't keep showing up here," Robert Gearhart spews. "I know my rights. Babe, put my attorney on notice that if these creeps don't stop coming around, I'm gonna sue." He stands in the doorway, blocking the hovel entrance with his body.

Cooper looks around the front porch. Sagging roof, scuffed, rotting wood where they plant their feet. *I bet you don't make house repairs because your money goes to supporting your attorneys in their fancy houses.*

"That's okay, Mr. Gearhart," Bellows says. "We can do this down at the Sheriff's Department if you prefer."

"What I prefer, is to be left alone."

"No problem. Just answer a few questions to clear your involvement," Bellows says.

Bellows wants this guy off balance, to sweat a little.

"I'm not involved in anything. I have nothing to hide. The sooner you fellas get that through your pig heads, the better."

Because he is clad in jeans and a dirty T-shirt, Cooper guesses Gearhart hasn't started his insurance calls yet. Or if he has, he schedules appointments for the evening. No one would buy from him if they knew how he carries himself, or where he resides. He does not project the all-important look of success. Cooper notes pungent smells emanating from inside, whiffs of fried bacon and weed.

"Stepping in or out?" Cooper asks, knowing they will not be invited in. *Does Bellows smell that?* He wonders.

"I'll give you five minutes. You can stay out there." He motions to two white plastic, stackable chairs at the side of the covered porch. One of them will need to rest his butt against the railing.

Bellows elects to stand. Perhaps it is to tower over the suspect, to maintain a posture of power, Cooper isn't sure. Bellows begins. "Do you have a prescription or is that recreational?"

"I told you I know my rights. Recreational weed is legal now, man."

Bellows smiles.

Of course, he knows, Cooper reminds himself. Bellows owns a reputation for his interrogations. *Sit still and learn how it's done. He's letting our man here know that not much escapes him. And a little paranoia favors us right now.*

"Tell me again, Mr. Gearhart, have you ever forced yourself on a woman?"

Bellows couldn't be more direct and to the point than that, Cooper thinks.

"I've enjoyed my share of ladies, but it is always consensual."

"Your relationship with a woman named Mandie was consensual?"

"It was business. She's a prostitute and I paid her for her time. That means I got to do what I wanted."

"So, you wanted to beat her, sodomize her and asphyxiate her?" Bellows takes out a 5 x 8 photo of Mandie taken at the hospital, displaying his handiwork of two black eyes, a broken nose, and purple bruises for a necklace. He passes it to the suspect.

"Business negotiation, that's all. Autoerotic asphyxiation heightens pleasure. You should try it sometime."

"She pressed charges."

"Business dispute. No big deal." Gearhart rubs his beer belly. "And the case is over, remember? Are we done here? I think we are."

Bellows and Cooper exchange glances with an almost imperceptible shrug. For multiple reasons, Robert Gearhart isn't CCK.

"One more thing, Mr. Gearhart," Bellows says. "Do you mind if we take a look inside your car?"

"You got a warrant?"

"I thought you had nothing to hide," Cooper says. "Do you want us to get a warrant?"

"Don't bother. Look inside my car if it will get you off my ass." Gearhart reaches into the front pocket of his faded jeans and hits the key fob to unlock the doors of his white Toyota Camry.

Bellows and Cooper saunter over and open all four doors, trunk, and hood. A formality, really. They are crossing the Ts to rule out Robert Gearhart as CCK. They discover no items usually found in a rapist's tool bag. Nor have they any carpet fibers from CCK's victims to match, but note the clean interior is 'cockpit red,' with no mold growing in the trunk or on the floor mats. Cooper notes no scratches or dents either, such as those that would indicate Gearhart liked to knock over women riding bicycles.

"Mr. Gearhart, we'll leave you now. Thank you for your cooperation." Bellows says.

The officers climb into Bellow's patrol car before either speak. "That's not CCK," Cooper says.

"Why do you think he isn't?"

A test. Walter is testing me. "For one, he enjoyed beating Mandie. If we keep digging, we'll find his fists connect with most of his women. That's not part of CCK's M.O. Sure, CCK waits a week to kill, but it takes longer than a week to hide a beating like that from the medical examiner."

"Good catch," Bellows says. "Why don't we drop in on Adrik Volkov unannounced?"

The long ride out to sleepy Melville, Oregon, an unincorporated part of Clatsop County whose post office closed in 1922 after 31 years of bustling activity, brings no new insights and minuscule discussion between the two law enforcement officers. Bellows inquires how Emmarie is getting along, adding that her parents' crash of their Beechcraft Bonanza V-tail is 'such a shame.'

When they pull into the driveway of Volkov's cabin, they see the blinds drawn down over the windows and hear a big dog barking in the backyard. A pole barn workshop with aluminum siding and roof dominates the other side of the house, all within the fence guarded by the chained animal.

"That's a serious building, even for a prepper," Cooper remarks. "You think he's home?"

"Only one way to find out," Bellows says, as they exit the patrol vehicle. When they get to the front door, he knocks with his left hand. His right hand rests on his holster.

Cooper follows suit. He unsnaps the strap securing his Smith & Wesson M&P 9 and places his hand upon the hilt.

The door opens a few inches. "Shit!" the occupant exclaims as he turns and sprints toward the back of the house.

Cooper experiences his own knee-jerk reaction, honed by law enforcement training. In a split second, he bursts through the semi-open entryway, tails Volkov around sparse furniture until he reaches the back door. Cooper leaps on him. Volkov twists and tries to grab Cooper's gun. He misses and ends up taking a swing at the young officer. He barely connects on his chin, but the red evidence springs up immediately.

His appearance is marred temporarily but the level of abuse bears no resemblance to Volkov's. His face is decorated with old scars through his eyebrow and cheek from a pipe beating other inmates dished out in prison for no apparent reason except Volkov's attitude, and the fact he's Russian.

Cooper executes a defensive maneuver and soon has the suspect flipped onto his stomach. He places his knee squarely on Volkov's back to keep him down while he places handcuffs on him.

"You a rabbit?" Bellows asks as he approaches, service pistol aimed at his quarry. "Rabbiting makes you look guilty. Stand him up, Cooper," he says. Ensuring that they have subdued the suspect, Bellows re-holsters his weapon. "Since you don't have any manners to invite us into your home for a visit, we're going to invite you to ours. Put him in the back seat and Mirandize him."

Down at the station, Cooper walks Volkov to Interrogation Room B and secures him to the table, facing the two-way mirror. Everything will be by the book, recording from two angles so no defense attorney can cry 'foul' down the road. There'll be no violence, no untoward manipulation, nothing that jeopardizes any case they can bring against him. Should they get lucky and Volkov confess, he'll have no grounds to claim coercion later. Bellows rolls that way, even when not everyone does. His busts are clean, or he doesn't make them.

Cooper leaves their man to stew in the barren room while he talks to Bellows. Bellows taught him never be in a hurry. Let the guy squirm and his nerves get on edge before you even start. This isn't a hot lead anyway. They lose nothing by letting Volkov sweat.

"So, Walt? What do you think?

"I think you better not be involved in the interrogation. I've got nothing on him now but assaulting an officer and resisting arrest. A good defense lawyer would chew you up if you were in there with me. Watch from behind the glass, son."

Disappointed, Cooper agrees.

"Relax. Grab a coffee," Bellows says. "I'm going to get one, then I'm going to see a judge about a search warrant for his place before I talk to him. Seems to me, a survivalist like him will have parachuting cordage someplace. If I don't already have enough for a warrant, they'll tell me exactly what I need from this fellow. He will cook enough by the time I get back."

Cooper sips his coffee while he scans back through Adrik Volkov's previous arrest reports, looking for links to information in the CCK files. When he finishes, he pours another cup of coffee even though the acid irritates his stomach. He mentally pats himself on the back for not being a smoker, but he understands why so many of his law enforcement brothers and sisters are. Smoking occupies the hands and calms the body during the ubiquitous waiting game.

"Got it," Bellows says, waving papers in his hand as he walks into the Clatsop County conference room where Cooper sits re-reading the files. "Volkov did us a favor by running and taking a swing at you. I got the department executing the search warrant as we speak." He grins, but not too broadly. "I say we have our visit with Adrik now. Rattle his bones. See his reaction to our search warrant."

This is a base hit, far from a home run, Cooper thinks. *But it's something.*

The two men walk down the hall together toward Room B. Cooper turns in to the first compartment where he can listen and watch the questioning unobserved, through the two-way mirror. He starts the cameras and the audio recording. Bellows takes the next door to enter Interrogation where his suspect waits.

"Good to see you here, Mr. Volkov," Bellows says, as he sits down opposite his subject with his back toward Cooper in the other room. "I know Deputy Cooper read you your rights in the vehicle when you were first apprehended, but I'm going to go over your rights again to make sure you understand them. English is not your first language, and we want everything to be part of the official record. Do you understand?"

Volkov nods.

"Good. For the record, today is May 12th. I am Detective Lieutenant Walter Bellows sitting here with Adrik Volkov, a legal Russian immigrant who was taken into custody today after assaulting an officer and resisting arrest. He was read his rights before transport and no questioning has yet taken place. Mr. Volkov both speaks and understands English as a second language, not his first, so I am going to re-read him his Miranda rights before we begin. Mr. Volkov, you have the right to remain silent…"

Cooper listens to the brief legal notification as if it is poetry, which it is, he thinks, in the hands of his uncle.

"I'm going to need a yes or a no, Mr. Volkov, not a nod because this is part of your official statement. If you need a Russian interpreter to ensure you understand your rights, let me know. We'll provide one. That might take a little time, so you would likely be held overnight while we wait." Keeping Volkov overnight is no idle threat. The nearest Russian interpreter authorized to work with law enforcement lives in Portland. "Let me ask you again, Mr. Volkov, do you understand your rights as I have read them to you?"

"Yes, I understand rights. I do not need interpreter. Get on with it."

"Thank you. Mr. Volkov. You have your own Internet business, is that right?"

"So? Lots of people do."

"Tell me about your business."

"I write blogs telling people how to avoid Big Brother. I sell survival books and gear. Completely legit."

"Your business allows you a certain familiarity with out of the way places, does it not? You live alone and you write about living off-grid and away from people?"

"So?"

"Have you ever been to Saddle Mountain?"

"Yes. I go many times. I like solitude, wildflowers."

"You're a regular Bambi, aren't you? Are you also familiar with Tillamook State Forest and Clatsop State Forest?"

"Is that crime? These places I go, too. Many times."

Cooper realizes Bellows uses these basic questions to determine a baseline. Understanding how Adrik communicates when telling the truth allows him to detect variants in his facial expressions, body movements, and tone of voice. Variations are Volkov's tells whenever he lies, so in effect, Bellows is a human-lie detector machine.

"When was the last time you took Highway 202 out near Neverstill?"

"I do not remember. Where is this Neverstill?"

"Do you remember what you were doing?"

"No. Probably something for Internet business. Article or blog piece perhaps."

"What size shoe do you wear?"

"12."

"Would it surprise you to learn that we recovered a footprint at a body dump near Neverstill?

"Having feet is now crime?"

"Why did you run when we knocked on your door?

"I am Russian. Conditioned response to police. Like Pavlov dog, I run."

"Do you like living in Oregon? Tell me about Utah. You used to live there, didn't you?"

"Utah was long time ago. I did not like so much. I move here for more freedom."

"That's right, Utah accused you of raping Melissa Ann Smith, a nursing student in Salt Lake City. Aggravated sexual assault. Pretty brutal stuff.

"I serve time."

"Do you know what I think? I think you enjoy hurting women. I think you reinvented yourself when you got out of prison when you should have gone back to Mother Russia. I think you want society to pay for locking you up."

"You think." Volkov says. "You know shit."

Cooper witnesses slight cracks forming in his tough-guy routine, not in what he says necessarily, but in the tells he reveals. Cooper watches their suspect stiffen and his eyes dart.

"That right? I know animal control is rolling up on your place right now for that guard dog of yours. I know law enforcement officials will be crawling all over your house, and your workshop. We have a search warrant to comb through your things. We'll see if you keep any trophies of your women."

"I want lawyer now."

"I thought you might. We're done here." Bellows leaves the room, and a uniformed officer enters to escort Volker to a holding cell. Assaulting an officer and resisting arrest is small potatoes, but enough to convince the DA to hold him. It also bought them a search warrant and the time to see if they can link him to CCK.

He opens the door and sticks his head into the room with Cooper. "I've got my fingers up his nostrils. Do you still want to talk to Sparks?"

CHAPTER 32

Sewing Up Loose Ends

Bob gifts most of his furniture to several thrift stores he passes on his way into Portland. Since he furnished his place in Early American Goodwill from these same stores or ones just like them, he amuses himself with the idea of donating the same shit back. Dishes and a chair here, a couple of twin beds there, sans mattresses, of course. He sprinkles them at the Saint Vincent de Paul and the Salvation Army, all without any overt attention. Slipping in and out unseen is his special power.

He pulls his gray Chevy pickup up to an old factory. He thinks he and Mason should lay low there while he figures out what to do. Moving everything out of the house on such short notice aggravated his whole body. His leg hurts and his side hurts, not to mention his head. He could use a few days rest at a minimum, and stitches, he thinks, but opts not to go to a hospital or urgent care center. He can't be certain his description hasn't been blasted to every facility in a 200-mile radius.

The boy, thank goodness, is subdued. He is sleeping as if nothing changed.

Bob rolls up to the 8-foot high, galvanized steel chain-link gate to the warehouse. He lowers his driver's window, leans out so the security camera tracking him can zoom its lens on his face, then he enters a series of numbers into a box that orders the gate to roll back, granting him access. As soon as he drives forward, the gate rolls shut again behind him with a clang. He drives a little farther to the backside of the distribution center and punches a different set of numbers onto the control panel box. Begrudgingly, the massive roll-up door begins to squeal and clank as it rises enough for him to drive inside, away from prying eyes, CCTV cameras, and satellites. Once inside, the big door reverses direction and settles down with a thud. He parks next to another van.

He off-loads only enough remaining items from the back of his pickup to camp out indoors. He drags some bedding to a corner. Mason can sleep in the truck's cab until he wakes, then he'll move him to a corner out of the way.

They have food stocks here and plenty of water. He can make himself useful too, if the boy stays under control. Granted, he has more difficulty keeping Mason in line now that he is 16.

Satisfied that going to the warehouse is the right move, he takes out his phone and punches in a number.

"What are you doing calling me?"

"Do not worry. It is a burner phone. I am at the facility" Bob says.

"You son of a bitch. You're hot, and you're at my warehouse? Can you be any more stupid? Don't leave, I'm on my way."

Bob prepares his explanation for when his boss arrives. He knows every detail of what he will say, how he will make this right.

He doesn't wait long.

Two men enter by way of the front door and walk past sound-proofed rooms and through the open bay where they manufacture animal cages for zoos and such. Bob can hear boots on the cement as they draw closer. As soon as they burst through the swinging doors the shorter man speaks.

"I've got product awaiting shipment. Staying here is out of the question."

"You do not want me out on the streets. Here is the safest place. For everyone."

"I can think of something safer." He's deadpan. If the man they called Snake is joking, Bob can't tell it.

"No, too many loose ends. I owe you another package. No worries — I will bring you two instead. Let me stay here."

The boss, with tattoos rising high on his neck above his suit and past the shirt cuffs on both wrists, remains silent, looking around the large dock, evidently thinking. Finally, he turns back to Bob, looks him directly in the eyes, and speaks.

"I have rules. You disobeyed them. I find myself now in the unenviable position of deciding whether to let you continue to break the rules for some gain or call your marker due now. It may already be too late. I stand to lose considerable money and my reputation. So, you see the predicament you've placed me in?"

"I am sorry, Snake. There is more. I need your help getting stitched up." He raises his shirt to expose an ace bandage over areas of seeping gauze. "My leg too."

"I see." The man's glance shoots over to his companion then back again. "Well, I'm nothing if not understanding. People make mistakes. You've made yours, and if being too kind and generous is mine, I'll live with that. Lars here will see that you are sewn up."

He gestures to the tall man dressed in jeans and a black tee standing next to him. "See to it that he's taken care of and able to secure those packages. By the way," he says, turning back to Bob, "I'm moving up the normal timeline for shipment. I want both in three days, by midnight. Do you understand? I have no more tolerance for mistakes. Any error will be dealt with speedily."

"I plan to—"

"I don't care what your plan is." He lifts his hand in dismissal as he heads back the direction he'd come. "In fact, I don't want to know. You know my requirements."

Lars sucks his front teeth as he moves to the gray concrete wall and takes a large first aid kit down from a peg. He grunts at Bob to follow him over to two chairs positioned next to one of the inner doors.

The kit holds standard first aid stock. Gauze, bandages, iodine, and antibiotic cream plus everything one needs to remove a bullet: Tweezers, tongs, alcohol, needle and thread, a hypodermic needle, a bottle of morphine, and a bottle of Rocephin, a heavy-duty antibiotic. Instead of giving him any pain medication, he sticks a short piece of dowel into Bob's mouth, telling him he can bite down if he needs to as the needle pierces his skin in football lace fashion. Bob will bear scars as a reminder.

Two packages in three days. One package, sure, if the order isn't too specific. He's done two in three days before; he knows he can do it again. As Lars tends to his stab wounds, he plans his strategy. *If I can, I'll go young. They tend to be stupid yet profitable.* His real concern is not the second package, it is the main package he wants to deliver.

He winces as Lars makes no effort to be gentle.

She'll be cautious. She'll be watched. The smart move would be to go for the sure play. Delay the inevitable, savor his revenge. Let her think she's safe. Go for easy now, while Snake's clock ticks. She can be another shipment, later.

That's the smart move, yet his blood boils when he considers it. *No bitch plays me.*

She's risky. Family and reporters will be all over her, he knows that. So how can he get her to come to him?

The answer dawns on him like the sun breaking over the horizon. *That slut has a soft spot.*

CHAPTER 33

Irrational Times

"Emmarie, would you be able to come down to the Sheriff's Department today? Ask Danny to drive you so you're not alone." It is Dash, not Bellows, even though the number isn't Dash's. The call comes from Bellows' department.

"I suppose so. You're not interrupting anything here, except World War III," she says.

"Sounds important."

"Not really, just family matters regarding the estate and my financial future. As usual, everyone has an opinion, and mine doesn't count."

They settle on meeting that afternoon then Emmarie returns her attention to what Danny and Aunt Julia are discussing.

"Mom and Dad have a will, which they updated recently, so probate shouldn't be a problem," Danny explains. "Now, I am no lawyer, but I've had enough accounting classes to know that we want to handle our inheritance with some additional pre-planning to mitigate the financial hit. All I'm saying is that it would help to decide what we want before we try doing it."

"That's right, honey," Aunt Julia says, directing her words to Emmarie. "Talk to the attorneys and to the accountants. That's all we're saying. Get information then decide."

"No, that's not really what Danny is saying, Aunt Julia," Emmarie says. "He thinks we should sell the house and diversify. And I don't see the hurry."

"Danny isn't saying that."

"No, I kinda am," Danny agrees. "Neither of us can pay the taxes or the upkeep on this big house without dipping into cash on hand, stocks, bonds, and whatever other investments they have. Life insurance will pay, but not immediately. I expect they'll wait for the crash investigation report, so who knows when that will be."

He continues reiterating his rationale with the speed of a semi-automatic weapon. "I don't yet know how badly inheritance taxes will hit us. Income from mom's books will continue to come in, but that stream could dry up faster than we anticipate. Even in the best-case scenario, I'm at Harvard. Emmarie will be in college. Neither of us will want to live here after we finish school, and it isn't a blue-collar rental you keep as an investment. So why keep it at all? The housing market is good now. We should sell before a down cycle starts."

Emmarie hears their practical father in her brother's voice and arguments; even sees his mannerisms. But the ground has not yet settled on their graves, so why rush into anything this big? This, too, is practical advice that her father could just as easily be channeling through her, she believes.

The house phone rings. Danny answers it. After a few seconds of saying 'Hello?' and getting no response, he hangs up.

"Look," Emmarie says, "I am willing to hear professional advice, but that's all at this juncture. I'm 18 now so I get a say."

"And I am the executor of the will," Danny inserts. "All the same, I prefer we see eye to eye and not fight. I am shelving this for now, but you know I'm right."

"What I *know,* is that my usually thoughtful brother has lost his mind over the prospect of his inheritance. None of this even feels real to me and you want to strip me of my home!"

Aunt Julia pipes up. "Now, honey, none of us have had time to process. Let's not say anything we'll regret."

"You are already upset at me, Em, and I understand that," Danny says. "So, this is either the perfect time to tell you, or totally the wrong time, but there is something else you should know."

"I'm listening." Emmarie runs through her mind all the things she loves about her brother, reminding herself this is only a hiccup in their relationship. Isn't it normal to act irrational in irrational times? *Try to remember that,* she tells herself, bracing for whatever else he's preparing to say.

"After you went missing and the FBI came, I flew out to be with the family. We were all so worried about you."

"I know."

"Mom was angry. Angry at the people who took you. Angry at the situation. Angry at herself. She was never angry at you."

"Why are you telling me this? Why was she angry at herself?"

"Mom told me something that she regretted not telling you." He drops his eyes from her stare and rubs his knuckles. "Her cancer returned. She was opting only for palliative treatments. She knew she should have told you. She didn't want you to worry, I guess," Danny says.

Aunt Janet gasps in surprise. "So that's the secret my sister kept from me? She was acting so strange, and I thought it was her marriage!"

His news stuns Emmarie. Back to numb. But angry too. Angry at her parents for hiding this. Angry at them for leaving her. Angry at her brother for once again enjoying an inside track.

She tosses her hands up in mock surrender. "This is too much. I'm going to meet Dash." She stands up, grabs her purse, and walks toward the keys hanging in the foyer.

"I thought that was this afternoon." Aunt Julia calls after her. "Why leave this early? Why don't you stay and have lunch with us?"

"No. I need time to think. Alone. I'm going for a walk on the beach.

"Do you think that's wise? They haven't found the guy who kidnapped you yet," Aunt Julia says. "What if he's still out there?"

"Wise? I don't know. Don't care. I'll *explode* if I stay here with you two."

One thing Emmarie can always count on, to help clear her head and put life into perspective, is the beach. Better yet, a walk along the beach. It calms her. A gentle breeze, seagulls screeching overhead, the rhythmic crashing of the waves, in and out, reminds her of the rhythm of life. The ocean makes her feel small in a good way; it makes her problems smaller too. *One person in the company of a universe unto itself. Somehow this equals balance.*

She's here to sort through her feelings and her thoughts, thoughts about her parents, about the liquidation of their estate, about Bob, and about everything that keeps the ground moving beneath her. She hadn't planned on thinking about Jack.

Jack, I miss your smile and your quirky sense of humor. You made me feel like a goddess to your Hercules. Why aren't you here with me now, with your strong arms around me? I need you.

He didn't call after the funeral as he promised he would. He hasn't explained himself, but small wonder. When she saw Amy slip her arm around him at the funeral, she knew Amy's web would be too sticky for him to resist. They had consoled each other in her absence; she's sure of it. *They might be somewhere, now, consoling each other.* It is painful to think about. But Jack has his locker room stories now. And she cannot give him what he wants.

He deserves to be free. What's one more smashed dream among all the others?

The water laps her ankles. She looks up to the dunes. A line of reporters had followed her. Now they stand along the crest with long-range lenses. *My new normal.*

Her mother had been fond of saying: "Whatever doesn't kill you makes you stronger." *If that's true, I'm Captain Marvel.*

CHAPTER 34

Easy Peasy

A white van rolls out from the gated backlot and onto the street. Bob turns right, away from the industrial buildings whose constant whirs and whacks, and buzzing and grinding, provide cover for the operation. He heads away from busy intersections, malls, schools, theaters, and other places where people congregate. Those are obvious places for finding quarry, but only fools would do that, he thinks. He prefers getting away from the city altogether, away from traffic cameras and porch lenses. He prefers the countryside where girls are less hardened, less suspicious. He loves the single dog walker, bicyclist, jogger, or stranded young driver with her first flat tire, out in the middle of nowhere, far away from prying eyes.

Young girls often come in pairs or packs, but their ease of acquisition makes biding his time well worth it. A spin on the 'help me find my lost dog' ruse rarely fails. Plus, he always has his handy hypodermic of ketamine at the ready, if necessary. The street drug, known as Special K, isn't in short supply. It's easily obtained with the right contacts. In far smaller quantities, Special K is a party drug.

By trial and error, based on estimates of height and weight, he learned exactly how much to dose to put a girl solidly out with only a hallucination or two dancing in her head. Even if she gains consciousness too early, her disorientation keeps it from being a problem. Older girls bring a tad more complexity to the table. They are stronger, smarter, or savvier, and better able to put up a fight. He almost always uses ketamine then.

Bob has standard orders, 'requirements' his boss calls them. Attractive young girls, no older than twenty if he can help it, with a freshness to them. No whores, but that's difficult for him to judge. *What is the difference between a whore and a slut?* In his mind, whores charge, sluts don't. That means no working girls. Just as well. Street girls look out for each other so the chances of being identified soar, especially if he fishes in the same pond too often.

He thinks girls 14 to 17 are ideal in that they are blossoming in that special way, still learning what being a woman means in its entirety. Occasionally he has requests for younger girls, which he doesn't mind on principle unless they haven't budded at all yet. Damn perverts, he thinks. May as well give them boys. He chuckles at the thought, knowing his company would supply pre-pubescent boys if enough market exists. He, himself, would not dabble in inventory like that. He has no interest in sampling such wares. As it stands now, he enjoys the perks assuming he isn't blatant about it or damages the goods. *What is that adage about not muzzling the ox which grinds the corn?*

Sluts want it any way. Everyone knows that. Men always respond to low-cut dresses, mini-shorts, see-through blouses, and lacy underwear. The way they paint their eyes, gloss their lips, toss their hair. The way they talk, all suggestive like, then act all prim and innocent. He knows damn well every one of them wants it. *They ask for it in different ways, that's all.* It is the game they play. Hard to get.

He rather likes it when he controls the game. Too easy isn't much fun. He likes the hunt, the conquest, the power over his quarry. He just wishes he understood the difference between sluts and nice girls. He's been wrong so many times.

The problem with this type of acquisition is the hit or miss nature of it. He can drive around all afternoon or evening and have nothing to show for it. *Mistakes happen when you take shortcuts,* he tells himself. He has three days.

He decides on Charbonneau, south of Portland, as his hunting grounds today. Ample rural roads, golf courses, riding academies, plant nurseries, and homes dot his route. There are businesses like cookie stores within walking distances of houses and he can reach agricultural land and housing projects spaced far enough apart to have both the prey and privacy he needs.

He pulls the van over at a wide spot to dig out a picture of a dog from the glove compartment, along with his leash prop. He might not use that technique, depending on the age of the girl he finds, but when done right, it's easy, fast, and fun. When he finishes making ready and assembling his tools, he looks up and sees a girl, perhaps 13 or 14 years old unless he misses his guess, walking a dog down the road toward him. At a distance, the mutt appears to be a terrier of some kind.

Damn, I am good. He chuckles. *This is meant to be.* He slips on a pair of surgical gloves, double checks the nearby light poles for traffic cameras, and checks traffic. There isn't any. He hops out, raises the van's hood, acts like he is peering into the engine, and waits.

As she approaches, he says, "Hi there! What's your dog's name?"

"Pumpkin."

"Hi, Pumpkin. You remind me of a dog I used to have when I was a boy. May I pet him?

"What's wrong with your hands?" she asks when she sees his gloves.

"Oh, I have a skin condition. Don't worry. It is not contagious, which means you cannot catch it. But it looks bad, so I wear gloves. My name is Bob. What is your name?"

"Angelica."

"Angelica, do you want to see a picture of my dog? He died two days ago and that makes me very sad."

He pulls an old Polaroid from his pocket. Most kids see photos on telephones these days, but a photo is a photo. It will do the trick, he figures. He shows her an old picture of him holding a poodle. In truth, the dog isn't even his.

"What was your dog's name?"

"That is me with Curly. I sure miss him. Hey, Angelica, do you think Pumpkin would like a bag of dog treats I have in my van? With Curly gone, I have no need for them anymore. Pumpkin can have them. Your dog would like some treats, right?"

"I suppose so. But I don't want to carry a big bag."

"No worries. It is a little bag, not heavy at all. Think we should give him one now to see if he likes it?"

"All right."

Bob takes another glance to the left and right and sees no one. *Perfect.* "Let us get that treat for Pumpkin, shall we?" He moves to the passenger side of the van and opens the panel door. "Bring Pumpkin over here. It will only take a jiffy."

In a jiffy, Angelica is inside the van and Pumpkin jumps in after her. Bob subdues her like an expert calf roper. In seconds he has the wide-eyed girl's arms and legs secured by plastic cable ties and her mouth covered by duct tape. When he finishes, he has a decision to make. He doesn't want to stay by the roadside any longer than necessary. So far, he's lucky, no one drives by.

What should he do with the dog? He can dump it out here, with collar and leash like it got away from the girl, or he can remove those items, so the animal looks like a stray. On the other hand, he can transport the dog elsewhere using either of those conventions or kill the damned thing outright. Small decisions like this should be thought through with the utmost care. If he transports the dog to throw the police off, then he risks being seen doing so.

Well, that's the answer. Easy-peasy. He finds her phone in a back pocket, turns it off, and tosses a stray Pumpkin into the brushy ditch before driving off. He smashes the phone then decides to ditch it elsewhere. No ketamine necessary.

CHAPTER 35

Roadblock

The State's forensics department enhances the ATM clip. They have CCK evidence to process too after the warrant turns up potential evidence against Adrik Volkov.

Portland still has chain of custody for most of the evidence in Emmarie's case. Portland PD has the pearls, the manacle, and the blood-stained clothes Emmarie wore. The antique pearl necklace has no documentation for having been stolen or purchased from a pawn shop, so that's a dead end. They find nothing but smudged fingerprints from the steel cuff, but they did retrieve DNA from the blood and saliva traces taken from her dress. Nothing to match it yet, but already they have more than they had before. Cooper is sure they'll find the creep who did this.

"You're looking good today. Where's Danny?" Dash asks as Emmarie enters the conference room where he temporarily works major crimes.

"I know saying 'thank you' for the compliment is the appropriate social convention, but I don't understand why," Emmarie says, void of a filter. "Why does how I look matter? And who made you the judge?"

"Whoa. Same side, remember?"

"You're a man. I've had quite enough of your type."

"Just for today, I hope." Dash smiles and motions her over to him. "I take it you didn't have Danny escort you, as I asked."

"We have differing agendas right now."

"You and Danny, or you and me?" He looks at her and longs to be able to kiss away her pain. He'll settle for helping her realize the importance of taking safety precautions. "Emmarie, I don't think it's wise for you to be unattended with Bob still out there. I don't have the power to assign a uniform to stand guard."

"I appreciate your concern, but I don't need a baby-sitter.

"I'm not suggesting you do."

"Did you know that Officer Lupe Díaz came to see me? I believe you know her. She, Carol Carlisle, and I had lunch yesterday. Sort of a girl power thing. She even said you suggested it."

"I don't remember recommending lunch, but I did tell her she might want to talk with you." What Emmarie says next feels like a hot load of bricks being dumped on him.

"Did you know she wants to use me as bait? She thinks I can help them break a white slavery ring by agreeing to let them track me all the way to New Orleans if need be. With my permission, so they don't need a warrant to track actual suspects, which by the way, they don't have. She said this wouldn't be like trolling Burnside looking for tricks at midnight or anything, but I told her Bob would be crazy to come after me again. The media bird-dogs me wherever I go."

"Crazy can only be counted on to act crazy," Dash says. "You are a loose end to him."

"Is that why you asked me here? To warn me? You could have done that on the phone and saved me a trip."

"No, not exactly. I'd like you to look at something. It might be uncomfortable but tell me if you recognize anyone."

Dash has footage of ATM man cued up on his computer. He's watched it a dozen times if not more. The image is cleaner and sharper after the technical wizards enhanced it. The mysterious man is the reason she is here, the focal point of their meeting, but Dash finds he can't keep his eyes off the helpless young woman on screen, whose life hangs precariously in the balance. He worries it still might.

"This was taken by an ATM camera the night of your accident," Dash explains.

"My God, that's the guy. That's Bob," Emmarie gasps. "Or at least it looks like him. I can't see his teeth, but that must be him! He told me we'd met before, but I couldn't place it."

"If you're sure, Emmarie, this is huge. I'll print the best frame and show it to businesses around Tillamook Street and Peter Iredale Avenue to see if anyone recognizes him. We have the police artist's sketch, so we can release both, side by side, to the news media and ask the public to help identify our person of interest."

Emmarie pulls back from the screen and from Dash. "Do what you want. I won't have any part of it."

"What?"

"The media invades my privacy enough. I can't relive what I went through. I won't. If you find Bob, kill him. Otherwise, there'll be a trial. I won't keep things stirred up by testifying."

"Not testify? Emmarie, you have the power to put him in prison, to get him off the streets so he can't hurt Mason or any woman ever again. Besides, a trial won't occur for months, even if I find him tomorrow. You'll feel differently then."

"I don't think so. And you don't know me well enough to tell me what I will and won't be feeling."

Dash is certain his chin rests only slightly above his belt buckle. He feels gobsmacked, as the British say.

Yet he watches real color drain from Emmarie's face as if she's reliving what she promises she wouldn't be willing to do. Tears well up, obscuring her lovely light brown eyes, but not the fear in them.

He wants to tell her she never needs to hear the name 'Bob' again, but what kind of promise is that? He knows she'll encounter daily reminders of her ordeal and will have to find a way to thrive despite them…or else risk folding in on herself, becoming a scared shadow of the woman she once was. He can't stand that idea.

"What's happened to you, Emmarie? You came in here feisty, ticked off at men, probably for good reason. Now, you're shrinking from a challenge. What then? He wins, and you're letting him?" Indignation burns in his gaze.

"Stop judging me. You weren't there. You can't know."

Her venomous words hurt as much as if she'd sucker punched him in the balls.

"You're right. I can't pretend to know what you went through. Or are going through now. But I do know you found amazing strength. *You* did that. *You* survived because you are a survivor. Bob couldn't change that. That comes from inside you, the part he didn't touch. It's still there, I can see it all over you.

"You have no clue what you think you see all over me." Her voice trembles and wavers, either through constrained anger or apprehension, he couldn't tell. Her hastily erected protective walls now sever him from her in every way. "I wish you would focus on your other work and leave me out of this."

Dash wishes he hadn't said those particular words: '*That part he didn't touch*' — He meant only to remind her that she'd found a way to prevent Bob from totally violating her. Instead, he feels he's only succeeded in making her relive Bob's unwelcome probing.

"I get it, I do. I'm sorry for pushing you," Dash says. "I respect your choices, and I respect you."

"Thank you, but you sound condescending," Emmarie says.

"Now who's judging?" He pauses, then lowers his eyes in full apology. "I don't mean to condescend, Em."

"Do you really respect me?" She asks as tears begin to subside.

"If you knew me, you'd know I don't lie. I think you have amazing strength and depth of character." He subconsciously puts his hand on her shoulder then rubs her back gently. Only then does he remember that he should have asked her permission to touch her, especially in the day and age of 'me too,' and especially after what she's been through.

Normally, he would view this kind of touching as non-sexual compassion, one human being reaching out to console another. *Would she view it the same way? She does not flinch or shrink away, so perhaps she does.* Still, he removes his hand and continues speaking, "You've received some punishing hits lately. I'm wrong. I won't push you anymore."

She nods acceptance and appears to quiet herself.

"Look, I am fulfilling my commitment to Detective Bellows, with your help or not. If I find Bob, I'm not going to kill him unless I have to. I'm in law enforcement. So that would be tacky, not to mention *illegal*."

She rewards his gentle teasing with a brief softening of her expression.

"Testify or don't testify, Em. I do hope you'll change your mind though, as I'd like to remain on your good side."

Emmarie nods again, her sniffles almost gone.

"Now, tomorrow I'll be in Portland with Officer Díaz. Why don't you come with me?"

"As exciting as that doesn't sound, no thank you. I have no desire to expose myself to whispers or pity or pressure. I have enough on my Pfaltzgraff right now."

CHAPTER 36

That's a Lot of Ifs

⟿

Dash's drive from the Sunset Empire into Portland the following day is uneventful despite intermittent rain showers. Unfortunately, he is only able to pass cars ahead of him occasionally on the winding, mostly two-lane road. The closer he gets to Portland, the better the roads become to accommodate significantly heavier traffic. The 2-hour drive affords him plenty of time to stew, turning over in his mind what Emmarie told him. By the time he parks and hoofs it into the police station, his pressure valve is set to explode.

"What exactly did you ask Emmarie to do?" Dash blurts out as soon as he sees Officer Díaz in the conference room.

"Well, good to see you again, too, Deputy Cooper," Díaz says.

He raises his voice even more. "I know why you think Bob is involved in your sex ring. Hell, I brought the idea to you. But to ask a civilian to be an active participant in a sting operation is foolhardy!"

"Really? Have you thought that through?" Díaz steps close to Cooper. He feels her body invade his personal space as she continues: "*You* told me you don't think Bob is the type who can leave things be. *You* think he would consider her a loose end, or at the very least, a reminder of his bruised ego. That means she *already* isn't safe. And if that's true, at some point in time, he'll find her and take her. If that happens, and granted, it's a big 'if,' wouldn't you rather have a tracking device on her so we can find her?" Díaz lets that sink in for a few seconds.

"If the breaks fall right, and Bob is involved in sex trafficking, we save Emmarie. We might locate the other missing women and get an opportunity to cut off the head of this thing. If he isn't involved, or if he doesn't come after her, she hasn't risked a thing. I see no downside."

Cooper lifts a hand signaling permission to stop. He shakes his head from side to side, fighting his own feelings. "God, I hate that you're right. It sounds so dangerous, so cloak and dagger. Emmarie is fragile right now. She isn't up to this."

"It isn't your decision," Díaz says flatly. "Besides, it only feels riskier to you. Since risk exists whether she wears a tracker or not, she's actually safer."

"Does Randall know about this plan?"

"Unlike you, I have the full support of my department superiors and my team. Look, this is happening if Emmarie agrees to it. You don't have a say in the matter, but you could help if you decide to stop being such an ass."

"Okay. Tell me how this works."

"It sounds a little James Bond-ish, but GPS technology gives us massive leaps forward. All Emmarie needs to do is have the tracker with her. We'd consider chipping her, but that's a little too Orwellian." Lupe smiles at her feeble attempt to break the tension. She continues explaining.

"If we have reason to believe he has her, we use a computer and satellite to track her movements in real-time. In a perfect world, we would do a Trackimo 'slap and track' on the vehicle too, but that gets messy. We'd have to have a suspect, a vehicle, and a location to obtain a warrant or risk the court telling us we violated a citizen's 4th Amendment rights.

"Of course, if we observe her being kidnapped and have one of our agents disguised as a bicycle messenger slap a device on his vehicle at a traffic light, we could claim we are tracking a kidnapping victim, not a suspect. I don't know if you noticed or not, but that's a lot of 'ifs.' Emmarie carrying a tracker by consent is less risky for her and better for everyone."

Cooper looks at Lupe Díaz and realizes the officer knows her stuff. She's been doing this, or something like it, for more years than he's been a cop, and he isn't even a cop with any experience in this arena. No, this isn't a plan cooked up in the middle of the night during acid reflux. He believes Díaz's years with Portland's police unit gives her insights and gadgets, even 'cojones,' he wouldn't have. *She's sharp. She could be in line to have Randall's job one day. Good on her.* But first things first. *How can I make sure Emmarie stays safe?*

"On what other busts have you used this technology successfully?"

"Female officers acting as prostitute decoys mostly. We surround our female officers on the street with other officers disguised as sanitary workers and homeless people. Their job is to keep watchful eyes on the operation. The tracker is an adjunct part of the plan in case something goes wrong. We're still trying to figure out how to use this technology on a larger sting operation like this. If you don't mind, can we get to work now?" Lupe asks.

"I appreciate your honesty, but what I'm hearing doesn't warm the cockles of my heart. The technology doesn't prove you can reach Emmarie in time."

"You want a guarantee? Ship Fed-Ex."

"I need fresh air!" Dash storms out of the room and finds an exit door that won't alarm if opened. *Even if it's raining, a walk around the block will do me good.*

He finds the gray skies softer than when he'd arrived, withholding their moisture for a spell. The air smells clean and promising, even if mixed with the scent of diesel exhaust. A half-hour and several blocks later, a re-darkening of the heavens end the downpour's reprieve. Raindrops start falling before Dash gets back to Officer Díaz to apologize.

"No apology necessary, Dashiell. It's an occupational hazard to become involved. But since you are, try harder not to let it affect you."

With his head clearer, he hunkers down for the real reason he's in Portland. He wants the police department to run facial recognition on his photo of Bob, a.k.a. ATM man. Clatsop County has no such resources. He hopes for a full name and address. If he gets that, next he wants the department's cooperation to roll up on the guy if he's in their jurisdiction.

In exchange, he brings a box of Voodoo Doughnuts from Old Town and the forensic reports from the vacant house outside Keasey. Turns out, Bob did leave a few clues behind.

CHAPTER 37

Indigestion of the Worst Kind

⤙⤚

Emmarie remembers sharing everything with her brother, much like twins do, even though he's three years older. At times when they were younger, they'd enjoyed what others call a psychic link. Not so much anymore, although she does feel she knows exactly what he would say now, and frankly, she isn't interested.

What is it about men? Especially fathers and brothers, that make them think they are better at making important decisions? Knowing he loves her, that he only wants the best for her and wants to protect her, complicates things to be sure. She prefers staying mad.

This decision is mine and mine alone to make. And as far as selling the house goes, she'll continue balking at that as well, gambling that she and Danny can find a suitable solution that won't tear them apart.

The house telephone rings. Most likely some solicitor or reporter looking for a scoop, she thinks. She decides not to answer it but changes her mind with the incessant ringing. *"Even salespeople know when to move on to other calls."* Exasperated and ready to tell the caller off, she picks up.

A young man's voice says through tears, "Emmee, I wanna go with you. Bob ain't been nice since you left."

"Mason? Honey, is that you?"

"I miss you. Please come." His crying makes it difficult for Emmarie to understand what he's saying.

"Mason, how did you know to call me here?"

"Number in Bob's wallet. Come now."

"Honey, I will come as soon as I can, but I don't know where you are. Tell me and I will send help."

"Don't trust nobody."

"Okay, tell me where I can find you."

"Portland, near 2nd or 3rd, um, near Burnside. Building is for sale. Hurry. Rats scare me."

"Mason, listen to me. It'll take me a couple of hours to get to Portland. I'm not even sure I can find you. Hang up and call 911."

"No. I want you. Only you."

As soon as she hangs up from Mason, Emmarie wraps both arms around her middle, doubles over and breathes a long sigh, hoping the expelled air takes with it her anxiety over the boy. *At least he's alive.*

With her next breath, she sucks in resolve and considers her options. She picks up her smartphone.

"Detective Carlisle? Mason just called me. He told me where he is and wants me to come get him."

"That's not a good idea, Emmarie. But if you are going, let me come with you."

"I'm the only one he trusts. I need to go alone." Emmarie knows that Carol coming with her makes sense. She would invite Danny, but he has taken Aunt Julia to Portland International Airport and won't be back until late. Dash isn't an option either. He would already be in Portland, but she isn't sure she wants to see him either.

"There's nothing to discuss. I'm 'back up' in case you run into trouble," Carol tells her. "I can also expedite help for Mason. He's going to need medical and psychiatric care based on what you've told me."

Emmarie protests. The last thing she wants is to involve the police in a potential wild goose chase. But this might be exactly what Carol and Lupe discussed over lunch.

"I'll be there in 15 minutes to pick you up. I'm driving," says Carol, who hangs up before Emmarie can argue any longer.

By the time Carlisle arrives, Emmarie has sent innocuous texts to both Danny and Dash updating them on what's happening and telling them not to worry. As though texting the words 'don't worry' makes a difference.

Emmarie hears a car honk. She pulls the curtains back and sees Carol in her personal vehicle. *Does every police officer drive an SUV?* She grabs her purse, along with an insulated bag she fills with a couple of waters and heads out the front door. She pauses on the stoop to take in a deep breath, to smell the faint saltiness of the ocean breeze that wafts to their house when the wind blows just right. She savors the headiness briefly.

As she settles into the front seat and buckles her belt, Carol volunteers the information. "Driving this won't attract attention like my police cruiser would on the streets of Portland. The area around Burnside has enjoyed significant urban renewal, but it can be a rough neighborhood. Especially at night." With the vehicle's transmission still in park, she reaches into the glove compartment and brings out a box.

"I have something for you. Lupe left it. A Saint Christopher medallion."

"Isn't that the patron saint of Catholic travelers? I'm not Catholic," Emmarie says.

"No, but Lupe is. And, in a manner of speaking, yes, I think you're right. But this Saint Christopher necklace is special. It has the protection we talked about already built in. Keep it on."

As they exit the driveway Emmarie gives a little wave to the reporters hanging around on the street. They head south on the 101 to take the Sunset Highway, Hwy 26, into Portland.

Two hours pass with neither of them saying much. They both know what's at stake. For Emmarie's part, she spends the time looking out her side window at sheets of rain drenching the passing landscape, listening to the rhythmic swish-thunk, swish-thunk, swish-thunk of the windshield wipers, and eyeing her companion. Finally, when they get downtown, Emmarie asks Carol, "What's wrong?"

"I'm distracted. I didn't sleep well last night. Indigestion, I guess," Carol says. "I don't feel great now either, but that doesn't matter." Carol talks as they drive around the block between 2nd and 3rd Avenue and Burnside, looking for the spot Mason described. "You know, Emmarie, I have no jurisdiction in Portland.

"Dash says the same thing."

"However, I do have my gun as a private citizen. When we find the place, I'll park and wait for you. If you aren't back in five minutes, or I don't get a phone call from you explaining your delay, I'll come in after you." They locate a building resembling Mason's description and snag a parking spot directly across the street.

"Lucky," Emmarie whispers under her breath.

"Emmarie, are you sure you want to do this? I can have the Portland police here in two minutes. Their department is only a couple of blocks from here."

"No, I'm good. Mason needs me."

"But you can't be sure Mason is alone."

"No, but that's why you're with me, right? Besides, Bob works late in the day and evenings. If he left right before Mason called me, I'll be fine. He'll be gone for hours, and it won't get dark for a while yet. I'll get in and get out with the boy. Then you can decide our next step."

Carol acknowledges the plan non-verbally while Emmarie draws another deep breath. She fingers the new Saint Christopher medallion around her neck while she waits for a cloud burst to slow a little. When it does, she reaches for the door handle and says, "See you in a few." She checks for traffic both ways then jay-runs across the street to the advertised edifice.

Standing under an aged awning, Emmarie jiggles the handles on two massive front doors, each with turn-of-the-century etched glass, trying unsuccessfully to get one to open. *Locked.* She spies a side alley with a simple metal door, so she decides to try that. They have come too far to give up, and this is the only building matching Mason's description that they saw.

The building has no gutters on the side. Rainwater shed by its roof hits her straight down the back of her neck as she tugs at the latch. The old door gives way with a creak. Since the building is technically for sale, Emmarie figures it has working electricity, but she doesn't want to turn on the lights. She does not want to draw attention to her presence. What if a cop comes by and charges her with illegal trespass? She knows how ludicrous her story sounds at face value.

Remnants of light from the gray sky enter through the west-facing, floor-length windows. Emmarie sees a massive oaken bar with a brass foot-rail running the length of it against the wall opposite her. Wallpaper, yellow with age, peels in spots. Dirty outlines where pictures had hung now reveal cleaner, lighter square or rectangular voids. She crosses wood plank flooring, once economical and commonplace, now a sign of authenticity and value. A door in the back of the old saloon leads to small offices and a bathroom, and stairs downward. She takes these and descends into a smaller, unlit room.

Groping along the wall, her fingers find a light switch. She turns it on yet sees nothing at first. After her eyes adjust, she notices old tables, a barrel or two, and a door in one direction. A dark, low passageway beckons before her. She loses her sense of time, having forgotten to note when she left Carol. Is it time to call her? She should at least check-in, she thinks, so Carol doesn't worry. She draws her phone from her back pocket, locates 'Recents' and calls.

"Carol, I'm in the basement but I don't see Mason yet. I wanted to let you know I'm fine. I'll be out shortly with him or without him. There's only one more place for me to look." She hangs up and realizes she's whispering. Is she worried someone else will hear?

The whole place reeks faintly of sewer and stale history. Emmarie prefers to stay in the well-lit room but that's not an option if she wants to find Mason. She tries the door, but it doesn't open, leaving her with only the unlit, dirty opening before her. She berates herself quietly for not bringing a flashlight until she remembers the flashlight feature on her phone. She finds the app and turns it on. Peering across the cave-like tunnel before choosing to enter it, she observes exposed pipes, loose bricks, and old boards littering the floor along the sides. The farther she ventures, the more she invests in continuing, *just a little farther.*

She is uncertain how far she's already covered. Occasionally, the passageway reveals side doors badly in need of paint, naked stairwells, and larger rooms with sagging beams and pipes above her head.

A rat scurries before her, making her squeal and jump. Discouraged, she is about to look for an egress, when beyond her beam, she thinks she hears someone. She travels a few more feet, expecting to find Mason. No one is there.

"Mason?" she calls out.

"I know what you are thinking," a familiar voice says as it slips in behind her. "How could a place as delicious as this not be on the Shanghai tunnel tour?"

Emmarie whirls around, panic striking her like a falling cement wall. Bob, not Mason, stands within a few feet of her. *Carol!* Her mind screams, willing her to appear.

"Where's Mason?" she manages.

"As you can see, he is not here. Not that it matters."

"Is he okay?" Getting no answer, Emmarie demands: "You, you need to let me leave. I didn't come alone."

"If you mean that woman who drove you here, I saw her when you arrived." He withdraws a 9 mm pistol from his belt and points it at her. "I am prepared to handle your friend if she tries anything. But you can avoid that by obeying. Turn around. Follow the passageway."

Stuffing her panic to keep it from climbing into her throat, Emmarie has her phone in hand, using the flashlight beam to navigate and survey her options. With her back turned to Bob, she wonders if she can dial 911 without him realizing it. Will she even have a signal here?

It is as if he reads her mind. "Drop your phone. I will light the way for you," he says, coming up close behind her. She can feel his breath on her neck. His body odor mingles with her fear, sickening her with claustrophobia. The short ceiling and narrow walls press in on her. The diffused, low light generated by his flashlight creates tall shadows from old boxes and timbers. Rats scurry over her feet. As he edges her around debris in the twisting corridor, she can no longer breathe. The urge to bolt engulfs her.

"Freeze!"

Emmarie and Bob both stop suddenly and pivot to see Carol has silently crept up behind them. Her flashlight and her service weapon aim squarely at Bob. A gunfight could be a draw, Emmarie thinks, except Carol won't shoot without a clear shot. And she won't have one while she stands behind Bob.

Carol is in trouble. I must find cover, to get away so Carol has a chance. But she has nowhere she can go. In two steps she'll be out of Carol's extended beam but not out of bullet range. She can't run down pitch-dark hallways with no way of seeing obstacles and sharp turns.

"I believe I have you at a disadvantage, friend of Emmarie." Bob gloats. "I know this tunnel and you do not. And there is nothing behind *you* that prevents me from shooting. Good-bye." He squeezes the trigger.

His shot rings out as Emmarie throws herself into Bob, trying to seize the gun from him. She succeeds only in causing him to miss his mark. The bullet pierces Carol in her left shoulder. She screams clasping her chest and slumps down.

Bob leaves Emmarie in the pitch-black inkiness. He moves cautiously over to the fallen officer and kicks her gun into a dark crevasse beyond her reach. He steals her phone and her flashlight before returning to Emmarie. He then drops the phone, stomps on it, and says, "Get going."

It has all happened so quickly. Should she have tried to run, feeling with her hands along the corridor walls? *What about Carol?*

"You can't leave her here like that!"

"I'd say your friend has a 50-50 chance. Would you rather I plant a bullet in her face?" He grabs Emmarie by the arm and drags her down the passageway to a predetermined spot where they exit the tunnel unobserved.

CHAPTER 38

Unfinished Business

They emerge at street level into an alley not far from the other side of Burnside, the iconic White Stag sign in the distance. The fresh air relieves feelings of being light-headed and queasy until Emmarie spots a white van parked nearby. Memories flood in like a tsunami, causing her to retch. Bob opens the side panel and tells her to get in. If she screams or runs, he warns her, "I will go back down and kill your friend."

Emmarie does as he instructs. Bob locks the door from the outside and nonchalantly saunters to the driver's side and gets in. No one on the street pays any attention whatsoever to another delivery van parked outside a shop. Bob edges out of his perch and squeezes himself between the seats to reach the cargo area. He brandishes a cable tie and secures her hands together in front of her, then he takes another one to attach her to a D-ring embedded in the bottom of the vehicle.

"And one more little encouragement for you to behave," he says, dropping a hood over her head. "We will get to where we are going soon enough." He pushes through the seats again and plops down behind the steering wheel. He checks his mirrors, turns the key in the ignition, and the engine starts rumbling. Before pulling out into traffic, he punches in his Led Zeppelin IV CD, turns it up and asks, "Ready?"

Trapped. Old resolve rises with the bile from her stomach. She will get through this or die trying. She listens to blinkers turn on and off, to honks and loud radios, engines that backfire and other vehicles with screeching, metal on metal brakes. Try as she might, she loses track of stoplights, left turns and right turns, although for a stretch she is sure they are on one of Portland's many bridges. *Bridges make a certain clacking sound as tires cross metal plates.*

Now, Emmarie has no confidence in Saint Christopher. She worries about her friend, not knowing if Carol has the strength to find her way out of the tunnel to safety. Emmarie isn't even sure she hasn't bled out.

Díaz and Cooper discuss recent progress on her human trafficking investigation. The deputy shares what he's learned about Bob, including a definite photo of him. "He did a good job wiping the place clean where he held Emmarie and Mason, but you can't catch it all," he says. Forensic technicians located a couple of smudged fingerprints and one good one under the counter lip at the kitchen sink. They also used luminol and found blood exactly where Emmarie said she'd stabbed Bob. Bleach can destroy evidence; however, it can't keep the truth from exposure. But neither officer could know for certain if any of this brings them closer to stopping a ring of deviants from preying on young women.

The more Cooper discusses the case with Díaz without reference to Emmarie, the more he remembers that he likes the female cop. He's always been attracted to strong women and what she lacks in subtlety, she makes up for with competency and pluck. He warms to her plan.

"Please demonstrate your tracker technology, if that's not against the rules."

"Nothing to show yet. Carol says she will notify me if Emmarie accepts. I have not heard from her," Lupe says.

"You haven't? Emmarie texted me a couple of hours ago that Mason reached out for help. She and Carol were going to find him."

"Well, they haven't," Díaz says. "Nothing to be concerned about."

Cooper opens an application on his phone that allows him to ping her location. It shows her only blocks away, not moving. "Look here, Lupe. Emmarie is already in Portland."

"Okay, then let's see if I show anything on my system," Díaz says. She logs in to the program installed on her laptop. "Not everyone can access this specialty software. Vice uses it almost exclusively, but we are learning other applications for it." After a few moments studying her screen, she says, "That's interesting."

"What?"

"This shows the tracker on the move, up I-5, which wouldn't be notable except you think Emmarie is stationary, near here."

"She ditched her phone. Get your guys on this and find her. I'll find her phone," Dash commands. Lupe orders a junior officer named Michaels to escort Cooper for official business. Together the two men rush to 1st Avenue near the Skidmore Fountain MAX light rail station, where Dash's phone app shows she should be. They arrive and see people coming and going, some hustling and people-watching, but they find no phone. No Emmarie.

"Is there a subway underneath us?" Cooper asks Michaels.

"No. But this area is full of old Shanghai tunnels if you choose to believe the rumors. Many of the tunnels have collapsed and fallen into disrepair except for the ones on the tourist routes. They were built for dockworkers and merchants to move goods back and forth from the riverfront. In fact, this area was notorious in the 1860s for liquor and card rooms. Burnside's reputation for saloons and sailors made it almost impossible for respectable businesses to thrive here."

"Sounds like you know your history. Are there any tunnels directly underneath us?"

"They wouldn't be safe unless they are maintained as part of the tour."

"How would I get down there?"

"You'd have to find an opening. I'd start by canvassing the managers of some businesses around here; see if they have basement access that hooks in."

"Fine. You start across the street, and I'll start there." He points to the Burnside Shelter, part of Portland's Rescue Mission.

A van rolls up to the manufacturing facility and warehouse. Motion-sensitive cameras on the building's roof and corners and at other key locations follow all activity in and around the yard, and on the street. After the driver enters codes at the keypad near the front gate, the razor-wired chain-link gate rolls open, closing behind as soon as the vehicle passes.

The driver punches in a different set of numbers for the access door of the warehouse and waits for the massive roll-up door to yield. That door clangs shut too once the vehicle moves past the sensors.

Two men with assault rifles leave their posts inside to oversee the unloading. Bob recognizes Lars, the one who stitched him up.

"You can tell the boss, I have made his deadline with time to spare," Bob says.

Lars grunts. He doesn't smile or acknowledge Bob, giving him nothing when Bob expects to be congratulated. *Well, at least Snake will appreciate the job I have done.*

Lars opens the van's side door.

"Hey, what is your hurry? I have personal business with this one before you put her with the others."

"No. Snake's here now. He wants to talk to you." Lars sucks his teeth and hops into the back of the vehicle. He snips the cable tie that secures their latest captive to the D-ring inside the van. He leaves intact the zip tie that binds her wrists in front of her. With Emmarie still wearing the hood, Lars assists her out of the van and leads her through the building.

The other guard grabs Bob by the arm and escorts him as well. "What the hell did I do wrong?"

They walk through the distribution area, into a large, dusty room with saws and presses and machines of every sort, past a smallish, guarded room, and regular offices to enter a security room filled with monitors.

Shuffling along without giving his consent, Bob's confusion grows.

CHAPTER 39

Tail the Donkey

At first, the manager of the Rescue Mission denies any stairs or trap doors leading to the underground labyrinth from their building. Sure, it's common knowledge that tunnels once existed in this area, but buildings old enough to have them in Portland's underground heyday have undergone multiple renovations since then. Walls knocked down, torn up, bricked up. History sealed over.

An abundance of ingress and egress no longer exists to the underground passages and holding cells of old. Used by merchants for shuttling goods to and from the docks; nefarious hands procured forced labor. Their victims enjoyed themselves in saloons and boardinghouses one minute and in the next, found themselves falling through trap doors. That is if they were lucid at the time. Usually stone drunk or drugged, they knew nothing of their predicament until they awoke at sea with no recourse.

The receptionist suggests to Cooper that the Historical Society might be able to produce a few access tunnels for him, but he has no time. Something is wrong and he needs to find out what.

Before leaving the mission, Cooper asks if he can look around. He isn't wearing a uniform and they have no reason to allow a law enforcement officer from a different county any leeway, but he tells them he will call the local authorities, if need be, which to him means Michaels.

The Burnside Shelter itself has nothing to hide, even if some of its temporary residents might, so they grant him permission, putting the residency area upstairs off-limits. He has no reason to search upstairs anyway, and since the basement isn't taboo, he agrees.

Down a hallway, he stops to talk to a resident janitor. "How long have you been here?" Cooper asks.

"Me? I've been 'round these walls for almost 40 years."

"Seen a lot of changes, have you?"

"A soup kitchen started near here in '49. Course I wasn't here to see that, but I've seen my share." The elderly man stops his mopping and extends a gnarled, arthritic hand. "Name is Dizzy."

Cooper takes the man's offering in both hands, careful not to squeeze too hard. "Dizzy, I'm wondering if you know of a way to access the underground tunnels."

"Why sure, you can catch a tour that starts at Hobo's Restaurant and Lounge, a few blocks from here."

"I want something closer, unofficial if you catch my drift."

"Well, can't say what it leads to, but there's a trap door in one of my closets. Ain't been down there myself, so I can't say where it goes if it goes. Can't say it's safe, either."

"Would you show me?"

"Your poison." The janitor walks Cooper back to a room, larger than most walk-in bedroom closets at home, filled with an old commercial sink, shelving, chemicals, step ladders, tubs, buckets, and brooms. The word 'closet' fits. "Right over here," Dizzy says, as he moves a few squeeze buckets on rollers aside. Cooper sees a panel cut into the old linoleum flooring, about the size of a modern side-by-side refrigerator with a pry hole large enough to insert a couple of fingers.

Dizzy tells him that many of these tunnels were boarded up to keep people out of them for liability reasons. He also explains that Portland sports earthquake fault lines running deep below them. Many residents believe the soil in areas of the city will liquefy when the expected big one hits. As it stands now, even minor earthquakes and aftershocks create cave-ins in the tunnel system.

Cooper's heart beats faster. He phones Michaels even though he isn't sure the underground access he's found will lead anywhere. Then he sticks in his fingers, grunts, and pries open the lid. It resists at first then years of grime and expansion gives way. Dizzy takes a flashlight from his belt and illuminates the hole for him. They see a set of steep two-by-four stairs descending into the abyss.

"You stay here, Dizzy. Officer Michaels will be here asking for you shortly."

"You ain't gotta worry about that." He slaps Cooper on the back and expresses his doubt that he'll be able to keep that fine suit of his clean, even if the tunnel fizzles out.

With Emmarie uppermost on his mind, Cooper drops down into the hole, tentatively at first until he's sure the old stair boards will hold his weight. Within a few moments, he pops back up and asks Dizzy if he can borrow his flashlight.

The first thing Cooper does when he reaches the bottom is to shine the light in a 360-degree sweep. The second thing he does is consult the locator app on his phone. Does he still have bars? Does his phone still register her location? Yes, to both questions, barely. He sets off in the direction of the flashing red dot, winding and twisting his way through arches and narrow passages, around rubble and exposed water and sewer pipes, lumber supports, and rubbish long ago discarded. He isn't certain of heading east, west, north, or south.

He feels like a kid playing a game of pin the tail on the donkey, blindfolded, and spun around until he has no sense of direction. His disorientation suggests that if he had no light and no phone to guide him, he would be unable to find his way out. Fortunately, he enters the dilapidated underground system near the point where his app shows a signal coming from Emmarie's phone. Wherever the signal is, he's close.

In fact, he seems on top of the dot, yet he sees nothing but some dirty, corroded pipes in a pile off to the side. He hears something move ahead of him, beyond the beam of Dizzy's flashlight. Rats, he assumes, but it might be Emmarie. As he draws closer, his beam falls onto a crumpled body. He approaches it with his gun drawn.

It's Carlisle. He checks and, thank God, she's still breathing. Immediately he uses his phone to call 911, but he has no way of giving them a better location than a tunnel near the Skidmore Max station that he accessed through the Burnside Rescue Mission. Rather than calling Michaels to update him, he stays on the phone with the 911 dispatcher for what seems an eternity until paramedics arrive.

The first responders assess her quickly. She has a GSW to her shoulder and is bleeding extensively. Her vital signs concern them most, Dash gathers. They can treat neither her wound nor stabilize her in the dark, cramped, and dirty cavern. All they can do is hoist her onto a stretcher and get her above ground to initiate treatment. Prompt transport to a hospital is paramount.

"Better alert the emergency room," one of the paramedics says. "She's in bradycardia."

"Does that mean something's wrong with her heart?" Cooper asks.

"Can't officially comment, but it's either that or blood loss."

Carol is unconscious so Dash can't ask her about Emmarie or tell her 'Thank you' for putting her life on the line. Right now, Carol and Lupe's plan seems damned stupid.

After ensuring that Carlisle is in capable hands, he uses the flashlight to search around. He finds Carol's smashed phone another ten feet down the passageway. Rechecking his phone, the signal emanating from Emmarie's phone is now behind him. He retraces his steps to where he stood when he first heard the noise, back to where he thinks he was on top of the signal. This time, from his new angle, he sees it, Emmarie's phone, cast aside amid the loose pipes along the wall exactly where she was forced to drop it. With her phone now in hand, Dash uses his own to call Officer Díaz for an update on Emmarie's location.

Don't let me down, he prays.

CHAPTER 40

Street Justice

⟿

Snake sits behind an L-shaped desk with a plethora of monitors and wires running across the surface. Some screens show street views, others reveal images of the roof and yard areas. Others expose real-time happenings in the vehicle bay, the reception area, and the inner sound-proofed offices where product awaits shipment. Not a crow lands on the premises without them seeing it. Lars and the other guard enter the room with their charges, one hooded and the other wearing irritation. Snake rises to let a third security officer resume his rightful position in the chair in front of the monitors. He moves closer to examine his guests.

Lars removes Emmarie's hood. She stands motionless, as if petrified, except for blinking and darting her eyes around to see she is outnumbered by men with serious gun power.

"Son of a bitch," Snake grabs a roll of duct tape, slices off a long piece with his knife, and wraps it over her mouth and around her head. Then he pauses, looking at the shiny St. Christopher hanging around her neck. "Lot of good he's doing you." He yanks it off her neck and flings it aside. It hits the concrete floor with a clacking bounce and skitters off to a corner of the room.

Then he turns to address Bob. "Did I not tell you, Bob, that any further error would be dealt with swiftly?" Snake glares at the balding man, inches from his face, and then hisses, "Yet you bring her, the highest-profile young lady in the state right now, here to me and expect everything to be copacetic. Even as we speak, I've got a helicopter circling overhead and people, whom I can only assume are police, cueing up at my front door."

"I was not followed. I made sure of that." Bob says.

"Your stupidity is unforgivable. You are the reason this young lady is hot in the first place."

"They do not have a warrant. Just lay low for a while. It will blow over. It always does."

"Lay low while I have a shipment? You'd do best to keep your mouth shut and let me just *think* you're an idiot. You will fix this," Snake says.

"No worries. Tell me what you want done and I will do it."

Snake backs away so he can breathe fresher air. "You boast how the Coastal Cutthroat Killer provides you cover for your activities. Take her up into the hills somewhere and make it look like she is another damn CCK victim."

"Consider it done. So that extra package? I still owe you. You can count on me."

"Yes. I'm counting on you. Now, get her out of here before the police break my door down."

Bob grabs Emmarie by the arm, pushing her back toward the cargo area.

Snake turns to Lars. "Go with them. After he's finished with her, you know what to do. Personally, I'd love to read about an unidentifiable male floating in the Willamette River, but I'll leave the details to you."

Lars smiles.

Snake didn't. "Damn it!" he says under his breath. "Good thing we only have three to transport because we can't wait any longer. Get Oscar to back up the semi-trailer to the loading bay. We'll use that until we can swap vehicles. Then you'd better be about your assignment." Snake twists a silver ring shaped like a skeleton head around his right ring finger. *Suit or no suit, some business decisions require street justice.*

As soon as Cooper and Michaels leave to find Emmarie with the aid of his phone locator app, Díaz puts some eyes in the sky and goes with her team up I-5, following the tracker's signal emitting from the vehicle's dashboard computer. They take the off-ramp at Rosa Parks Way then head west to an industrial area. She radios for police from the North Precinct to join her. Before her unit rolls up and parks in front of where the tracker indicates, she hears from Dash about Carol.

She watches the gate open, and a van exit the grounds, making a left. She sees a lone occupant, the driver. She quickly calls Cooper back. "Dash, we think Emmarie is in a warehouse in northwest Portland. We've got the building covered, but we can't breach without a warrant. All we can do is watch from the street unless we have indisputable, probable cause. We don't have enough yet to ensure whatever we find in there won't get thrown out in court. But one of our guys thinks he spotted a guy with an assault rifle on the roof. If we can confirm, we're calling in the Special Weapons and Tactics Team as a backup."

"Are you sure Emmarie is there?"

"Yes. We tracked her here and she hasn't moved. We've got her."

"Then you need to be damned careful that they know Emmarie is in there before SWAT takes them down. No civilian gets hurt, remember?"

"We'll do our best. Two vehicles have left the premises. One of my units reported seeing a gray pickup leave and I saw your white van exit moments ago. Both appear to be solo. I've ordered a helicopter to follow the van until you can pick up the trail."

"Thank you. We need that van for evidence. But unless he drives through Columbia or Washington County all the way to Clatsop, I'll need an assist."

"My hands are full here. Coordinate anything you need through the chopper pilot. I'll have him radio any agency you need. Hey, Dash?"

"Yeah?"

"Stay safe, okay?"

"You too."

"That's my plan." Lupe loves the adrenaline rush of fieldwork. Yet every veteran knows there's a multitude of ways things can go wrong, and often do. The thrill isn't in planning a perfect mission or in perfectly executing a plan. The thrill's found in the chase, the outwitting, the outmaneuvering to bring the mission to a successful conclusion. Of course, sometimes it means redefining 'success' as necessary. Plans are fluid anyway.

Officer Díaz hangs up with Cooper as one of her men confirms sighting assault weapons. They spot snipers on the roof and heavily armed security in the reception area. These aren't the weapons of regular building security. Based on the abundance of cameras, razor wire around an 8-foot-tall security fence, and roof snipers, her team prepares as if it were breaching Ft. Knox. She notifies SWAT that they will have their hands full. She calls for ambulances and fire trucks to gather but stay out of range.

When SWAT vans arrive, the head of the highly trained tactical team, Markus Steele, checks in for a status report. Lupe Díaz does not have as much information as either would like. "We know of at least one high-profile civilian in the building. We tracked Emmarie Kelso here and have reason to believe she's being held against her will. Unfortunately, we have no idea how many hostiles are inside, but two vehicles have left the premises. You can see weaponized guards posted on the roof and around the building."

"Coadunate Industries?" Steele asks. "Anybody have a clue what they do?"

"Naw, vague business license. Something to do with zoology equipment."

"Heavily guarded for manufacturing animal cages, don't you think? This sounds straight-forward, but has anyone knocked on the door to request access?"

Barry Smith, Lupe's second in command, speaks up, "We didn't think they'd let us in without a warrant plus we didn't want to tip our hand."

"Seems to me, your hand's been tipped. They know we're coming. And your team is less threatening than mine. What's the word on your search warrant?"

"The warrant hasn't come through yet," Díaz states.

"We wait then. Let them make an aggressive move. You get your warrant, and we'll help you enforce it," Steele says.

"As long as they don't move Miss Kelso and we think she's safe, I'm okay with that," Díaz says. "I want your team ready, however, to breach at any moment."

"In the meantime, let's widen the perimeter," Steele says. "The last thing we need are more civilians in the way.

Reporters put their lives at risk trying to get too close if we don't keep them back farther."

Steele's right, Díaz thinks. *If it bleeds, it leads.* Reporters smell blood and vie for positions from which to air a story on the local news at 11 p.m. That is unless something exciting happens first and they interrupt scheduled programming for breaking news. Viewers hate missing their favorite shows until they realize lives hang in the balance. Just like the fascination of watching the infamous O.J. Simpson white Bronco chase, people crave out-of-the-ordinary thrills.

"Steele?" She calls him back over after getting her people to move the perimeter back. "Still no word on the warrant, so let's try the direct approach you suggested. Your men hang back and cover ours. I'll take Smith here and knock on the front door. Have your guys prepared for anything."

She turns to Smith, a father of five and the most experienced man over whom she holds seniority. "Are you ready? Let's see if they'll let us in."

"They'll buzz us in if we're welcome." Smith agrees. "I'm game."

They proceed cautiously from Díaz's patrol car across the street and up the sidewalk to the main glass door. A rain awning covers them from being in direct line of sight with the roof. The big glass doors displaying the company's phone number and hours of operation are locked, not uncommon anymore even during regular business hours. A keypad for employees and a buzzer for all others hangs nearby.

Smith engages the buzzer. It announces their presence, but no one comes. He buzzes again. "I think we've got our answer," he says. "How long are we going to wait here?"

The radio crackles and one of her team members announces, "Officer Díaz! We've got our warrant."

"Well, that answers that," she says, turning to Smith. "I say we let SWAT knock now, shall we?" She and Smith retreat to defensive positions behind the patrol vehicles, waiting for Steele's team to encircle the building as much as the fence allows, then break the door down.

CHAPTER 41

A *Combustible Situation*

On Steele's orders, several of his men crouch with weapons to their shoulders, ready to fire. They move forward. The action triggers a hail of 5.56 NATO ammo fire from AR-15's hidden behind various vantage points. One cartridge grazes the top of a patrol vehicle, bounces, and pierces Smith in the neck above his bulletproof vest. He dies instantly. Díaz screams.

With officers on the street pinned down, Steele orders Collins, a tactical officer, to shoot a smoke cannon through the window. They follow the smoke with gas. The team dons their gas masks and Steele is the first to breach, followed by Collins. They enter quickly, away from the roof sniper's line of sight. He employs hand signals to direct his men down hallways, clearing each room as they advance.

317

Even with the smoke and gas, they encounter sporadic gunfire slowing their offensive maneuvers. The assault team drops two suspects almost immediately and kick away their guns. While one SWAT officer checks for pulse and breathing, securing with zip ties the suspect who still lives, the remaining tactical assault team members continue their sweep of the building.

Collins approaches one of the sound-proofed inner rooms, its holding cell inside empty. "Clear!" He moves on to the next one, "Clear!" Beyond him, a door leads to a manufacturing area that houses metal grinders, circular saws, welding torches, and tanks of oxyacetylene, as well as raw stores of zinc alloys, magnesium, aluminum, and iron. Coadunate Industries has high-tech cages in various stages of assembly. A thick film of manufacturing dust coats every surface in the room, as well as the equipment, shelving, and rafters.

The effect of the gas weakens in the back of the building. Gunfire increases. Steele, Collins, and several other SWAT members enter the manufacturing and assembly area to more live fire. The team cannot advance without clearing the gunmen. And so far, they have found nothing that explains this level of resistance.

Steele sees a flash before him. A stray bullet from an attacker's weapon ricochets off the circular saw and ignites the combustible dust. A fireball explodes in every direction, rattling windows and felling Collins, setting his uniform on fire. Steele grabs Collins and drags him back to safety from the gunfire before smothering the flames with his bare hands.

A roof sniper tosses his weapon to the ground and jumps to avoid the fireball. For his efforts, he receives a broken leg — and the muzzles of three guns in his face before officers drag him off.

"Call for more ambulances!" Lupe shouts into her radio.

Not knowing what is happening inside, Díaz knows the plan has gone to shit. She scrambles to get what is left of her team together to decide what's next. SWAT has yet to finish clearing the burning building. Above the din of fire trucks and shouts, she hears a metal clanking sound coming from the parameter fence.

Almost simultaneously Officer Díaz and four other Portland police focus their weapons on the electric gate. Then they hear a big diesel engine roar to life over and above the squeak the gate makes as it slides open.

The passenger in the front seat hangs an **AR-15 out the window, laying down scatter fire while the truck speeds up to make its escape.**

"Aim for the tires!" Díaz orders. She, herself, aims for the windshield, first at the shooter then at the driver. Indecision costs her several seconds before she squeezes off several rounds. The scatter fire stops abruptly then the driver slumps, foot on the accelerator, propelling the semi into stacked concrete barriers that are manufactured and stored across the street.

Two officers keep a bead on the cab's occupants while two others check on their welfare. The shooter took a bullet between his eyes. The driver is seriously wounded, but alive.

Díaz moves cautiously to the back of the cargo container, gun drawn and calls more officers over to cover her. They open the door to find Snake with an AR-15 guarding three young women sitting, arms tied behind them. Accepting the situation, the man lays down his rifle and raises his hands in surrender.

As soon as they cuff Snake, they sit his ass down in the back of a patrol vehicle. Díaz announces over the radio: "I've got four suspects in custody and three hostages. Hostages are safe, I repeat, hostages are safe."

Lupe Díaz still has her hands full. The raid thus far has produced one dead officer and several injured tactical team members, suffering burns and minor gunshot wounds mostly. Add five dead and four captured suspects, two of whom are wounded. She's amazed at the paramedics' ability to keep up.

Díaz and the other officers help the three frightened young women out of the truck. With no ambulances available, she places them in protective custody in the back of patrol cars for transport to the nearest hospital. When she realizes Emmarie is not among them, she checks her laptop's tracking program.

It still shows Emmarie inside the smoldering building; her whereabouts unmoved. "My God, she's been dead all this time," she whispers to herself.

Firemen, attired in full gear, rush in with water cannons to curb the fire as soon as SWAT allows. It's a matter of saving lives as well as evidence. They know by radio chatter men are down in there, both police and suspects. As soon as the fire department squelches the flames, the mop-up crew moves in to ascertain if any more bodies are inside. Their job makes it safer for others to enter.

Díaz hopes for no more surprises. The tracker reports a person's location, not their condition. *Emmarie could have died before the assault and fire ensued. Hell, she may have died before we even got our warrant.*

Nevertheless, having a high-profile civilian killed on her watch, while executing her plan, negates all the good she's managed.

There's only one way to spin this raid now as being successful. At least they rescued three women and shut down the Portland tentacle of the operation. That should equal a lot of currency with her superiors, but she knows it's not enough. Politicians and Monday morning quarterbacks in the media don't understand the necessary, split-second decisions that are required as things can happen so quickly, things over which leaders have no control.

"Officer Díaz?"

"Yes?"

"All people accounted for. There are no more inside."

"What about Miss Kelso?" she asks the officer who approached her. "The tracker shows her still in the building."

"I don't know ma'am. You're cleared to enter if you wish."

Díaz nods and shows the officer her tracking app. "Take me here," she orders.

She walks through the blackened rooms and notes that the Fire Department did a good job combatting the flames. The combustible dust fireball and ensuing smoke charred several rooms but mostly damaged the manufacturing room where it started. The security control room with the computers and monitors remains intact, with a few blackened monitors blown over by the suck of air. The amount of water on the equipment shouldn't present a problem for forensics once it dries.

Díaz looks around without touching anything. *I bet that tattooed man wishes everything had been destroyed in the blast.*

But the state forensics department has a great reputation for retrieving information, even from crispy equipment. If anyone can retrieve it, they can. Of course, technicians will need to get past any privacy firewalls. But once they do, they should be able to harvest rich information and evidence to help the Feds shut this whole ring down; that is, if that's what they have here. It's too early to tell just what they've got.

In the corner, under a table, Díaz spies what appears to be a broken silver-colored chain. She takes a handkerchief out of her pocket, squats down and picks it up. Scratched, darkened, and wet, Saint Christopher's image rests in her hand.

A momentary sigh of relief escapes her lips. *Kelso didn't die in the warehouse with the others.*

But it also means she has no clue where she is. Nor what she'll tell Cooper.

CHAPTER 42

When a Plan Comes Together

⌁

"You know what to do, right Bob?" Snake's muscleman grills him as he crawls forward to sit in the front passenger bucket seat. "I'm getting nauseous back there with no air. Don't see how the girl can stand it, myself." He buckles up, lowers his window by four inches, and settles in. "That's better."

"Yes, I know how to make it look like CCK," Bob says. He keeps his eyes on the road and the traffic ahead of him. "I cannot have you contaminating the area with a second set of footprints. You will have to stay in the van and let me do her the way I want."

Lars sucks his teeth. "Fine by me. Just see that you handle it as CCK would."

Emmarie strains to listen to their chatter, appreciating the wafts of fresh air reaching her from Lars' open window. The air helps keep her head clearer, her mind better able to focus. An escape plan requires she remember as much as she can from the news reports of the Coastal Cutthroat Killer's victims.

What does he do to them? Where are the bodies found? What are Bob's weak points? She hopes he will still be vulnerable in his leg and stomach where she stabbed him before. She hasn't fully healed so he probably hasn't either. She'll go for these areas again, but with what? Her hands are bound in front of her with cable ties. Perhaps she can still pick up something to use as a tool. But even if she gets lucky taking out Bob, can she take out the other man too? He is larger and looks tougher.

Bob turns on his Zeppelin music. Lars reaches over and shuts it off. "Keep your mind on what you're doing."

The bigger man's in charge. Can I play the two men against one another? She doesn't see how.

Finally, Bob speaks again. "I am thinking Clatsop State Forest. I happen to know that area pretty well."

"Whatever. Just make sure it's in CCK's stomping grounds."

"My knife is not right. Not the same one he uses."

"How do you know? It will do the damned job, won't it? Keep her from blabbing what she knows."

"Yes, but even if they blame CCK at first, they will not after their investigators comb the scene. Snake overestimates my ability to shake the police on this."

"He knows what he's doing."

Bob heads up Highway 30 through St. Helens and Rainer. He chuckles out loud. "You know those little communities named themselves after mountains that are not even in Oregon?"

Lars grunts and sucks his teeth again. "Haven't you noticed the view of Mount St. Helens from St. Helens?" he asks. Then he turns to look back out the window. Under his breath, he murmurs his agreement with Snake. "Idiot."

Distracted, the two had hurried to leave the warehouse so Bob had simply clipped her bound wrists to an eye bolt on the van's floor with a carabiner. As the two men in front ignore her, Emmarie maneuvers her fingers to open the coupling link and slip the zip tie off the carbineer, effectively freeing her from the van but not the cuffs in front of her.

Perhaps I can throw my arms over Bob's neck while he drives and strangle him properly this time. Emmarie doubts that'd work with the big guy free to pull a knife or a gun on her. All her efforts would accomplish, she figures, will be messing up the ruse of CCK's involvement. What could she lose by trying?

By the time they reach Westport, back in Clatsop County, Bob is musing out loud about where he might take the girl to do the deed. It should not be difficult to find an out-of-the-way place in any direction in the rugged hills off Highway 30 even during the day, he tells Lars.

Lots of old logging and access roads exist to choose from, he says. While most have old gates across backset entrances, he tells Lars, 'No worries, I have bolt cutters.' They won't need them though, he says, because he knows a few old roads whose gates only appear to be closed by the casual observer driving past. "That will actually help conceal us from prying eyes. Remember the old television reruns for *A-Team*? I love it when a plan comes together!"

They pass the Gnat Creek Fish Hatchery on their left and drive another mile farther before slowing at the road that leads to a trail for the Gnat Creek Campground on the right. He turns left and lets the vehicle crawl and rock slowly down the unimproved road until they are way off the beaten path.

Lars rolls his window all the way down before Bob shuts off the engine.

"Remember, Lars. You stay here. CCK plays with his victims, so if Snake wants me to make this look like CCK done it, I must not skimp on that. Besides, Miss Kelso owes me, and I am going to take what is mine." He grins, exposing his dead tooth.

"I know what my damn job is, and you should secure her better," Lars says.

"She has to walk. I know what I am doing, too."

Bob leaves his 9 mm pistol under the seat and plays with the grip on his 6.5" Frontiersman blade. He wields the knife in his right hand and opens the sliding van door with his left. He sees that she is no longer secured to the van. "Come out, you bitch!" He picks up a coil of pliable rope and ties one end around her waist before ordering her to "Move." He pushes her out forward, away from him, prodding her to take what looks like a deer trail through the forest.

Even if she didn't have duct tape around her head, she doubts anyone would hear her scream this far off the beaten path. She remembers Dash telling her that CCK likes to display his victims and place them where they are usually found within a couple of days. Maybe they will eventually find her, but she can't imagine hikers or people out fishing stumbling over her in time to help.

The helicopter pilot stays on the white van longer than Cooper expects. The pilot doesn't peel off until the van reaches Clatsop County. Unorthodox perhaps, but it pleases Cooper that no one is willing to take chances on losing track of that vehicle. He believes the vehicle contains critical evidence.

Even though he is back in his own territory where he has the authority of the law, Cooper calls for backup and stays well behind the van trying not to reveal himself to the driver. He lets the van dictate the pace along the winding road. *With Emmarie safe, I can take the time to do this right.*

He watches the van turn off the main road and waits before taking the same left turn. He doesn't want to be seen.

When he feels he can no longer continue unnoticed, he decides to park and hike in on foot. His timing is instinctual and moments later he witnesses the van slow then stop altogether. He watches as he sees the driver exit and remove a smaller person from the back, pushing the form down a trail leading farther into the woods. His pulse quickens.

Taking cover where he finds it, he uses his boyhood skills to close the gap and deftly sneak up behind the van, gun unholstered and ready. From the reflection in the side mirrors, he sees another man sitting in the front passenger seat. How many more might be in the van, he doesn't know. Clearly, he can't continue tracking the suspect without first dealing with anyone who might exit the van to flank him.

He inches forward on his haunches, underneath the mirror's line of sight, then pops up with his service weapon, aiming squarely at the suspect's head. "Stick both hands out the window where I can see them! Anybody else in there with you?"

"Nope," he grunts.

Keeping his weapon trained on the man, Cooper orders him out of the vehicle. "Turn around, up against the door. Hands behind your back." The man complies. He secures the man's hands behind his back with handcuffs then makes him kneel. While he trains his gun on his prisoner, Cooper opens the van's panel door to confirm no one else hiding inside.

When he's fully satisfied, Cooper walks the suspect over to a fir tree, three feet in diameter. He releases one of his wrists, has him hug the tree, then he re-handcuffs his free wrist. *Overdone?* He wonders. But he doesn't want the man sitting alone, handcuffed in his own vehicle. Who knows if he has a weapon stashed where he could still reach it? He refuses to take chances despite the urgency he feels to locate the other suspect before the man reappears from the woods alone. He knows the kind of damage that can be done in just a few minutes.

He must hurry.

CHAPTER 43

Vengeance and Evidence

I'm not going to make this easy! Emmarie vows to herself.

"No bitch gets the best of me for long," Bob growls. "I cannot tell you I am disappointed. Nor that I am not going to enjoy this. Come on now, a slut like you might enjoy it too. The first part anyway." Bob seems to be speaking for his own titillation.

"The Coastal Cutthroat Killer ties up his women, plays with them until they are not fun anymore, then he slits their throats. That might not be exactly right, you understand, but close enough."

Over a little ridge, they stumble upon four trees growing roughly in a square, about 15 feet apart. "This will do," he says. "I wish Snake had not put that duct tape over your face and hair like that. Tape captures fingerprints like crazy. Removing it requires cutting your beautiful hair. CCK does not treat his women like that. See? They give me impossible orders to make it look like CCK, yet they sabotage me. Assholes!"

Bob comes up behind Emmarie and sweeps the back of her knees with his own, causing her to fall forward immediately. He gets on top of her back and ties the loose end of the rope around her left foot. He holds on tightly as he removes the rope from her waist and loops it around one of the four trees. While he focuses on tying her to the tree, she manages to stand and kick the rope out of his hand. When he grabs the rope again, he tugs hard. Emmarie falls on her back, with no hands available to break her fall. Bob gives her about seven feet then ties the rope he loops around the large sapling. He cuts off the excess rope, then cuts that piece into three more sections, one for each limb.

"I am almost sorry I decided not to cut the tape off until afterward. I would enjoy hearing you beg."

Emmarie writhes and struggles to free herself. She can barely draw enough oxygen through her nostrils alone to feed her body's heightened demand. "Increase my pleasure if you insist, Emmarie, or just let it happen. You know this ends only one way."

She groans and rolls onto her stomach. Then Emmarie rocks to her knees before standing.

He carries a rope length and his blade as he approaches her.

Now or never. As he draws close enough to grab her wrists, Emmarie imagines a soccer ball and uses her free foot to kick him hard between his legs. He moves a thigh in defense at the last minute, preventing her from obtaining a solid hit, but he still falls to the ground, clutches himself, and vomits. In the few seconds she has stolen, should she untie her foot? Try to grab his knife? *Bob won't stay down long. He'll be back with a vengeance.*

She decides on the knife but has trouble with her balance since one foot remains tied to the tree with her arms locked in front of her by the zip tie. She drops to her knees but cannot reach his blade.

Bob groans, yells something unintelligible at her, and rocks to all fours. Spittle drips from his open mouth in one long, thin thread. He picks up the knife he's dropped and lunges at her with a swinging motion. A crimson line appears across her forearms. Emmarie sees rather than feels it.

Bob moves to grab her free leg tucked behind her, trying to tie one end of the rope around her ankle. The other end will go around another mature sapling. In the end, she knows he'll have her legs spread-eagled. Then it will be a matter of tying a length of rope around a wrist before cutting the zip tie that holds her arms together. He'll tie each rope to a tree, then it's over. Cutting her clothes off with the knife instead of his damned scissors will be easy for him.

She doesn't wait for Bob to recover from her kick. As soon as he goes for her foot, she lunges for a large stick. She picks up a dead but sturdy one, almost five inches in diameter and four feet long, barely managing to hold it with her hands cupped. She swings with all her might and connects on the side of his face, his temple catching the brunt of it. He drops the knife again. Each scramble for it, but this time, she reaches it first.

Now, with both on their feet again, she feels she has a chance to defend herself. The feeling is fleeting. He reaches down and yanks on the rope that holds her leg to the tree. She falls again and he dives on top of her, sitting on her legs and using his free hands to try to wrest the knife away from her immobile ones.

Being flat on her back on the ground limits her movements. With her arms tied together at her wrists, she can rock the knife from side to side or up the full extension of her arms. That's all.

Bob grabs her arms, sliding his hands up to her wrists, then to her hands, to get the knife as she flails, stabbing and punching the air. He misjudges and gets too close. She slashes his face with the blade. Instinctively, he balls his fist and rears back to hit her. In the moment of his swing, he exposes his right armpit long enough for her to jab the knife above it, slicing his artery and arm muscle in two. Blood spurts over her, spraying his neck and chest and running down his lacerated appendage. Now even angrier, Bob pummels her with his left fist until she extends her slippery hands and drives the knife deep into his gut and twists. He rolls off her with a groan.

She withdraws the wet knife, flips it around, and carefully cuts the plastic tie that binds her hands. It's difficult to keep the bloody knife from slipping out of position. After several attempts, she has her hands free then she tries to untie the rope from around her ankle. To no avail. She picks up the knife again and saws through the rope that secures her leg to the tree.

Your turn, asshole. She returns to Bob and plunges the knife through his neck.

Bloodied, heart racing, and lungs heaving for air, her brain has just enough capacity to think, *"What now?"* It registers that she can't return to the van because of Lars. Footprints or not, Lars will soon come looking for Bob, to see what is taking him so long. She must flee.

This time she has a vague concept where she is. Her plan is clear. She makes a sweeping arc to her left well away from the van, and heads back toward where she believes Highway 30 to be.

Cooper follows the bent-over tall grass until the trail enters second or third-growth trees. The trees and underbrush are not so thick that he can't pick a natural path he thinks they followed. In ten minutes, he spots a motionless form on the ground. Instinctively he drops down before being seen. Even though he detects no one else around, he still scrambles from tree to tree until he is close enough to get a better view. The body is laying on its back, pinned through the neck by a knife. He recognizes ATM man, his eyes glassy and fixed. Cooper approaches, gun still poised. He feels the man's wrist for a pulse and as he expects, finds none.

He scans the woods. He's alone. *Who got the better of Bob?*

Was it Emmarie? *No, Lupe said she's at the warehouse.* He finds fresh blood every few feet off to the left, so he follows it, calling out: "Hello! Sheriff's Department! You're safe!" He continues yelling every so often yet hears nothing in response.

A forty-something couple returning from an afternoon of picnicking and exploring the hatchery see a blood-soaked female wander into the parking lot of Gnat Creek. "Oh my God! Call 911!" the woman shouts to her husband. She runs up to the disheveled woman, attempting to console her. "Larry is calling for help." She directs the young woman to sit on the open tailgate of their Ford Ranger, but it's too high, so she grabs a plastic lawn chair and motions for her. "Here, sit."

"Help's on its way," the man says, joining his wife. He automatically hands the bloodied woman a bottle of water, which she accepts but cannot drink. Between the two of them, they discuss whether to try to remove the tape from her mouth or to leave it alone lest they contaminate evidence. The fact they cannot see how to remove it without hurting her or cutting her hair, decides the matter for them. They can do nothing for her but wrap her forearms in a clean towel to stem the bleeding and continue uttering comforting words.

Cooper exits the underbrush and enters a parking lot still following the trail of blood. When he looks up and sees a couple attending Emmarie, he lets out the breath he unconsciously holds. In that instant, he desires to run to her, to scoop her up in his arms, and never let her go. Instead, he limits his legs to a brisk walk as he calls 911. They inform him an ambulance and emergency medical technicians have been dispatched and should be arriving shortly.

"Emmarie, it's Dash," he calls out. As he draws closer, he resists his impulse to run and kiss her. Feelings or not, he's a Clatsop County deputy working in an official capacity. Instead, when he reaches the couple, he instinctively reaches to flash his badge. "I'll take over. I'm Officer Dashiell Cooper," he says before slipping his identification into his pocket and turning his attention to Emmarie.

"The ambulance is still a few minutes out, but they are going to stabilize you, then get that tape off your mouth, okay? Do you need to lay down?"

Wide-eyed, Emmarie shakes her head 'No' and somehow conveys that she understands: *She is safe.*

Dash stands guard over her, gingerly brushing a few leaves and twigs from her hair before remembering that everything could be evidence, the bit of rope around her ankle, the tape, the forest debris, all of it. He should be touching nothing. But to not touch her seems an impossible expectation.

The ambient air is cool but not cold. Yet Emmarie shivers. Shock. Dash asks the couple to get a blanket to throw over her shoulders if they have one. They produce an old quilt and are about to place it around her when Dash reaches for it. He gently wraps the soft, faded blanket over her shoulders and tucks it in at her waist, lingering to stand closer than he should. He'll have to relinquish care to the EMTs when they arrive but for now, Emmarie is his charge.

He makes her as comfortable as possible, then excuses himself when he sees Bellows drive up in his official vehicle. Dash opens the front passenger door and climbs in so he can speak to Bellows privately.

"Walt, I've got a suspect handcuffed to a tree a mile or two up the road. I also have a dead perp in the woods that Emmarie killed in self-defense. From the look of it, it was quite a battle."

"I'll call for more units and the forensics team," Bellows says. "Draw me a map to the tree hugger. I'll take it from here until you can join me."

"You can't miss it. Head west on Hwy 30 and take a left at the next intersection, away from the campground. Down a bit, you'll see my Jeep. A hundred yards beyond, you'll see a van. That white van ties this case to a string of missing women. I'm sure of it."

CHAPTER 44

Monkey Shoulders

"I appreciate you getting a uni to guard her hospital room," Dash tells Bellows as he hands him a new bottle of Monkey Shoulder, blended malt Scotch whisky. "It'll help us both sleep a little better tonight."

"That kid's been through hell. Feel sorry for her." Bellows says.

The two men sit on the elder man's back porch, feet up, sipping amber liquid from the freshly opened bottle. The younger man is a bourbon guy, but he knows his uncle's tastes. Monkey Shoulder fills the bill for both. Bellows lights the end of his ever-present Camacho cigar and puffs.

"I'm surprised you aren't at the hospital with her. This has all been about her for you, hasn't it?"

Dash removes his feet from the low coffee table in front of them and places them on the ground. He leans forward bracing his elbows on his legs and admits, "It started that way, Walter. And I'm sure glad finding her didn't take any longer than it did because I burned through my vacation." He takes a sip from his tumbler, looking off wistfully into the distance, thinking about Emmarie. Then he switches gears to answer the question his uncle asked.

"Her brother, Danny, showed up at the hospital. They deserve time together alone. I was a third wheel." He brings his gaze in from far away and looks down at his feet. He realizes his shoes need polishing. He takes another sip of Scotch.

"Give her time."

Dash nods. He changes the subject and brings his feet back up to rest on the long rattan coffee table. "I will tell you this rollercoaster ride will make going back to traffic seem pretty mundane."

"Hell of a way to use vacation. You should try fishing next time." Bellows chuckles and Dash smiles. They do not look at each other. The black man puffs on his cigar, does not inhale, and blows the smoke out slowly, to savor the draw. "I should tell you," Bellows continues, after taking another sip of Monkey Shoulder, "busts are still satisfying when your suspect's in custody on other charges. The raid on Volkov's place turned up parachute cordage in his workshop, with the same orange paint spray and the same sodium and chlorine contaminants found on Stanley and Samamoto.

"Forensics also assayed the same fungal spores they'd found on Martin and Gilbert, growing on a floor mat in a pickup in the shed. They uncovered a little dungeon where he kept his victims for the week. It's a good collar. Volkov might get the death penalty. Or plead guilty to his sadistic murders to get the prosecutor to take death off the table. Either way, we retired CCK."

"That's awesome news." Dash takes another satisfying sip of his Scotch. He savors the way it tantalizes the taste buds on the roof of his mouth and tongue before caressing his throat, warming him all the way to his stomach. He could become a Scotch man, just like his uncle.

"We've got to stop meeting like this," Danny says as he leans over and kisses his sister on her forehead. "I'm getting a complex because every time I see you, you look beat up. Makes me think maybe I'm the constant in the equation."

Emmarie would have smiled, but it hurt too much. She welcomes her brother's visit though. In truth, they haven't spoken much to one another since vehemently disagreeing over the settlement of the estate. She believes her brother still thinks of her as a little girl who needs others to make decisions for her.

She's grown a lifetime in a few months. And, despite lying in a hospital bed yet again, arms and hands bandaged from defensive wounds and the right side of her face swollen and purple, she feels confident and able to handle almost anything.

"I'm glad you're here, Danny. Later, can you sneak out and bring me some Bowpicker Fish and Chips? I'll die if I have to live on green Jell-O, no offense to kids everywhere, I hope."

"None taken, I'm sure." Danny sits down next to her bed and holds her bandaged hand. Fortunately, she has no I.V. drips or needles sticking out of her this time. For a while, they sit, lost in their own ruminations. *Being together is enough.*

Danny finally speaks again. "You should know that I'm not going to push you to sell the house."

"Really? What changed?"

"Don't get me wrong, I still think we ought to sell while the market is good, but the insurance agent called and said they won't be holding up Mom and Dad's life insurance. Upkeep money isn't a problem anymore."

"Thank you, Danny. This means more to me than I can tell you right now."

"Of course, Em. Stay as long as you need to. We can replace money; we can't replace family." He looks down sadly and pats her hand.

She does not perceive condescension or paternalism in his touch. Instead, his caress articulates volumes of love.

"So," he says, "we'll divvy the inheritance fair and square, together. I'll come up with an investment plan you can follow if you want, but it's your money, no strings attached."

"I need some time, Danny, that's all. I won't hold on to the house forever." Emmarie wishes she could offer her brother something tangible in return. She thinks of nothing. All she ends up saying is, "Consider yourself hugged. It hurts to move."

He moves his arms to embrace himself in an exaggerated fashion, complete with sound effects of a loud, slobbery sister kiss.

"Oh, don't make me smile," she pleads, "It hurts!"

"I do want to head back to Harvard by mid-August. I assume you will go to Juilliard?"

"Oddly enough, I don't know. A career in music and acting doesn't seem all that important right now, but I'll figure it out." She looks off into the space above her toes, grasping for words she thinks he'll understand. She can't find them because she, herself, does not understand.

"Danny, I don't know what to think about anything. It's like some cosmic rug has been pulled out from underneath me, and things I once was sure about, I can't even wrap my brain around."

"Any chance you won't be ready for me to leave in August?"

"None. I'll be fine. You don't need to sacrifice anything more on my account. Mom and Dad wouldn't want you to. And I don't want that for you." She endures the pain to smile at him. "Hey, I'm getting tired. Why don't you scrounge up that Bowpicker's, while I busy myself not moving a muscle?"

"Beer-battered Albacore tuna and steak fries, coming right up!" He lifts the television remote and clicks it on. "Watch a little news if you want. I'll be back as fast as I can." He kisses her on the forehead and departs on his mission.

The television blares, and she almost shuts it off but instead, a news story catches her attention. The broadcast airs aerial footage showing thick, black smoke. She reduces the volume a little to listen as the female anchor's voice announces:

"A huge fireball erupted at Coadunate Industries today after being stormed by Portland SWAT who had reason to believe the manufacturing plant that makes zoological equipment was actually a cover for a human trafficking operation. One officer died and several were wounded in the raid that netted the release of three missing girls. Several suspects also died in the attack and four suspects are now in custody. Police aren't confirming, but some say this operation may have ties to a criminal front based in New Orleans.

"In a related story, Miss Emmarie Lynn Kelso, the daughter of the late Dr. Janet Brooks Kelso and her husband, Roger, is back in the hospital this evening. Apparently, she was attacked again by her obsessed fan. Reports indicate that Miss Kelso may have killed the suspect in self-defense. One police officer, who declined to be named, said that the abduction of Miss Kelso had its roots in the sting operation at Coadunate Industries."

"That's a wild one, Jennifer," the older male co-host says. "We all look forward to hearing more as that story develops."

"I'm just happy to report Miss Kelso is safe, and it's over," Jennifer says.

"Yes, indeed. Speaking of safe, young women across the state can now breathe a little easier because a suspect in the Coastal Cutthroat Killer case is behind bars tonight. CCK suspect Adrik Volkov has been charged in the brutal rape and deaths of six young women since last September. Volkov was already in custody under assault charges when authorities obtained a search warrant for his property near Melville, Oregon. Authorities say they seized several boxes of evidence during the execution of that warrant. More on that story as it comes in. Now stay tuned for the weather…"

Emmarie clicks off the television, imagining what must have happened after the police followed her to the warehouse. At least she knows Officer Cooper isn't the law enforcement official who died, but she worries about Díaz and Carlisle. The reporters didn't mention Carol at all. Is Carol still alone, somewhere under the streets of Portland, or did they find her?

The deputy isn't her only concern either.

Now that Bob is dead, Emmarie worries about Mason. *There are ramifications to killing Bob after all.* Mason will die a lingering, horrible death ankle-cuffed in a tunnel or cellar somewhere. She cannot stand the thought.

She can't reach her phone, so she pushes the nurse-call button. A young male nurse enters and retrieves the cell for her. Should she call Díaz to inquire of Carol, or should she call Dash? She chooses Dash.

CHAPTER 45

The Bargain

National and local news reporters re-assemble at the base of the broad lawn in front of the Kelso home as soon as they hear she is being released from the hospital. In truth, she thinks the hospital kept her longer than necessary, to give her time and space to rest, un-harassed. This time, she does not mind.

Danny serpentines the Mercedes through the throng to deliver his sister inside the garage so she does not endure long-range lenses and prying eyes.

"Do you think I'll ever get my life back?"

"Of course, Em. But if you want that any time soon, you'll need D.B. Cooper to walk out of the forest arm-in-arm with Bigfoot, or for a jetliner to crash onto the front steps of the governor's mansion. Reporters will dump you like the plague, taking off on the scent of their next big story."

Danny means well, but the mere mention of a crashing plane was an unfortunate example. He must know it too as he diverts his eyes and tries to change the subject.

"It's okay, Danny. You don't need to tiptoe around me. I expect triggers everywhere. I'll handle them. In fact, I'm thinking about negotiating with those reporters."

"I don't follow you, Em. Stay away from them."

"And wait it out? You as much said it yourself. Who knows how long it will take this sleepy berg to come up with enough dirt to draw their attention away from me? I'll offer them a bargain," she says. "In exchange for going away, I'll give them a formal statement and answer their questions."

Emmarie brushes past Danny, who is still in the garage, to enter the kitchen through the utility room. "Think that will work?"

"Oh, they'll agree. But I don't think they'll keep the deal if they think you're still a story. That's why," Danny says, catching up to her, "you need to convince them what a boring little sister you truly are. That all you do is stay home and bake cookies for your big brother."

"Chocolate chip still your favorite?"

"You betcha, but I'm branching out, educating my palate. Whatever you bake, I'll enjoy."

"Your advice sounds a little self-serving."

"Look, all I'm saying is that waiting couldn't hurt. Why don't you sleep on it tonight and see if it still makes sense tomorrow?" Danny opens the refrigerator door, grabs a carton of orange juice, and sets it on the counter. He retrieves a juice tumbler, pours himself a glass then points the carton of juice at Emmarie to offer her a glass. Receiving a 'no, thank you' headshake, he puts the jug back into the refrigerator and downs his juice.

"To clarify," he says, "wait on the briefing not on the cookies."

Reporters from all the news stations, KATU, KOIN, KGW, and others short of TBN, huddle around a makeshift podium and a half dozen microphones, waiting for the promised statement by Emmarie Lynn Kelso. The blue sky and faint sea breeze settle over the proceedings much like a new mother bathing a newborn. The placid weather stands in contrast to the energy of the moment, where curiosity and excitement over what juicy new details might be exposed, reminds Emmarie of a hound with a gopher down a hole.

"Ladies and gentlemen of the press," Danny starts. "My sister, Emmarie, and I appreciate your interest in our family over these past few months. We also appreciate all your prayers and support, and the prayers and support of your viewers and of our entire community. We can feel the love.

"We would ask, after today, that you would let our family process everything that's happened and to continue to grieve the loss of our parents in private. That means we are asking you to respect our privacy, not as national public figures, which we are not, but as private citizens, who must continue to work through an ordeal no one should have to face.

"We ask that you allow us, especially my sister, to have her dignity and space. With that, she would like to make a statement. Afterward, she agrees to answer your questions. Please keep your questions civil and appropriate. Otherwise, I will end this interview. Now, I don't want to do that, but I'm sure you all understand my sister's wellbeing and safety is our primary concern. Thank you." He steps back from the bank of microphones. "Emmarie?"

Cameras continue rolling amidst a barrage of still photography flashes.

"Yes, thank you." For her debut on television screens across the nation, hoping she has only a few moments left of her '15 minutes of fame,' she wears some foundation and a touch of blush to help hide the yellow and purplish bruises remaining on her face. She accents her eyes with a little mascara and fills in her lips with a rose-gold lipstick to bring out the highlights of her freshly bobbed, auburn hair. Having chosen a blue stripe, cropped wide-leg pantsuit, she has fashion magazines buzzing about her as well.

Emmarie takes her notes from her pocket and begins to read. "Thank you all for being here today. I will endeavor to keep this simple, and to the best of my ability, review the events of the past several weeks. Some points I won't be able to comment on due to legal advice, and other points due to the private nature of what occurred.

"As you may know, I was abducted while riding my bike along Fort Clatsop Road and kept manacled to a bed in a basement outside Keasey. I was not alone. There was another prisoner, a boy named Mason, who was kept in a leg iron. I was held captive for a week before I managed to escape. After more than 24 hours in the wild, lost, and suffering from exposure, two hunters found me and brought me to the attention of the authorities. I was hospitalized for my wounds at OHSU. Shortly upon hearing that I was safe, my parents took off in the family's Beechcraft Bonanza to join me in Portland.

My father is, or rather was, a qualified, licensed pilot, cleared for both VFR and IFR flight. I do not have information from the NTSB's investigation, so I cannot speak to what went wrong. I only know that while I was hospitalized, their plane crashed in the coastal mountain range, killing my parents. I did not have the opportunity to see or to speak with them or to tell them I love them. Fortunately, they knew I was safe before they passed. I believe their love for me was uppermost on their minds at the time of the crash.

"Given the obsessive nature of the man who abducted me, and another criminal investigation involving activities at Coadunate Industries, which to my knowledge was figured out by Deputy Dashiell Cooper of Clatsop County, I was approached by law enforcement officers from both Clatsop and Multnomah counties and asked to wear a tracker on my person.

That tracker idea was the brainchild of Officer Lupe Díaz of the Portland Police Department and our own Carol Carlisle, a deputy here in Clatsop County, who was shot trying to protect me. I do not know any details regarding that on-going criminal investigation.

"Approximately ten days ago, I received a call from Mason, my fellow captive. Wearing the tracker supplied to me, I went to help him. I did not find him. I now believe Mason's cry for help may have been a ploy of the maniac who took us. However, due to the success of the tracker program, the Portland Police knew my whereabouts and initiated a rescue mission.

"My assailant took me to the Coadunate manufacturing facility in Portland. Believing I was still there, the Portland police raided the building. That's where they found and rescued three missing girls and captured several suspects. I was not in the building at the time. Two men had orders to remove me and kill me.

"Fear is a great motivator. I was forced to kill one of my assailants in self-defense before he was able to carry out his plans. The other suspect was apprehended by Deputy Cooper.

"I owe an extreme debt of gratitude to Lieutenant Bellows from the Clatsop County Sheriff Department as the lead investigator on my case, as well as Officer Díaz and deputies Carlisle and especially Cooper. Indeed, I feel I owe these brave and courageous men and women my life.

"I will now accept your questions." She folds her notes and puts them back in her pocket.

The gaggle of reporters clamor for her attention. "Miss Kelso! Miss Kelso! Over here, Miss Kelso!"

Emmarie points to a reporter close to her.

"As I understand it, Miss Kelso, you were not actually raped. Is that true?"

"I was violated. He attempted to rape me on two occasions. He was not successful. Next question, please."

"Did you think you were going to be a potential victim of CCK? If so, how did you feel?"

"When I was first abducted, I had no clue who held me, or why. It is petrifying to think that you might meet the same fate as the victims of the Cutthroat Killer. My heart goes out to his victims and their families."

"What do you regret most about not being able to see your parents again?"

"Just that. Not being able to see my parents and tell them I love them."

Seriously? Do you reporters understand how inane your questions are? How would YOU feel?

"Emmarie, nice haircut. Are you re-inventing yourself?

"I am sporting a new hairstyle because my kidnappers wrapped my head in duct tape before trying to kill me. The tape could not be removed without damaging evidence unless I allowed my hair to be cut. Hence, we cut my hair."

"Would you comment on the 'two kidnappers' angle?"

355

"Yes. The second abduction was my first clue that my situation involved a larger criminal enterprise. Given my notoriety, my attackers were given orders to kill me rather than have me jeopardize their operation."

"What can you tell us of this boy you say was being held prisoner with you?"

"I only know what he told me. That is, our abductor kept him for years. As a young boy, he watched his mother murdered by her boyfriend. He entered child protective services, but the system let him down. I do not know which state is responsible for that. Now that his captor is dead, I worry about him, not knowing where he is or what has happened to him. Any more questions?"

"Yes! Emmarie, what will you do now?"

"Right now, I might bake some cookies. Then I plan on taking a long, hot bubble bath, and crawl into bed with a good book. If you are asking me to speculate on the rest of my life, I won't. I am taking it day by day, at least until I chart a new course. That is all. Thank you." Emmarie turns to her brother for support. He joins her and they walk away from the microphones together while the reporters yell out more questions behind her.

She leans against him and whispers, "Think they're satisfied?"

Danny shakes his head almost imperceptibly and puts a protective arm around her. "Naw, bottom feeders must eat constantly," he whispers back. "But you did great. Perhaps you should go into politics."

CHAPTER 46

Sleepless in Clatsop City

With reporters gone, the days warmer and sunnier, Emmarie places no demands upon herself other than doing what she feels like doing. She spends hours talking with Danny about nothing, skirting the real issues when she lacks the energy to face them. With each passing day, she feels like doing more, talking more, and tackling more.

The void her parents left means that life can never be the same, she knows that. Still, these days remind her of riding through the countryside, catching glimpses of a destination, speckled by sunshine through the trees because she can't see the whole vision of where she's headed. Nevertheless, what she sees gives her hope. She's making progress.

She makes her peace with the house, every room, except for the office off the kitchen where the great doctor wrote her books and consulted on cases with colleagues. That door remains closed. She cannot yet bear to enter there, to sit in her mother's chair, to rifle through her desk. It would feel like a violation of privacy.

Much of this day she spends sitting in the back yard, appreciating the flowers and sorting through memories…the Japanese Maple, which she and her dad planted together when they first moved to Oregon…the patio furniture she helped her mother select during better times…and the lawn statues. Her mother's outdoor tastes ran toward the classical, statues of Greek gods and goddesses, urns, and topiaries. As a child, how she begged her mom to incorporate some whimsical, colorful garden gnomes and fairies. The gardens, still void of these things, now seem right.

"I thought I'd find you out here," Danny says as he joins her. "Can anyone sit?"

She isn't relaxing in one of the comfortable Adirondack chairs but on the stairs leading down to the patio and barbecue unit. "Pull up a step."

Danny hands her a tall glass of iced tea, no lemon, no sugar, the way they both like it. He takes a sip of his own. "Penny for your thoughts."

"With inflation, I'll have to charge you a nickel."

Danny fishes in his pocket for a nickel and hands it to her.

"I was thinking we should get the gardener out here. The grounds could use a manicure."

"A nickel doesn't buy much anymore, does it?"

Emmarie takes a long draw on her tea, letting it trickle down the corners of her mouth like a child hastily gulping cherry flavored Kool-Aid. "I hadn't realized how thirsty I was. Thanks."

"It's a bribe. I'm wondering if you'll be okay tonight if I have a few beers and shoot a little pool with old friends from high school."

"Hard to believe you have a better offer than watching chick flicks with me. No popcorn for you. Go."

"I might be late."

"It's a double feature for me then. Don't worry." As kids, they loved watching movies together. *The Princess Bride, Goonies, Stand By Me,* and *Young Frankenstein* were classic favorites they'd watched with their parents multiple times. As much as she would enjoy his company, she urges him to go. Life needs to get back to normal, whatever that looks like. For Danny too, she thinks.

Her brother leans over and kisses her on the cheek, then stands up. "Need a refill? I'm headed out early to run a few errands, then I'll meet the guys."

"No thanks. I'm headed into the house anyway. So much time and so little to do. Wait a minute. Strike that. Reverse it."

"Willy Wonka, right?"

"Gene Wilder, not Johnny Depp."

Danny walks back into the house and as the door begins to close behind him, Emmarie calls out, "Danny?"

He turns around and walks back. "Yes?"

"Have fun storming the castle," she says with a broad smile.

That evening, Emmarie does a perimeter walk around the interior of the house and makes sure all the doors and windows are locked. A formality really, as Danny and she both make a habit of locking doors behind them. This isn't new behavior, either. Satisfied, she makes popcorn for dinner and paws through their collection of old movies. She is in the mood for something light-hearted, perhaps a romantic comedy. Something requiring only a few brain cells.

Her first thoughts include re-watching *The Princess Bride* for the umpteenth time but decides to save that for when Danny can watch it with her. They know it by heart and quote their favorite lines to each other a split second before the actor recites them. Instead, she decides on a Nora Ephron film, *Sleepless in Seattle.*

She changes into her comfiest pajamas and curls up on the couch in the family room with a few pillows, a lap blanket, her popcorn, some more tea, and the remote. The movie in the player is not a typical romantic comedy because the couple remains strangers, never getting together until the end. She finds that satisfying, realistic even, because life rarely works out as you expect it. For her second feature, she selects *Maverick* with Jodi Foster and Mel Gibson, filmed on the Columbia River. But she closes her eyes one too many times and falls asleep before the big poker game.

She wakes with a start as a hand covers her mouth. She opens her eyes to see Mason squatting on his haunches beside the couch. He holds the index finger of his other hand to his mouth in a 'shushing' gesture. Alarmed, she nods her head in assent. She will not scream.

Thoughts rush like water over a dam. *You're alive! Wait, what are you doing here? How did you get in?* As soon as Mason removes his hand from her mouth, she speaks.

"Mason, you shouldn't scare a person like that. It isn't polite." She expects him to say he's sorry, or to act remorseful or sheepish. He does not. She tries to sit up, but he doesn't let her. He pins her down with his arm.

"I saw you on TV. You say you worry about me. No need. Bob taught me stuff." Mason eyes her in the same way Bob had looked at her.

"I-I'm glad you are not chained up, unable to care for yourself. But you should not be here."

"Why? I missed you."

"Yes, but it's late. You can't come into someone's house uninvited. Didn't Bob teach you that?"

"Bob taught me to pick locks. He taught me to drive. You surprised? I told you Bob is nice. You were not nice. You killed him."

"He kept you chained like an animal! You need to leave. Now."

"Nope. You're not the boss of me. You're alone."

"What do you mean, I'm alone? My brother's here. Danny will come down those stairs any minute and call the Sheriff. He will make you leave." Emmarie does her best to act normal. Even though she lays on her own leather couch, surrounded by her own familiar household items, everything appears foreign and fuzzy. The only light comes from the television.

Her eyesight falls onto the glint of three long knives from the butcher block in the kitchen which now lay on the coffee table next to him.

"Liar. Your brother ain't home."

"Mason, you do not want to do this." *Keep him talking.* "How did you find me?"

"Bob knew about you. I have his truck. It's mine now. I have his scissors too."

Emmarie's thoughts flash to Bob using the scissors to cut off her clothes. How many times had Mason watched while he did that to a woman? He was turned on too, more than Bob. She tries to distract him. "Why are you here?"

"What else did you lie about? Did you lie when you said you worry about me?"

"No. Of course not. I tried to get you to leave with me, remember?"

"Bob said you're a slut. You should get what a slut gets. And a murderer. Whatcha think should happen to you 'cause you killed my uncle?"

"Your wha—?"

"I told you I had un uncle. The State threw me away to bad people. Uncle Bob found me. He looked for my sister too, but he didn't find her. He did his best."

"Bob kept you chained like a dog!" she repeats.

"Only when he brought a girl. For protection. For my sake." Mason clutches his groin. "Look, but do not touch," he repeats in a sing-song fashion. Soon, his clutching turns to rubbing.

"What are you going to do?" Emmarie asks the obvious question out of compulsion. She does not want to know.

"I'm grown now, so whatever I want. I watched Bob many times. Bob always starts like this…" Mason removes the scissors lovingly from his pocket and considers them. "Nope." he shakes his head. "I like knives better," he says, returning the scissors and patting them like he must have seen Bob do many times. He rocks forward onto his knees and picks up the middle knife.

Starting at the top of her pajama bottoms, he cuts the ribbon tie. Then he moves to the bottom of her top and with expert flicks of his wrist, he separates each button from the thread that holds it closed. He glides the knife tip gingerly up to her breastbone where he playfully traces the blade in figure eights without drawing blood. He adeptly applies enough pressure to leave white marks on her skin.

"Stop. Y-you don't want to do this."

"Stupid girl."

"Hold it right there!"

Surprised by the intrusion, both turn their faces in the dim light to see Dash bursting into the room. He holds his Smith & Wesson M&P 9 steady on Mason.

The boy stops his play, shoving the blade against Emmarie's throat. "Stay back."

Emmarie cannot move unless Mason allows it. She barely breathes.

"Can't do that, son. Put the knife down." Dash keeps his gun trained at Mason's head. He continues to close the gap between them. "More deputies are coming. You don't have a chance. Drop the knife and move away from Miss Kelso."

Mason begins to cry and rock back and forth on his knees.

Classic soothing gesture, Emmarie hears her mother telling her. *Rocking triggers the brain to release endorphins, feel-good chemicals.*

Emmarie swallows her fear. Still feeling the pressure of the knife against her throat, she speaks carefully. "Sweetheart, if you put the knife down, I'll hug you." She remembers how much she had wanted to hug Mason, to comfort the little boy inside when he told her how he hid under his bed watching his mother being beaten to death. "You'd like a hug, wouldn't you?"

Mason says nothing. He continues to whimper and rock. Slowly, he withdraws the blade and sets the knife on the floor.

"Let her up, Mason." Dash orders.

He continues rocking himself and does not resist Emmarie sitting up and quickly scooting off the sofa. She stands well away from the knives, keeps her shirt closed with one hand, and opens wide her other arm. "Mason, I'm ready to hug you."

He does not stop rocking. Emmarie breathes deeply to calm herself before approaching him. She kicks away the knife on the floor. Looking at Dash for reassurance and seeing he still has his gun aimed at Mason's head, she picks up the remaining two knives by their blades and tosses them over to a side chair, well out of reach.

She then drops to her knees in front of Mason and puts her arms around him. Mason stops his rocking. With his arms dangling limply at his sides, he lets her embrace him until Cooper comes up behind, clamps a handcuff on one wrist then the other. He stands the boy up and walks him outside to put him in the back seat of his Wrangler. Then he calls for the backup he had said was already on its way.

"How did you know to come?" Emmarie asks, using the lap blanket around her shoulders as a shawl to keep her pajama top together.

"I didn't. I ran into your brother at Chinook's Pool and Bar. He said you were home watching movies, so I thought I'd drop by. When I pulled into your driveway, I recognized the vehicle you'd described in your statement, the one you saw at the cabin. Your front door wasn't latched; it sat ajar. The situation didn't feel right." He offers an open arm to her.

She accepts and buries her face against the crook of his neck, her arms wrapping around him, holding on for dear life.

After a few moments of deep, slow breathing to encourage the adrenaline to fade from her body, she pulls back and asks, "Can we keep this quiet?

"We can hope."

"What will happen to Mason?"

"I'm guessing he'll be booked on breaking and entering, attempted rape, attempted murder, and for anything else they can think of. But given the circumstances, he's more likely to go to the Oregon State Hospital in Salem as a psychiatric patient. Either way, you're safe. You don't have to worry about Mason anymore."

CHAPTER 47

What the H?

⌒

In the two months since she'd seen Dash, Emmarie notices that time has treated him well. He's more handsome than she remembered, now seasoned with confidence judging by the way he handles himself. His success in helping capture CCK and breaking open Portland's human trafficking ring brought him to the attention of his superiors. When Carol Carlisle in the County's major crimes department retired due to her heart condition, his uncle hadn't pulled strings.

One of the perks of his new job with the Sheriff's Department is that he now works from a private office instead of a bull pit of traffic cops or a stray conference room. This suits him, she thinks. He leans against the side of his desk, finishing up a phone call when he motions her into his small office with a wave of his hand.

Emmarie acknowledges Cooper and tiptoes in. She sets her sweater and purse down on one of the cushioned chairs arranged a few feet in front of his small, utilitarian desk. She judges the personal space between them to be comfortable, or at least adequate.

What am I doing here? Aware she's trembling, she is grateful she can hide her nervousness from others. Of course, the last few months afforded her a little space and time to get her act together. But becoming the same naive person again is impossible. She settles for learning *to act as if* she manages her life with aplomb.

Emmarie chides herself for her nerves. She accepts that new experiences will threaten her when she lets them, but she chalks up these nerves to being bad at small talk. That latter revelation comes with its own frustrations because she remembers once being good at chit-chat. She could converse with anyone. Not so anymore. Non-important things are, well, not important in the scheme of things. *That, too, has been stolen from me.* Now, all strangers make her want to run.

Dash Cooper isn't exactly a stranger though. He's been in her life searching for her before she knew he existed. He has a protective way about him. He keeps her safe, plus makes her feel safe, two very different things. The latter is especially true, provided she isn't busy chafing at those who care about her.

No, Dash isn't exactly a stranger. He knows intimate details about her. Uncomfortable details. Embarrassing details. She's sure he has photographs in his files or remembers seeing them at least, of bruises all over her body after escaping from Bob, twice.

Yet what does she know about him? Not much.

He stayed with her in the hospital when she'd learned of her parents' crash. They spent time together in Vernonia and Columbia County looking for Bob, of course, but all their interactions and exchanges were about her case. Now that's over, it feels strange to imagine talking to him about anything else.

Dashiell Cooper smiles at her as he replaces the receiver in its cradle. His body language projects casual, welcoming warmth. Even his intense blueish gray eyes seem to soften upon seeing her she thinks. *If I could just melt into those eyes ...*

Emmarie urges her body to relax but it refuses. Every muscle remains on high alert, as they usually are whenever she does not sequester herself at home. It doesn't help that Dash hasn't yet spoken. Instead, he seems to be appraising her. *Bob and Mason did that too, but this is different.* She might even consider it pleasant to be noticed by Dash. *Yet why did he call? He must have some reason.*

Wait. Is my case not over? Does he know something? Did the D.A. decide I didn't kill Bob in self-defense? Did Mason break out? She recoils from the possibilities overwhelming her, yet she struggles not to panic.

In those few seconds, she mentally consults every movie she's ever watched for something that approximates 'normal' conversation, then settles on simply: "So, what made you decide to go into law enforcement?"

Dash smiles easily and lets out a brief laugh. He starts to answer her then shifts his weight. For the first time, he looks uncomfortable, as if he is about to relay a tragic event from a secretive past that drove him to pursue dangerous criminals. It must be a story he doesn't like to talk about much, she reasons. On second thought, *perhaps a guy like him prefers a story like that.*

"It's not complicated," Dash says before he pauses again.

Emmarie feels his eyes search her face, her frame, for some encouragement to go on. She gives it. So, with a resigned sigh, pregnant with all sorts of potential meanings, he explains. "My parents are English professors. I grew up with all sorts of literature. They made me read everything from Shakespeare to Mark Twain." His voice trails off. Feigning distraction, or lost in thought, she can't tell. He picks a piece of lint off the arm of his suit.

"I don't think they understood. As a boy, I yearned to get dirty like Huckleberry Finn." His voice grows softer. "I grew from wanting adventures to wanting to make a difference." There is a lightness to his voice now. With a small shake of his head, he chuckles again.

"It sounds corny, I know. Law enforcement seemed..." Dash stops himself. At that moment, he appears boyish to her. "Let's say my attempts at calculus didn't suggest being an astronaut."

Emmarie smiles. It's easier than she expected to talk to him like this. She notices how pleasant Dash's voice is when he isn't nailing a suspect or de-escalating somebody like Mason. *And didn't he deflect attention away from himself with self-deprecating humor? That's rare.*

She lets her line of sight drop from his face to the desk in front of her. The first thing she notices is a beautiful pen and pencil set with gold trim and his name engraved upon it.

He sees her looking at it. "A gift from my uncle when I took this job."

"It's beautiful," she says. "Why — Dashiell H. Cooper — you're a…"

She stops herself when a fresh synapse flashes across her brain, erasing all previous thoughts and halting even her autonomic reflexes. She collects herself for a moment, letting an 'ah-ha' moment sink in. A slight, knowing smirk commandeers her lips. She can't refuse it, nor does she try. "Do you mean to tell me the H is for Hammett or Hemingway?"

Dashiell averts his eyes from hers, which confirms her suspicions. "Hemingway" he admits slowly.

"Too cute," she offers.

Did he blush? Did she? Right then and there, she regrets saying anything. She doesn't mean to embarrass him. And she hopes she wasn't condescending either.

Am I trying to flirt with him? The rough idea surprises her, but she owns it. She feels new to flirting. She can't remember flirting with Jack. He was always there for her. Until he wasn't.

Emmarie doubts if she'll ever get flirting right, let alone master the feminine art form. She knows girls like Amy whose very existence centers on feminine wiles. For girls like that, flirting is first nature, not second. For her though, not being good at something as trivial as flirting never mattered before, but somehow, now with Dash, it matters a great deal.

A young deputy, not stopping to consider that he might be interrupting, barges through the open office doorway. He and Cooper exchange a few words that seem to satisfy the new detective, but Emmarie politely tries not to pay attention to anything they say. She busies herself by looking around the room at his ample awards and trying to imagine Dash outside of work. She sees a photo of Cooper from his Academy days. And one of him with the mayor and Lt. Bellows. *"Not bad for a man's office,"* she thinks, *especially in the Sheriff's Department.*

The deputy leaves and Emmarie tunes back in at the sound of Dash's gentle voice. He is saying something about a pet snake, then Emmarie figures out Dash is half suggesting and half assuming a longer social exchange to be their next step.

He picks up her purse and sweater for her. "Let's get some coffee, shall we? Unless you'll let me buy you dinner…"

CHAPTER 48

At Peace with Your Own Terms

⌐━━━⌐

Emmarie and her best friend Sophia sit outside the Bridgewater Bistro, having lunch in the shadow of the Astoria-Megler Bridge that connects Oregon with Washington. The unseasonably warm ambient air and killer views across the Columbia River could convince any visitor to linger.

"Danny left last weekend, didn't he? How are you doing with that?" Sophia asks while they wait for their food to arrive.

"I'm good. He's good. It was time," Emmarie says. Then she shakes her head a bit to signal that she's willing to explain. "I can't be a drag on Danny anymore. Besides, it's time I stop cocooning myself in the house. Whether I feel like it or not, I need to see friends like you and meet new people. I've even considered dating."

Even though Sophia is her best friend, she tries to keep her facial expression neutral so that she doesn't express her more private thoughts. But the idea of seeing Dash generates a smile she can't repress. She changes the subject before Sophia stops looking at the gorgeous view and notices. "Tell me about you. I understand you're taking classes at Clatsop Community College."

"For now. I'll be full-time but living at home, I won't have to work. I can focus on school."

"Makes sense."

"Why didn't you leave for Juilliard?" Sophia asks point-blank. "You could you know. It's what you've dreamed about." Sophia leans back so the waitress can place her pasta on the table in front of her. She takes a mouthful of the red wine dish made with Parmigiano and Dungeness crab and waits for Emmarie to answer. A seagull swoops and caws overhead.

The waitress sets Emmarie's scallops seared with bacon, served with purple Peruvian potatoes and a medley of fresh vegetables, in front of her. "Bon appétit," she says as she excuses herself.

"Yes, Juilliard is what I wanted," Emmarie says as she places her napkin in her lap. "And there's always next year if I decide to go. Passing on Julliard sounds crazy, I know…

"The last few months, I've enjoyed my music. But the idea of turning it or acting into a career doesn't thrill me the same way. I don't want fame or fortune. I prefer a private life." Her voice trails off, "Besides, think of the downside," she says.

"Downside?" Sophia scrunches her brows quizzically between bites.

"You remember, don't you? That crazed fan shot and killed The Voice's Christina Grimmie while she signed autographs after her concert. But let's say that didn't happen. Did you see Bradley Cooper and Lady Gaga in *A Star is Born*? Sure, that was Hollywood. But you've got to admit singing is a rough career even if you make it big. A string of hotel rooms, pawing fans, constant demands, and pressures, I don't think I want to make a living like that anymore."

"Like *you* need to make a living. I know you, Emmarie. You don't need to make a living so much as make a life. So, what do you plan to do?"

"Maybe music therapy. I don't know. I've also been thinking about social work or law enforcement, even some kind of business as Marta suggested." Emmarie devours a scallop and follows it with a sip of raspberry tea. "I don't think I'd benefit from going away to college until I know what interests me. Perhaps I should take a class or two at Clatsop with you and see what resonates. I'm in no hurry to leave."

Sophia sets her fork down and asks, "Have you considered psychology?"

"It hadn't occurred to me." *But now that you mention it, there is something I still need to do.*

Emmarie places a hand on the doorknob leading into her mother's private office. Is she ready? She enters and opens a window to let fresh air in for the first time since before her mother's passing. Hardback tomes by Dr. Janet Brooks Kelso line the built-in bookshelves, along with reference works and books by her colleagues. She scans the titles of each of her mother's books, running her index finger across the spines one by one as she recalls what was happening in her life at the time her mother wrote. It wasn't all bad.

Her mother's massive cherry wood desk graces the middle of the room. Emmarie pulls out the well-worn, high back executive chair from behind the desk and sits down. Her fingers and palms explore the desk's durable top surface and the ornate side carvings.

She's not sure what she expected. Perhaps to have the ghosts and memories in the room reject her, to rebuff her advances to understand her mom. Yet no presence seems to mind; none are as obdurate as she once believed them to be.

When she feels ready, she summons the courage and fires up her mother's MacBook Pro. She looks inside the desk hoping to find the password, and smiles. She sees that her mom used her only daughter's birthday to unlock her digital world.

Next, she scrolls down her mother's well-organized files until she notices the word 'current.' She clicks to open the manuscript of her mother's final book, *At Peace with Your Own Terms.*

Prologue

Everyone seems to be talking about taking time to invest in yourself, myself included. It has been an honor for me to walk alongside and help guide you, my dear readers, through life over these many years. However, you need to know the real solution to your problems comes not from me. Your solutions always come from within you.

You are the ones who make decisions to change your circumstances. You are the ones who find the strength to do what needs doing. You are the ones who find the courage to say 'no more' to bad situations and bad relationships. My guidance only helps you recognize your own power, your own ability, and your own value as human beings. No one can take your power away from you. You are always stronger than you think.

In this extremely personal book, I talk about my own struggles to live life with dignity. Not the life I would have chosen, but the hand dealt me, just as you must live the hand dealt you. Like some of you, this has been my most difficult year.

I would be remiss to give you platitudes as I share my journey facing the cancer I once beat, but that is now beating me. It ravages my body in stage 5. Rather than spend my last days grasping for a little hope, I am choosing to embrace life to the fullest every day I have left and to not worry so much about a clean finish. I would much rather slide into home plate sideways in a cloud of dust.

This book shares my honest ups and downs and insights that I hope will encourage you and help you find the superhero within yourself. My main message to you is: You are strong. Stronger than you think.

Gandhi said, 'The weak can never forgive. Forgiveness is an attribute of the strong.' Therefore, forgive yourself first, then forgive others. Freedom and happiness, indeed, all the ingredients that make life worth living start with the power to forgive.

I would also be remiss if I did not mention that the most difficult part of my final journey comes as I put the finishing touches on this farewell book. This manuscript was essentially complete when our not-so-little-girl went missing. She is still missing, and we have no guarantee of a good outcome.

Life offers no guarantees. As I write this, her kidnapping has been national news and our unfathomable nightmare. Yet, I cannot find it within myself to change a word in this book about encouraging you to embrace the cycle of life and to forgive.

To my readers, and my family: my husband Roger, my son Danny and my precious Emmarie, you have made this life journey of mine more than I could ever have hoped for. Thank you.

Emmarie stops reading and stares out the window, lost in thought. She is unaware of how much time passes before she gives herself permission to look up a phone number.

"Mr. Pamplin? My name is Emmarie Kelso. I am Dr. Janet Brooks Kelso's daughter. I understand that you were my mother's agent."

"That's right. Terrible shame what happened. How are you holding up, my dear?"

"I'm okay. I am wondering if you know much about my mother's last book?"

"We were eagerly awaiting it, but I'd assumed we'd never see it finished. It was so difficult for her to make progress when you were missing."

"Well, I'm calling because I'm reading it. I think Mom would still want you to have it. It may need editing, but it seems finished to me."

"Fabulous. Her readers will gobble it up; sight-unseen it will likely stay on the New York best-seller list for six months, maybe a year."

"Is she still under contract with her publisher?"

"No, actually. That means competition. We might get a bidding war."

"See what you can do. I'll send it over."

Emmarie unplugs her mother's laptop, goes into the kitchen for some iced tea, then walks out to the patio lounge to sit, digital manuscript in hand. She puts her feet up and begins to read.

The End